YE OLDE MAGICK SHOPPE

STORIES OF MAGIC FOR SALE

MISHA BURNETT   MICHAEL CONNON
STEVE COOK   L.C. GIBSON   JAKE LITHUA
WILL NEELY   J.S. ROGERS   AARON SMITH
MAX SPARBER   WONDRA VANIAN
ALYSSA N. VAUGHN   VANESSA WELLS

Edited by
OREN LITWIN

LAGRANGE BOOKS

ALSO EDITED BY OREN LITWIN

Liberty Island Media

The Odds Are Against Us: An Anthology of Military Fiction

Lagrange Books

Ye Olde Magick Shoppe: Stories of Magic for Sale

The Wand that Rocks the Cradle: Magical Stories of Family (coming soon!)

CONTENTS

INTRODUCTION

BY OREN LITWIN

Why sell magic?

Magic is the strange and unusual. Magic breaks the rules. Magic gives you power, sometimes power over others. Who would want to sell magic? If magic makes you special, what does it mean when you let other people be special too—if they pay?

Does selling magic make it a toy of the rich? Or is it available to all? What dangers are caused by letting ordinary people buy magic? What challenges would they face?

Many beloved stories involve buying magic, whether it be a handful of beans, an enchanted sword, or Potions of Vitality from the local adventurer's guild. A well-timed magical sale can change the buyer's life, solving his problems or throwing her into the middle of a hair-raising adventure. Pushing open the door to a magic shop can be like entering another world—and you can't always go back!

Most of all, the idea of a magic shop is simply *cool*. If browsing a bookstore is exciting, with each book offering new possibilities of wonder, what if the books were all spellbooks? If a hardware store suggests new projects you could undertake, new skills to conquer, what if the hardware inside broke the laws of physics? It was largely because of the concept's coolness that *Ye Olde Magick Shoppe* was born.

In this collection, twelve authors looked at the theme of buying and selling magic in very different ways. In "Polimancy," the owner of a magic shop is threatened with terrible peril, in the form of unsympathetic government officials. In "Rule of Three," two sisters in rural England introduce a new line of products in their shop, with surprising results. American soldiers invading Nazi Germany find themselves face to face with old legends come to life, in "Mud."

Even magical animals need medical care, and in "Alternative (Veterinary) Medicine," our hero seeks out rare ingredients before time runs out for a sick unicorn. A human surviving at the margins of a world ruled by elves goes shopping for forbidden goods, and finds himself "In Pursuit of Memory." A bizarre experience while watching a home video leads to a dramatic change of career, in "The Extra."

In "Highwaymen," a team of modern Knights Templar is hired to recover stolen goods, only to be waylaid by a deadly motorcycle gang of nightmarish faeries. In "Banishment for a Homesick Demon," an exiled witch is given a chance at enormous power. Zombies and vengeful spirits lurk beyond the borders of a small Texas town, in "Mind the Store."

Wish you could press a button and fix all of your life's problems? Well, "There's an App for That." Junkies looking for a magical high unleash deadly necromancy on an unsuspecting city, and the cops have to clean up the mess in "Grand Theft Nightmare." A merchant's son is plunged into a strange, dangerous world and must learn its magic or die, in "Trust."

I'm incredibly proud of the stories in this anthology. I know that you love reading them just as much as I did.

Last but not least, a huge thank-you to the talented authors who submitted their stories to the anthology; it was their hard work and creativity that made this book possible. Thanks as well to voice actors Adrianna Burton, Williamson Knox, and John Patneaude, who lent their voices to our promotional video during the submissions period.

Come on down to the neighborhood magick shoppe, dear reader. But remember: let the buyer beware.

Oren Litwin, editor

December 2018

POLIMANCY

WILL NEELY

Why is it that municipal offices everywhere tend to have the same basic feel to them? Whether it's in a squat brick block or a beautiful glass testament to modern architecture, the inside is inevitably the same: uncomfortable chairs clustered together, the smell of burnt coffee tainting the air, and of course the unavoidable haphazard collection of printed notices stuck up all over the place, brusquely declaring the policy-du-jour in all caps. It's like an angry copier exploded:

"PAYMENT IN CASH OR BY DEBIT CARD ONLY. NO PERSONAL CHECKS ACCEPTED!!"

"EFFECTIVE NOVEMBER 12, TWO FORMS OF I.D. REQUIRED WITH ALL BUSINESS LICENSE RENEWALS!"

"STAY BEHIND THE YELLOW LINE UNTIL YOUR NUMBER IS CALLED!!!"

It's the exclamation points that really sell it, if you ask me.

This particular office happened to be in a large room with taupe walls. The uncomfortable chairs in the waiting area were discolored from age, but had definitely started out as taupe. The woman sitting at the taupe desk just across from me wore a taupe sweater; behind her round glasses she eyed me with the curious mix of hostility and disinterest only a government employee can credibly pull off.

The nameplate on her desk read DOLORES. It was taupe.

"Can I help you," she said. Her words formed a question, but the tone in her voice didn't; it was one of those questions you don't really care about, such as "How ya doin'," or "What's up," or "How was your vacation."

Questions like that are like fishing without any bait. You just toss the line out and then whatever.

I smiled. "Uh, yes, I got this notice in the mail..." I held up said notice. She didn't glance at it. After an awkward second, I continued. "It says my business may be in violation of..." I turned the notice around and read the arcane gibberish off the front. "Code 722E-4. So, uh, I just need to come get it sorted out..."

Dolores grunted. She was good at it, too. Came right from the diaphragm, boom, just like that. Probably dislodged a few particles of microwaved noodle or whatever it was she had for lunch that day. "Okay, hold on..." She pulled a form out from a drawer in her desk, set it in front of her, and started filling out the bottom section—you know, the one that says "DO NOT WRITE BELOW THIS LINE! THIS SECTION FOR MUNICIPAL OFFICE USE ONLY!"

"What kind of business is it?" she asked.

"Oh, it's a magic shop," I replied.

Her tone communicated her complete and thorough lack of interest. "Uh-huh. Would you categorize it as Hobbies or Novelty Items?"

"Huh? Oh, no, no." I laughed, to try and build rapport. I failed. "It's a *magic* shop. I sell supplies for, you know, mages, wizards, other practitioners."

Her pen stopped. She looked at me with the first spark of life I'd seen in her eyes. "*Oh.*"

Like many words in the magical realm, that *Oh* carried a weight and meaning greater than a single syllable really should. I cringed a little bit inside.

Dolores sighed as she threw away the form she'd been working on. She leaned over, opened a different drawer, and pulled out another form, dropping it on the desk between us with a *THUD*.

The first form hadn't gone thud.

This form started off about an inch higher than the desk. Caught somewhere between shock and disbelief, I started to leaf through it.

"Number of items sold in the past two years, sorted by category," I said. "Demographic of target clientele, estimated number of customers of each race, human, magical, and exoplanar—*Estimated number of crimes* which may have been committed with my products?" I looked up, incensed. "Are you kidding me?"

"No need to get testy, sir," Dolores growled testily. "The Magical Responsibility Act requires all of this information to be on file for any business with a supernatural aspect. It's your responsibility to be in compliance with the law, sir."

"Well, sure, I understand that," I blustered. "And I try to obey the law, believe me, but this is just ridiculous! I don't have access to this information. Plus, I'm pretty sure there are some Constitutional rights being violated here... I can't just go around asking my customers what crimes they've committed!"

"Well, sir, if you don't want your business to be shut down, you'll need to get this form back to us by the date on your notice," she said.

"But that's two days from now!"

"Then you should get started." She turned away from me and clicked her mouse. "Number 42!"

For a second, I was tempted to enspell her computer. Just a little bit. But the law really wasn't her fault, and causing her trouble wouldn't accomplish anything aside from venting my frustration and vastly increasing the severity of my issues. Plus, I'd be in violation of the small sign posted outside the building: "By Federal Law: NO weapons, firearms, or active magical foci permitted on this property."

The sign wasn't magical or anything—it just told you what the rules were, in case you cared.

As I walked away, I heard Dolores greet another valued citizen. "Can I help you."

"I don't know, Morgon, maybe I should give it up," I said as I slumped into a chair in my attorney's office. "Things have been bad enough since that whole Impapalooza fiasco, and now this? I just don't know what to do."

"I hear ya," he Morgon replied, leafing through The Form. "This is pretty irksome." He chewed on his lip, thinking. Or maybe just enjoying the flavor, I don't know.

I should explain.

Morgon's a half-gnome. He was raised in a gnome enclave until he was twelve, resulting in a slew of habits that might be considered odd (or even disgusting) by human standards. Gnomes are... different. Reclusive. Mysterious. More than a little gross. But sometimes love crosses borders in ways we'd rather not think about—hence Morgon.

Fortunately for me, he was also a decent attorney, and his weird habits had put off enough straights that his rates were low enough for my budget. Not that it was doing me any good right now.

"*Irksome*? It's insane! I literally cannot get this information. I don't even want to get this information. This is outrageous! How can they even require this?"

"Well," Morgon started, cleaning underneath one oversized bony fingernail with another, "In point of fact, they're not actually violating any privacy laws that haven't already been nullified by the courts. Really all they're asking you to do is basically be a mandatory reporter for the city. Proactively, instead of after the fact. The bigger companies, Magicorp and them, they've been doing it forever already."

"Well bully for them," I snarled, "but this is freaking *impossible* for a one-man operation to pull off, especially going back for *two years*. And last time I counted myself, there was just one of me."

Morgon shrugged. "Welcome to bureaucracy." He paused. "There's not, like, some spell you could do..."

I rolled my eyes. "No."

He heaved a sigh and flicked the fruit of his labor into the corner, then went back to paging through The Form. "Well, I don't know how I can help you then. I..." He turned another page and paused. "Hold on now."

When you're sliding off a cliff, you'll gladly clutch the thinnest spiderweb if that's all you can see. "What is it?"

"Take a look at this section right here," he said, pushing aside the first few hundred pages of The Form. "Pretty much the entire thing can be exempted by the city councilman for your district if it's, and I quote, 'of well-examined and unquestionable moral benefit to the city and community.' That's imp-speak for 'because I want to,'" he added helpfully.

"Oh," I replied. The spiderweb snapped.

Seeing the expression on my face, Morgon paused in the act of scratching his chest under his shirt. "Who's your councilman?"

"Helfter," I said, groaning.

"Ah," he said. There really wasn't any need to say more, but

Morgon didn't let that stop him. "That would be the 'Go-on-TV-and-rant-about magic, Sponsor-the-Magical-Responsibility-Act, organize-pickets-outside-Magicorp-until-they-endorse-him' Councilman Helfter, then?"

"Yes."

"Ah."

We sat in silence for a minute before Morgon spoke up again. "So I take it you regret selling that summoning orb?"

I groaned again.

Look, here's the deal. Orcs get a bad rap in pop culture, okay? Sure, they're hulking, smelly, and not that bright, but they also tend towards gentleness, and I've never known one to go out of their way to pick a fight; they actually strongly prefer to be left alone. To be honest, most of them are just looking for their next fix. They're kind of like some Libertarians that way.

An orc's absolute favorite "fix" is imp. Boiled alive, cracked open, and eaten right out of the shell. Fresh imp tastes pretty much like fresh lobster, with the added benefit of producing a relatively intense euphoria—all with only the *slightest* risk of irresistible addiction.

Orc parties, needless to say, are *legendary*.

Most humans, however, will never properly experience those parties, because imps are wicked. Not morally; imps don't have any moral agency. They're not even that smart, falling somewhere between a cow and a monkey in raw intelligence.

No, what imps have is a vicious survival mechanism. By sheer reflex, they psychically tap into whatever sounds or actions would disturb nearby creatures—actual *intelligent* creatures—and mimic that behavior.

So if a gnome were to chase an imp that got into its garden, the imp would, possibly, curse the gnome's deceased mother with the *Ghushish Va*, the Forbidden Word. If an imp starts to feel threatened and has access to markers or paint, it will sketch out the disturbing nightmares of whatever poor unfortunates are nearby. And whenever an imp gets cooked while a human stands anywhere close? Well, in that case the imps will typically mimic the sounds of horrified screams as they plunge into the boiling water. I know that's what happens, because I've been there, and it did.

Geez, some people can't even boil a *lobster* without needing psychotherapy. Try exposing them to *that*.

Again, imps aren't smart. It's just a reflex they've developed, a method of survival. There's no malicious intent; they literally lack the capacity to intend you harm when they beg for mercy in your kid sister's voice (like I said, wicked).

Anyway, orcs are immune. Nobody knows why, but imps can't sense orcs' thoughts. (Cue the jokes about orcs not having any thoughts to sense, ha ha ha, see what I meant about orcs getting a bad rap?) So the orcs just keep on rolling, boiling hundreds of imps in a night, stuffing themselves full of psychotropic goodness and in general just having a grand old time.

Now I'll admit to having a soft spot for orcs. I tend to root for the underdog (what can I say, it's an American thing), and thanks to popular books and movies, the orcs are pretty much as "underdog" as you can get right now. So a few months ago, when these orcish teenagers came into the shop just bursting with enthusiasm for this festival they were having—"Impapalooza," they called it—I just smiled and nodded. Kids are kids, no matter their race, you know? They put up some posters, left some flyers at the counter, yada yada. No worries. Until a couple of weeks later.

I was in the back of the shop when I heard the soft electronic chime indicating that someone had entered, accompanied by a low, gravelly voice. "Ey bossman!" I walked out into the room to discover an orc with *multiple* multiple piercings, studs, and twin gauges in his lower lip. A conservative orc, in other words. "*Kahdz-eesch.*"

"*Kahdz-eesch,*" I returned the traditional orcish greeting. "How can I help you?"

He glanced around the shop, rattling the assorted chains spiderwebbing across his face. "Need... what is... *Bulrum-fahs*. Orb! Orb, yah."

"Ok, sure," I responded. "What for? We have a few different kinds." I led him over to a repurposed bookcase (I'm big on the whole secondhand thing) and indicated a couple of shelves of different types of orb: Glass, crystal, obsidian, even a couple that looked like precious gemstones but were actually much more exotic (i.e. exoplanar). "You want one for scrying? Seeing far?" I put my pointer fingers by my eyes and pushed them out to arms' length. When you run a shop popular with immigrants you tend to up your charades game pretty quickly.

He shook his head. "*Khu*. No. Need..." He scrunched up his face, giving me a fresh perspective on his eyelid piercing. "Eat. *Ehmfaz*. Grr... Imps! Eat Imps." His face split into a wide grin. It was frankly terrifying.

"Got it. You need a summoning orb." I picked up a milky white sphere about the size of a tennis ball. "How about this one? You should be able to get at least ten imps out of it." I spread the fingers of my other hand wide, closed them into a fist and spread them again. "What's the word... *Dhezhact*."

He shook his head again. "*Khu*." He ambled over to the counter like a miniature bulldozer and returned with a flyer, gesturing violently at it. "Imp! Imp! Palooza!"

It was a flyer for Impapalooza. (Side note: whoever taught orcs the suffix "-palooza" should be ashamed of themselves.) This guy needed something that would stand up to summoning hundreds of imps. Maybe thousands.

I raised my eyebrows. "Oh! Oh wow. Yeah." I set the white orb down. "I don't have one that big, but I can get it in a week. Seven days. *Schem*."

He sighed. It was like the exhaust from a garbage truck. "Fast? Fast?"

I tried not to wrinkle my nose. "Well, I could expedite it... but that's expensive." I hated to pass up on the business, but I did want to help the guy. "Have you tried looking at Magicorp?"

He snarled. It was almost as bad as the grin. "Magicorp... *Khu*." His voice ramped up past gravelly, acquiring a couple of boulders and maybe a dead armadillo. "They say... *Khu*. They say... orc... No good look." He scrunched up his eyebrows. "What is 'bad press?'"

Ah. Politics. Image. Public opinion. It's a realm far more confusing and arcane than that of magic, if you ask me. It's not something I've ever really been interested in.

"Well, I can get your orb for you. It will be expensive. Many..." I moved my hands in a series of wide circles, "...dollars."

He scrabbled around in his loincloth. "*Khu Dalsh*." *No worries*. "I have." He pulled out his hand. "Visa or Mastercard?"

Three days later, he walked out my shop door with an enormous smile and a jade sphere the size of a grapefruit.

Two days after that, all Hell broke loose.

To clarify: not literal Hell. That's an entirely different discussion, one which I'm more than open to having some other time. Imps come from the Netherscape, which—although it is frequently described as hellish—is not the same thing at all.

No, what actually happened is that somehow (and no one who knows how it happened would ever actually admit to it), Impapalooza got out of hand. *Way* out of hand. About a hundred fifty imps managed to escape, making their way to nearby homes, parks, shops, offices, and other miscellaneous non-orcish institutions, where they promptly panicked and terrorized the locals with sights and sounds from the locals' most horrifying nightmares. And that's not even the worst part. Several of the Nether-escapees managed to drown themselves in the reservoir, tainting the city's water supply with psychotropic substances. People of all races found themselves unexpectedly in a very, *very* good mood (well, the ones not being terrorized by imps). Now, that's great if you're sitting quietly at home, but not so much if you're working with heavy machinery, or driving a school bus, or performing open-heart surgery.

To sum up: More than five thousand citizens wound up needing medical attention for some reason or another due to Impapalooza. I don't think anyone actually *died*, but a few did suffer severe injury from what authorities benignly termed "secondary effects." Many more came down from their involuntary highs only to blink stupidly and then demand to know what had just happened.

Like I said to Morgon, it was a fiasco.

The magic words here (not literally) are "Something Must Be Done." Whenever something salacious happens and the public puts down the gossip rags long enough to pay attention to the news for a brief second, Something Must Be Done. Whenever emotions run so high that intelligence is dumped in favor of reaction, Something Must Be Done.

Whenever there's political hay to be made, guess what? Yep. Something Must Be Done.

"Something" in this case had been the Magical Responsibility Act, an intrusive and far-reaching move by the City Council to keep closer tabs on the supernatural sector of the economy—and to give greater power (and funding) to law enforcement in order to "combat the new magical threat facing our region." It was cheered on with lots of overwrought fanfare and fawning publicity. Ringmaster to the whole circus was Councilman Dennis Helfter, the sponsor of the Act. It was great for him; it catapulted his reelection campaign to the forefront of every local discussion, and everybody was asking him to run for mayor next term. Problem was, it was also choking the life out of the local independent magic shop owners. E.g. me.

I'll be honest, I didn't follow the news of the Magical Responsibility Act closely before it passed. I tried to read it a couple of times, but the language was so dense and arbitrary I mostly couldn't even tell what it was saying. Now I can read magical literature in English, German, and Gnomish, so it's not like I'm stupid or anything. Politics just has an arcane vocabulary all its own, and the average schlub doesn't have enough time to figure it all out. And like I said before, I've never been interested in trying to figure out the whole political scene.

Not to mention, at the time I was mostly concerned with whether or not I had any liability for Impapalooza.

"Absolutely not," Morgon had said. "*You* sold the orb lawfully, totally in compliance with all regulations, et cetera, et cetera. *They* used it in full accordance with all legal guidelines... it was totally legit, even if it was totally gross."

Considering what I'd seen him doing with his nose earlier that day, I didn't figure he had much room to talk about *gross*.

He continued, counting his points on each gnarly fingernail as he listed them: "The city gave them all necessary permits for the festival, *including* a guarantee of security. The orcs even paid off-duty cops to watch the perimeter, eh? Lastly, and most importantly," he grinned, "No one knows you sold it to them, right?"

"Well, no..."

"There you go, then." He turned his hands palm-up. "You have nothing to worry about."

But that had been months ago. Today, I was worried.

I was still worried as I sat in the waiting room outside Councilman Helfter's office. Whichever interior decorator had inflicted the multi-taupe travesty on the municipal building down the street had not been allowed within spitting distance of this one. The chairs were plush and comfortable. The walls were a very elegant combination of deep blue paint and tasteful wallpaper. The desk was certainly an antique; rich varnish and dark wood lent it an air of refined opulence. Behind the desk sat an attractive young woman. She was playing with her iPhone.

In this room, brash capital letters had not been allowed to band together and colonize individual signs. Rather, they had been forcibly dispersed and sent to live on separate notices, maximum one per word. Even then, their harsh, blocky edges had been chipped and smoothed away until what remained were genteel, refined capital letters more suitable for a councilman's waiting room.

There was not a single exclamation point to be found anywhere.

I had been sitting in plush comfort for the past forty-five minutes, growing progressively more irritable as the digitized sounds of flying birds and exploding candy assaulted my frazzled nerves. More than once I almost stood up to leave, but I never quite got there, mostly because I literally had no other option if I wanted to keep my shop open.

I had tried to fill out The Form. It was impossible. The questions —the few that even made intelligible sense—were so comprehensive and intrusive that I couldn't even get through the first section. That would be section One of Thirty-Seven. If I wanted to stay in business, I had to somehow convince the Councilman to help me out.

Finally I stood up and wandered over to the young woman behind the desk. The brass nameplate sitting there read *Marcie*.

I cleared my throat. "Excuse me—"

She didn't even look up. "The Councilman is busy. Please take a seat."

A set-up line like that? I couldn't help myself. "Where should I take it?"

Yeah, *then* you bet she looked up, annoyance in her expression. "Hmm. You're the magic shop guy, right?"

"Uh, yeah." I coughed. "Yes, I am."

She just watched me for a second, then shrugged, going back to her phone. "You're wasting your time."

I was taken aback. "What?"

"Whatever it is you want, you're wasting your time." She sniffed, swiped at her screen. "The Councilman doesn't like all the messed-up stuff you guys do. There's, like, zero chance he'll listen to whatever you want to say."

I bristled; this was exactly the kind of prejudicial crap that had helped lead to the passage of that stupid Act in the first place. I took a couple of deep breaths before trusting myself to respond.

"That's an interesting point of view," I said levelly. "So, what kind of messed-up stuff are you talking about now?"

"Oh, you know," she waved a hand briefly before tapping her screen. "All that crazy voodoo and messing with dead body parts and stuff."

Okay. *This* is one of the reasons I started my shop in the first place.

Here's the deal: The universe is a big, incredibly complicated machine. It's got a jillion whirling parts all mixed together, bashing against each other. You hit *this* thing and it moves *that* direction, do *this* and get *that* reaction, etc. Magic? It's just a handy way of pushing the universe's buttons. If you want a certain response from your machine, you just push a certain sequence of buttons. That's literally all there is to it.

That being said, of course the universe is complicated. So throughout the ages different people have discovered a bunch of different random button combinations to get more-or-less the result they're after. Some of these combinations can be... distasteful.

You know, crazy voodoo. Messing with dead body parts. "Stuff."

The kicker is, everything that can be accomplished with all of that "stuff" can also be done via much simpler and cleaner methods. Burning a ton of incense and dancing widdershins around a mulberry bush in your skivvies at midnight *might* protect your turnip crop from beetles... but I can sell you a six-inch statue that will do the same if you just bury it anywhere in your yard, at whatever time of day, wearing whatever you want. It's not even an *obscene* statue. (Those cost extra.)

Anything more complicated is like super-gluing a butter knife to a weedeater, then trying to use it to loosen a screw. Why even bother, when somebody like me can just sell you a screwdriver? Or even teach you how to make your own?

Making magic simple is kind of my passion. So whenever I run into superstitious ignorance, I try and correct it. Gently. Usually.

"I can see how you would think that," I replied. "Actually, I don't really know much about voodoo" (this was technically a lie), "and dead bodies gross me out" (absolutely true). "But magic doesn't have anything to do with all that. Really, it just comes down to knowing how to push buttons."

Marcie was looking back up at me, interested in spite of herself. "Buttons?"

"Sure." I indicated her phone. "You want to call somebody with that thing, you just press the right buttons in the right order. Magic is the same way, only with the entire world instead of just a phone. Watch."

She leaned back, probably more than a little nervous as I tapped my glasses and whispered. "*Oculus.*"

(Forgive an aspirational geek.)

Immediately, wavy colored lines of light appeared to my eyes, gently flowing back and forth as if blown by an invisible wind. These were streams of aether, the source of magic in our plane. Red, Blue, and Green were the most prominent, and the only ones that I typically used. Other colors were for more specialized stuff that I didn't usually bother with.

I contorted the fingers of my right hand into the specific shape that would attract the essence of Green aether. Slowly at first, but picking up speed as they moved, several lines of glowing Green gathered around my hand. I extended a finger and began to trace a matrix in the air, creating a frame to hold the construct I had in mind. I glanced over at the desk. About six inches tall, almost three inches wide, slightly thicker than a piece of paper. Got it.

With my left hand, I formed another specific shape, drawing Blue aether on that side. Once I had enough, I applied it to the matrix of Green I now held in my right hand.

Marcie gasped. I smiled to myself, just a little. From her point of view, she just witnessed what appeared to be motes of light coalescing in my hand, transforming from a nebulous cloud into a familiar shape.

I finished off by calling just a touch of Red to my left hand and igniting my new construct with a trace amount of light. I whispered "*Obscura,*" and the streams of aether faded from my sight.

Marcie was staring, eyes wide with wonder, at what I was now holding—a near-perfect replica of her iPhone, complete with glowing screen and gold glittery case.

"I can't believe that!" She looked at me suspiciously. "Is it real?"

"Well, it's not an illusion," I told her as I thumped the case.

"But no, it won't work the way a real iPhone would. It's basically a fancy brick." I tossed it up and down, pleased at how solid this one was. "Yours has a ton of fancy microchips and whatnot in it, plus all the programming. I could spend years of effort replicating all that, but it would be stupidly expensive and time-consuming. It's easier and cheaper just to buy one made in the factory in China—"

"Marcie, what's going on out here?"

Councilman Helfter stood in the doorway to his office, the perfect portrait of a politician, right down to his pinstripe suit and American flag pin.

And the hair. A half-gallon of product, combed all the way over to one side. I don't know what it is about politicians and used-car salesmen that causes them to gravitate towards that hairstyle.

And he was tall. Of course.

He smiled, but his eyes radiated suspicion.

Marcie flushed. "Oh, nothing, councilman! This is just—"

"I know who this is, Marcie. Come on in, son."

I pulled a tab of Green aether I had intentionally left dangling from the corner of the construct so that I could find it without reactivating my glasses. The faux-iPhone dissolved into a glowing cloud, dissipating back into the aether streams.

I followed the Councilman into his office and he closed the door behind us.

"What you're asking is impossible, I'm afraid." Councilman Helfter had barely let me get my request out. "My constituents, you understand, are quite concerned about the growing influence of all this mumbo-jumbo in our city. How could I explain to them that I was not only not protecting them, but I was actually making an *exception* for someone to flout the very letter of the law? No, no, it's quite impossible." He never stopped smiling throughout the vicious onslaught of oratory.

"Councilman, please," I begged, "I provide a valuable service to the community. My tools and charms have helped many practitioners and their families—"

"Yes, yes, I know, families, workers, etc." He interrupted me, smile still plastered on his face. Was that a nervous twitch under his eye? "But mine and my constituents' concern is how many *others* could gain access to the services of under-the-radar shops like yours, hmm? I'm sure you've heard of the Warlock problem we face?"

I gritted my teeth. Some genius gang-bangers had decided that magic was the next great weapon in their turf wars. So far, pretty much all they'd accomplished was blowing themselves up, but to hear the mayor and police chief tell it, our city was one spell away from becoming ground zero for magical Armageddon.

Seeing the expression on my face, the Councilman sighed. "Listen," he said. "I'll be frank. Months ago we had that terrible imps escapade, you may remember..."

I nodded guiltily.

"As a matter of fact, I myself was affected by that tainted water. It's all I can do to forget it..." He trailed off looking into the distance, then appeared to remember where he was. Glaring at me, he continued. "We *cannot* risk another catastrophe like that one! So I am sorry if the requirements of the law seem onerous to you, but there will be no exceptions for *any* magical business!"

His phone buzzed. Marcie's voice on the other end: "Councilman, your package is here."

"Ah!" He practically leapt up from his seat. His eye twitched again. "Thank you for your time. Good luck in your future endeavors."

And my shop was dead.

"Maybe it's for the best," said Morgon from the other end of the phone. I was slumped in the front seat of my car outside the City Council offices, too depressed to drive. "You can get back into practicing, maybe some consulting?"

"Meh."

"Hey, has it occurred to you that it's super ironic that you're the one who sold that orb, and without that orb this Magical Responsibility Act thing would never have happened?"

Most people would know better than to ask that, but that's Morgon for you.

I hung up on him.

I'm not sure how long I sat there, but it was approaching sundown when a man emerged from the Council offices hefting a medium-sized wooden crate.

Despite myself, I was intrigued. Doubly so when he turned his head and I realized it was Councilman Helfter.

I'll be honest, I'm not sure what I was thinking. Some part of me was straight-up refusing to let it go; I'm still a little hazy on the details. What I am sure of is that while he was wrestling that crate into his trunk, I gathered Green aether in my hand and formed three small constructs, tethering them to me, then flinging them out my open window and towards his car.

They sunk into his bumper and door, enspelling his car with a simple tracking function I had built into them. As long as I stayed close, I would be able to sense the direction and distance of the car—which I did, as I followed him for the next fifteen minutes.

Councilman Helfter lived in a pretty nice house in a pretty nice neighborhood. I mean, not *too* nice; after all, he was in my district. Still. Two-story, full brick, wrought-iron fence. It was a nice house.

I drove past while he was struggling with that crate. He froze when he heard my car and looked up, glaring; I was hunched up in my jacket, so I was pretty sure he couldn't recognize me. To be safe, I drove around for a few more minutes before going back.

When I got back, his car was parked in the driveway on the other side of the wrought-iron gate. There were no lights on in the house. No one appeared to be present—just me and my failure.

I sighed. *This is stupid.* I just needed to let it all go. I called to my constructs, pulling them from the car. I activated my glasses to make sure no trace of magic remained in the Councilman's car—and froze.

Over the house, an *enormous* vortex of Black aether swirled madly, forming a funnel cloud, which tapered down, down—directly into Councilman Helfter's garage.

Okay, so Black is one of those colors I don't use much. There's not a lot of it, and what little exists is all entangled with energy in the Netherscape, so unless you have business on that plane you're better off leaving it alone.

It's also the *last* thing you should find pouring into the home of a notoriously anti-magic politician.

The gate was locked, but that was no problem. A simple construct of Green and Blue let me float right over the fence. I approached the side door of the garage with caution, but I needn't have bothered. The door was unlocked, and as I opened it I saw that the good Councilman was quite preoccupied.

Seriously. It was pathetic.

He was wearing a black robe, streaked with what could've been meant to be blood, but actually looked more like red paint. He was holding a twisted dagger in one hand, and a grimoire in the other— one of those absolute trash spell books that pick the single most convoluted and ineffective method of doing magic and present it like some Secret Truth.

On a small table rested a most unpleasant collection of paraphernalia: a skunk pelt, a Pyrex bowl filled with what looked to be chicken innards, a sputtering yellowed wax candle. Helfter encapsulated the complete caricature of everything I most hated: the mindlessly ritualistic, meaninglessly complicated wizard.

Even worse, he *sucked* at it.

While I watched, he bent in close towards the grimoire, trying to pronounce the Latin-ish strings of gibberish that passed for magic among the mentally weak. "*Quot peedes viva...* Uh, *viventem in ten- ten- tenebris, ita ex,* ah geez, *su... supermundanae! portal...* Um."

He was so caught up in trying to read that he bumped the table, knocking over the candle and spilling wax everywhere. He just looked at it forlornly. "Aw, crap."

I swear, I would have busted out laughing except for what I happened to notice right at that point. On the floor, next to the spilled candle wax, sat a large sphere, somewhat bigger than a basketball. It had the color and opacity of a black pearl, but I knew it for what it was: a *very* powerful summoning orb. The one I sold the orcs was capable of pulling in thousands of imps; this one could pull in a *hundred* thousand. Easy.

But that's not the bad part.

This orb had a much larger limiting threshold, meaning more exoplanar material could be summoned at once.

Meaning the Black aether was manifesting as something much bigger than an imp.

And Helfter had zero control over the thing.

We were in serious danger.

"Helfter!" I shouted, just as the orb pulsed, a single wave of deep purple.

Helfter yelped and sprang for the table. He came up with a Smith & Wesson 9mm, which he promptly aimed at my chest. I mean, I'm flattered, but I was not the biggest threat in the garage just then. "What are you doing here!?" he screeched.

"Forget that! Look!"

I pointed frantically at the orb, just as a horrifying shadow jumped from it.

Like an imp, this thing had nine legs and jointed carapace.

Unlike an imp, this thing had enormous jaws and sharp fangs. It was also roughly the size of a horse. It approached us, snarling in harmony with itself.

I *really* hate monsters with multiple voice boxes. They just sound creepy.

Helfter yelped and spun, emptying the Smith & Wesson into the monster. Well, *near* the monster. He wasn't a very good shot. I sincerely hoped none of those rounds hit any of the neighbors' houses, but I wouldn't have bet a dollar on it.

Still, a few bullets managed to bounce off the creature's carapace. "What is that thing?" he screamed while repeatedly pulling the trigger. At least I think that's what he said. By the time the jerk was out of ammo, I was pretty much deaf from the gunfire.

Regardless, I wouldn't have had time to explain before we died. We were stuck in a garage with a *shattenhund*. A fearsome hunter, always hungry. Virtually indestructible. Also incidentally one of the reasons you don't go vacationing in the Netherscape. (Other good reasons: poisonous atmosphere, boiling-point temperatures, no room service.)

Loves human flesh. *Yum.*

So, there was no time to explain, as the *shattenhund* leapt for us...

...but there was plenty of time to press buttons.

I had summoned my little constructs before the monster even appeared. While Helfter had been doing his Stormtrooper imperson-ation, I took the opportunity to siphon off a little of the Black aether swirling through the air, enspelling my own constructs with a very specific piece of magic.

Now, as the *shattenhund* prepared to make us monster-chow, my constructs penetrated his carapace, activating the core spell integral to every summoning orb.

"It's all about knowing which buttons to push," I whispered to myself.

Time froze. I could see the horrified expression in Helfter's face, the slavering maw of the *shattenhund*, so desperate to make a meal of us...

...the tiny ripples of my magic diffusing throughout the monster as my little constructs flitted away...

Time returned.

Instantly, the *shattenhund* fractured into a hundred tiny splinters, each one frozen in mid-air for a split second before streaking towards the summoning orb and disappearing with a loud, echoing screech. I gasped and bent over, panting with shock and effort. The ringing in my ears subsided. A couple of seconds later I stood upright and turned to face Helfter.

He had the gun pointed straight at my chest.

I sighed. "Don't be a moron, Helfter. It's empty."

He blinked a couple of times, looked at the Smith & Wesson like he'd never seen a firearm before, and looked back up at me with a snarl on his face. "What are you doing here? Get out!" His hair product was failing him; that perfect part was flopping down into his eyes.

I gestured at the orb. "In case you just missed it, I just saved your life, Helfter. Now tell me *very quickly* what you thought you were doing here." I called the constructs to my hand, infusing them with Red aether until they glowed like fire, letting them hover there menacingly. Well, it probably looked menacing. I'm assuming. "Before I have to ask again."

He tried to stare me down, but he had no other play here, and we both knew it. His gaze dropped to the floor.

"I... just... needed some more." He said. "I could only ever get one or two, so I thought if I had a better orb..."

I looked over at the massive dark sphere. Ah-ha. "It was the imps," I said. "After you got a taste from the water..."

He looked back up, shamefaced. "After that, well, I got curious," he sighed. "But once I had the real thing... I just couldn't forget about it. But if the voters ever found out, I'd be through! Finished! My reputation, tarnished forever!" His voice became, well... wheedling, I guess. "Please, you can't tell anyone!"

I held up my hands, letting my constructs dissipate. "Councilman Helfter, I'll do you one better. I'll make you the deal of your dreams. You can hire me on contract. I will supply you with a dozen imps each week, using that orb right there. I'll charge you fair market price for my labor, plus a twenty percent fee for my 'special services' in the area of discretion. You will never touch that orb or try *any* sort of magic without my direct supervision. Fair?"

He breathed deeply. Seen up close, he wasn't really that tall. "That sounds superb." He extended a hand.

I met it with a thick roll of paper. He looked up, puzzled.

"I just need your signature on a couple of things," I grinned.

After he wrote his name in a few very important places, a thought occurred to me. "Councilman, do you need help preparing the imps?

They're going to say and do some extremely disturbing things every time you cook them. You might be a little bit, ah, repulsed."

A sly look crept into his face. "Son, I'm in politics. I do repulsive things with a smile on my face every day of my life."

The next morning at 8:37 A.M. I dropped The Form back onto that taupe-colored desk with a *THUD*. "Here you go, Dolores," I said with a wide smile. She just stared at me. "Fully exempted, signed by Councilman Helfter himself."

As I walked away, my phone rang. It was Morgon. I answered.

"So?" he asked.

"I worked it all out," I replied. "It turns out that politics is actually a lot like magic. If you want to get anything done, first you have to figure out which buttons to push."

RULE OF THREE

MICHAEL CONNON

Christine definitely had a spring in her step today. The wheels of her suitcase rattling behind her heels on the brittle November pavement, she steered a course for a small row of shops on a very ordinary street in her small country town.

Not yet five o'clock but a brooding sky was making its intentions clear and the streets were almost empty. Only the Mini Mart on the corner was doing any business, serving last-minute supplies to stragglers before they scurried home to barricade themselves in for the night.

She came to a stop outside one of the shops, nestled between a vendor of confectionery and one of ladieswear, and looked on it with new eyes. No lights were visible; in fact the place looked closed, but she knew otherwise. The display in the dingy window seemed designed to be as unappealing as possible: faded books, thick tallow candles and vials of essential oils, poorly arranged and barely visible in the gloom. But that would change. She pushed on the door and entered with a jangle of Tibetan wind chimes.

Inside, greetings cards, handmade writing paper, candles, oils, incense, dried herbs and cheap jewellery jostled for space with rails of colourful, hippyish clothing. A bookcase at the back of the shop supported a broad selection of titles ranging from simple self-improvement to the deeply esoteric. Witch dolls on broomsticks hung, suspended in mid-flight, from the ceiling while a basket of stuffed black-cat toys made up the rest of the stock. The shop's sole occupant barely stirred, just continued reading her gossip magazine by the light of a small lamp in the corner by the till, the requisite huge mug of coffee to hand.

Christine forged a path through the clutter, ploughing through rails of pashminas and scarves, ducking beneath dangling dreamcatchers while steering a course between boxes of unpacked stock on the floor, step by careful step.

'Shop!' she called out sarcastically. 'Anybody here?'

Shirley didn't rise to the bait any more than usual, just muttered a greeting and turned a page without looking up.

Having successfully navigated her way through the sea of clutter, Christine felt on the back wall for the light switch.

'How was the course?' asked Shirley drily.

'Brilliant!' Christine flicked on the lights. 'I'm chock full of ideas.'

Shirley winced, whether from the unbidden brightness or otherwise. Her severe countenance and severe jet-black bob contrasted sharply with her younger sister's curly, strawberry-blonde locks and ready smile. (Those visiting the shop invariably hoped to be served by Christine and it wasn't unusual to see potential customers loitering outside to see exactly who was at the till before daring to enter.)

'We're doing loads wrong, Shirl,' Christine observed mournfully. 'That course has really opened my eyes.' She made to move a display stand only for the top half to come away in her hand, a crusty rind of dry tape at its end testament to a long-standing repair.

The two Madeley sisters had opened the Krafty Koven a decade ago with money left by their grandmother, most of that time turning a profit - but only just. Formerly a glass and china shop, now listed in the local trade directory under both 'New Age Paraphernalia' and 'Craft Supplies', it offered a wide range of items – it just didn't sell that many of them.

Like all of the town's traders, the Koven depended heavily for its survival on the bus trips which ran from March to September, daily depositing their cargoes of hungry, thirsty passengers – mostly women of a certain age – with plenty of money and insatiable appetites for cream teas and knick-knacks.

In the off-season, locals looking for an unusual birthday card or the impulse purchase of a fragrant-oil burner made up the typical daily sale. Teenage goths from neighbouring villages made Saturday pilgrimages in search of something different or a cheap occult thrill, but as for passing trade, mostly it just passed.

'We'll soon get this place back on its feet,' Christine said, 'but things are going to change. They *have* to,' she added decisively and headed for their living quarters behind the shop.

· · ·

Change. Shirley shivered. Fair enough, something had to be done and if anyone could turn this place around it was her little sis. But that said, she didn't have to *enjoy* it, did she?

Pulling her cardigan tighter, she took a comforting sip from her mug and turned another page. In the pages of these trashy magazines (for which she maintained a sizeable standing order at the Mini Mart) Shirley found the evidence she needed to confirm her judgment on humanity. When she insisted that most people were a waste of space, it was from precisely those pages that she accrued the ammunition to fight her corner, to add bite to her bile.

As for Christine, she insisted on believing that a grain of good lay at the heart of everyone. *Even in the face of bitter experience.* Shirley curled her lip at the thought. Christine's school days had marked her for life - unhappy, troubled years they'd been. If not for Shirley, who knows what might have happened to her? And yet still she suffered a crippling lack of confidence that savagely clipped the wings of her true potential.

'Kettle's boiled,' she called over her shoulder.

'Yes, Shirley, I know,' came the voice from the kitchen. 'It always is, isn't it? It always is...'

That evening, ensconced in her favourite armchair with fresh magazine and coffee, Shirley knew something was up. After showering and eating, Christine had been a whirl of activity. Although Shirley pointedly refused to show any interest as her sister repeatedly passed through to the shop or to retrieve something from a drawer or cupboard before disappearing back up to her room, she was quietly pleased. For long hours the clatter of a computer keyboard and occasional whir of a printer made their way down the stairs while Shirley read on. When around 10.30 she decided to call it a day, Christine showed no sign of slowing.

Lying in bed, Shirley was lulled by the gentle hum of quiet intensity from the next room. She'd known the course would do Christine the world of good, had even exercised her subtle steering hand more than once to ensure she attended despite the customary self-doubts. *At least* one *of us believes in her,* she thought. As she drifted off, it was with a satisfied smile that Shirley listened to a wind of change blowing outside her door.

On a crisp midwinter's morning such as this, no-one was expecting to do much business. Yet Christine brushed past a half-woken Shirley at the foot of the stairs on her way to open up, a huge cardboard box in her arms. It looked like she'd been up for hours already, making good her promised start on re-arranging the stock and displays.

'What do you think?' she asked breezily of her blinking sister.

The change was dramatic. The whole shop was much brighter for a start and far less stuffed with the unsold and the unsellable. A carpet had revealed itself between the display stands, allowing customers the chance to actually browse for once, and the overall impression was of a much larger space than before. In the air the familiar overtures of mould and patchouli had been superseded by furniture polish and Windolene. The improved illumination came courtesy of the removal of the age-old heavy grey curtain between window and till, revealing for the first time in many years the street beyond.

'I'm sending the kaftans to charity – we're never going to shift them – and I'm going to do the window out this afternoon,' Christine went on.

Shirley peered carefully over into the newly-exposed realm of dust and dead flies; at the candles and the uninspiring spread of inspirational texts with badly-faded covers. Cobwebs at least added an unintended touch of authenticity.

'But Chris, who's going to see it? It's the middle of November; the bus trips don't start till Easter, nobody's got any money and we're stuck on a back street in a shitty little town.'

'Ah, no, actually, our location's perfect,' Christine corrected sharply, determined to head off any defeatist talk right from the beginning of the new era. 'We've got a line of sight not only from this street but a lot of Market Street as well, thanks to the Square. We just have to make the most of it, get a new sign made and have an eye-catching display.' She smiled encouragingly, as though in possession of all the answers. Nothing was going to burst her bubble today.

Shirley squinted out across the newly-unveiled vista. If nothing else, her perch at the till would now command a superb view of the town's comings and goings.

'Besides,' continued Christine, 'we need a nice clean showcase for our brand-new line – the one that's going to make us a fortune!' She giggled fit to burst as she set down the box she'd been carrying onto the counter and opened it.

'I've been dying to show you these all morning! You see, what we need are new and unique products, so I thought to myself, what can *we* offer that no one else can? – it's what they call a Unique Selling Point – and then I came up with these!' She promptly pulled out two bags from the box and held them up triumphantly, the *Ta-dah!* unvoiced but implicit.

'Spell kits! Everything you need's included. There's three varieties to start with: Love, Luck and Money.'

Shirley took one and turned it over in her hand. A polythene bag of small bits and pieces hung from a brightly decorated card stapled across the top. Among the colourful shooting stars and hearts were the words "KOVEN KITS – D.I.Y MAGIC!" and below that, "LOVE POTION". The whole package looked thoroughly professional.

'You see, it fits in with today's culture; people want quick and convenient,' Christine enthused, 'It saves people buying the products separately and having to have the books and all the know-how. It's magic in a bag! Hang on, I like that,' and paused to make a note in an open jotter on the counter.

'Well, maybe as a novelty....' Shirley sniffed, belying how impressed she truly was. 'They might catch on, I suppose.'

'It's not a *novelty*, Shirley, it's a serious product!' Affronted, Christine snatched back the bag and held it protectively for a moment before opening it carefully and spreading out the contents across the counter: a little bag of herbs, a green candle and some pieces of paper.

'Look, everything you need's in the bag. You just recite the incantation from the card,' she held up a piece of green card bearing a Latin inscription, 'while you burn the herbs and then the card in the candle provided. Full instructions are here,' she unfolded a sheet of paper. 'Completely foolproof!'

'It'll need to be,' sneered her sister, 'Some of them round here don't know their left from their right.'

'If they can use iPhones and Facebook, they can light a candle, Shirl. And it costs us nothing to try it out because we stock all these things already.'

'But £8.99?' Shirley picked up the packaging again. 'Isn't that a bit steep?'

'It's a premium product. If you price too low, people lose faith in the quality.' Thus did Christine neatly summarise the theory of price placement.

'But what's to stop someone knocking them out cheaper?'

Christine sighed patiently and leaned across the counter, carefully dropping her tone and casting a meaningful look into her sister's dark eyes.

'Because *ours* will work, Shirl. That's our USP,' and she tapped the back of the header card in Shirley's hands. Sure enough, there were the words "GUARANTEED TO BRING YOU LOVE OR YOUR MONEY BACK!"

'Think about it,' she went on, carefully holding Shirley's gaze. 'You and I put the kits together. So as long as the customer follows the instructions, they'll work, because it's our *will* and their *intention*. You should know that.'

If the penny had dropped any harder, Mrs. Hickson would have heard it next door. A comprehending 'Ah...' was about all Shirley could manage as a list of objections began building in her mind but these she quickly shook off in the face of her sister's determination and obvious enthusiasm. *Actually*, she thought, *little sis could be onto a winner here*. But she certainly wasn't going to admit it and so made do with a non-committal, tight-lipped smile.

With impeccable timing the wind chimes chose that very moment to herald the entry of the day's first customer. Casting a playful grin at her sister, Christine picked up a 'Money Magic' kit and approached Mrs Daly who it seemed was in search of a birthday card for her granddaughter.

It was a delight to watch Christine handle the old lady, discussing the hand-made nature of the cards, the well-being of the grand-daughter and the changes to the shop before pressing upon her the kit, with their compliments, amid a glittering spiel about exciting new products. Shirley watched, silently impressed, outwardly impassive, as her sister displayed all of her natural gifts and charm. But by the time the chimes tolled Mrs. Daly's departure, Shirley simply couldn't help herself.

'So *that's* what they taught you, is it? Giving stock away?' she chided.

'Yes, actually, it is. Endorsement by word of mouth is like free advertising – better, in fact – because people trust their friends and neighbours more than adverts. Mrs Daly goes to the bingo, the social club, the day centre; there's nowhere she doesn't get to.' And with a shrug that suggested it was all so obvious if only you put your mind to it, added brightly, 'You'll see!'

And she was right. When Mrs Daly won a modest amount on a scratch card she told everyone in the Mini Mart about Christine's gift and by the weekend it was the talk of the town's extensive network of senior citizenry. Three days after purchasing a 'Lucky Stars' kit, Miss Davison won a year's supply of cat food in a magazine competition. Such things do not go unnoticed in a small community. By the time Helen Davies bought a 'Love Potion' and met a nice young man at a night class, not a person remained who didn't think something was afoot.

～

By the following Friday the first batch had sold out – even at Christine's premium price – and best of all, they didn't have one single return. Christine immediately decreed that every spare moment was to be spent making up kits on tea trays, something observed only in the breach by Shirley, but at least the sisters began to spend an enjoyable hour together before bed each night working away at the dining table building up stock.

After the first phase, Christine had explained at length, it was necessary to capitalise on their initial success by quickly expanding the range of kits. She spoke with the zealous passion of the convert, an initiate into the hidden doctrines of the Chamber of Commerce. You had to keep it fresh, she insisted, in order to keep people interested. Know your market. Do your research.

During Christine's abundant evangelical outbursts, Shirley had taken to muttering, 'Yes, boss,' with a tug of her neat fringe while remaining thoroughly engrossed in true-life tittle-tattle. She thought her sister was sounding more and more like a PowerPoint presentation by the day, her every pronouncement delivered by bullet point.

Still, she'd never known Christine so happy. Lately she'd been completely irrepressible, seemed to bounce everywhere she went, emitting ideas in all directions with every bound. In all of this Shirley took great but silent pleasure, not least because Christine's success was well-deserved and long overdue. She even looked on with approval at her sister's purchase of the odd little luxury – one day a tasteful blouse, another a small CD player – nothing extravagant of course; that just wouldn't be Christine.

In the run-up to Christmas they sold hundreds of kits and the range stood at eight varieties. One day in late December Christine conceived the idea of a hangover recovery kit – 'Hair of the Cat' – which had them both beavering away late into the night but which sold immensely well over the New Year period.

As the year turned, the range expanded to twelve with yet more lined up for a Spring launch. One of these was to be an exam success kit, a variation on the existing luck kit; soundings from the Saturday teens and a few free samples around the time of the mock exams boded well.

Meanwhile, several well-placed magazine adverts had been attracting numerous enquiries from overseas and an eBay presence had doubled sales overnight. As a result, a website of their own quickly became a top priority.

'I think Gran would be proud of what we've done,' Christine announced one quiet January afternoon. She sat with a tray on her knee, making up kits, periodically gazing out of the window dreamily while Shirley sat at the till, customarily occupied.

Christine particularly valued these afternoon conversations; the chance to talk, to flesh out her ideas, her feelings and thoughts. Invariably one-sided affairs, she found in them all the benefits of talking to herself with none of the attendant embarrassment.

'We're only doing what she used to do, really. People came to her for help; we've just updated it, haven't we?' There was no reply. Shirley seemed to be having one of those difficult days, common enough, when the sarcasm was turned up to eleven and her sporadic utterances seemed more enigmatic than usual. Things had moved quickly, Christine understood, and she was worried her sister might feel a little left out.

'Of course, you were always Gran's favourite, Shirl. You took it all so seriously, read all the books and practiced all the time. She liked that. I was never very good at... well, that sort of thing.'

A group of children passed on their way home from school and a couple of them waved at Shirley who, colouring noticeably, discreetly returned the greeting. Christine laughed. 'Ah, you're going soft!' Shirley snorted derisively and went back to her magazine.

It was an open secret that the Saturday crowd of goth and emo kids quite liked Shirley, were much less afraid to approach her than many of their parents might have been. A small number of them were drawn to her, the more sensitive ones usually, sharing her penchant for black cardigans and her dry wit. Then there were the practitioners amongst them, the keen students in awe of her rumoured proficiency.

And though Shirley would never admit it, Christine knew that she liked them. Each had the blessing of a blank canvas, she would say, free to sketch out whatever destinies they could imagine for themselves so long as they could avoid the spoiling strokes of lesser talents. For these were important years; get them wrong and the cost could be great, the instabilities created injurious to both innocent and guilty alike, generation after generation. Which was why, in Shirley's creed, the inviolable principle was *balance*.

'They're not a bad bunch on the whole,' Christine offered with a smile.

'Better than the shower we had to put up with,' Shirley spat, more fiercely than intended.

She'd spoken recklessly and instantly regretted it, saw how Christine seemed to shrink before her eyes; knew that two decades on, emotions were still raw. Christine's schooldays at the hands of that Taylor girl had taken her to the brink; dark days that tested them both and proved the seat of today's insecurities.

For a long moment the silence owned them both, transporting them to another – almost certainly the same – place. Oddly, it was Christine who pulled out of it first.

'It's a more frightening world, mind,' she decided eventually. 'So many more dangers out there now... I just hope they've all got someone to look out for them.'

'Like a guardian angel?' Shirley suggested carefully.

Christine barely heard; she made no direct response, merely set down her tray and stood abruptly, drawing herself to her full height with a deep breath before sauntering casually to the far wall. By the time she got there the bounce was unmistakably back.

'I've been thinking...' she stroked the wall contemplatively as she spoke. 'Why don't we put an offer in for next door? We could knock through and do coffees; no-one does proper coffee around here. And little cakes – we could do a deal with Debs at the bakery – and if people like the cakes we can send them to her and she can send people to us. We could call it the Kauldron Kafé!' she giggled. 'What do you think?'

'Yeah, could do, I suppose....' Shirley shrugged coolly, 'if you think so,' and went on with her reading.

'Poor Mrs Hickson must be getting on. This way she could retire and enjoy herself. And obviously I'd make her a fair offer.'

Shirley casually flicked a page. 'You'd have to find her first. She hasn't been seen since 1986.'

'And *you'd* have to pull your finger out!' she retorted.

'I do my bit,' her sister asserted tetchily. 'I'm more of a back-ground presence. The silent partner.'

'Yeah well, whatever you are, I'm going to the Post Office with the international orders; there's a load of them and that's without a web site. Imagine what it'll be like when we get online!'

She waited briefly for any echo of her own enthusiasm, but finding none, simply collected her coat. *Time alone might be just what she needs.*

Buttoning up the warm, woollen coat, Christine looked down at the top of her sister's head, propped on one arm, the other hand nursing the requisite mug, and hesitated.

'Will you be alright on your own?' she asked kindly.

'I'll cope. If there's a rush I'll send for you.'

'Fine!' Christine picked up the orders brusquely and made for the door. 'Have it your way!'

Shirley did indeed have it her way for a good while, enjoying a blissful fifteen minutes of peace and quiet untroubled by the unso-licited intrusion of customers.

When finally she *was* disturbed, the huge man was at the counter before the chimes knew what had hit them. Planting a pair of meaty fists on the counter, he leaned in menacingly. 'Alright, love?'

Shirley uncurled from her reading with all the controlled indig-nation of a somnolent python poked with a stick. Through narrowed eyes she took in the shaven lump of a head, the lack of any discernible neck and, beneath a quilted jacket, the sort of pit-bull frame that suggested he pumped more than just iron.

'Yes?' she hissed. 'Can I help you?'

'I want one of them kit things,' he said impatiently, 'you know, the lucky ones.' The accent was pure South London.

He seemed on edge. Perhaps it was discomfort with his unfamiliar surroundings of candles and essential oils; it could just as easily be that congenital anger she saw in so many, but most likely it was the result of something entirely self-administered.

'Sorry, sir. All sold out,' she announced with an all-too-obvious pleasure, even thought of adding, 'Looks like you're out of luck!' before having a much better idea. 'Tell you what, though. Call back on Friday morning and I'll set one aside, especially for you. How's that?' - adding her very best attempt at a helpful smile.

Unimpressed by either effort he merely tugged at his nose and sniffed tellingly. 'Yeah, alright. Cheers, doll,' he turned his enormous back and left.

Very few people had the ability, not to mention the temerity, to make the elder Madeley uneasy but this visitor most certainly had. She'd recognised, although never previously met, Eddie Brunson, recent incomer, ex of the capital's criminal fraternity it was said, dealer in this and that, but mostly that. Of course she knew all the talk, of his relocation at haste and, some whispered, under a cloud to a cottage on the outskirts of town with land and stables, how he harboured ambitions of running a riding school and delusions of squirarchy. As usual, gossip provided all she needed to know.

She'd driven past the Brunson property several times, seen the grounds full of cars and vans in various states of disrepair, his own S-Class Mercedes standing out like a highly-polished black marble monolith in an auto graveyard. Already there was talk of altercations with neighbours over land use and even dark murmurings of involvement in the town's embryonic drug trade.

Such were Shirley's musings as she carefully gathered the components for Eddie's kit. Just then Christine returned, her arms full of purchases: a carton of milk, biscuits and what looked like a box of cream cakes. 'A little treat from Debs,' she explained brightly but Shirley was already hungrily eyeing the virgin copy of *"That's Life!"* which lay beneath them. 'Who was that?'

'Eddie Brunson,' Shirley replied shortly.

Christine frowned. 'Eddie Brunson? What did *he* want?'

'A Get Well card for some poor sod's kneecaps. I sent him packing,' Shirley turned to conceal the items she was holding.

Christine didn't pursue the matter, just deposited her purchases on the counter. She clearly had something more pressing on her mind.

'Eurgh!' she began with a grimace. 'Guess who was in the Mini Mart? That bloke you don't like. What's his name?'

'I'll draw you up a shortlist, give me a week.'

'Oh, you know, the sleazy guy from the carpet cleaners. You're always on about him.'

'Dirty Dave? The Beast of Brimley?'

'Yeah, that's him. Well, I think you might be right.'

'I'm always right, it's a gift. Was he wearing that suit?'

'Yeah, the beige one,' Christine sniggered, 'and *gallons* of Brylcream. But Shirl, you know what he did?' At this point she paused to steel herself for what she had to impart. 'He only got one of those dirty books down from the top shelf and starts looking through it in front of the part-time girl, Lauren. She's only seventeen, you know? Anyway, he's flicking through it on the counter and he's going "Hey, you should be in here, you're much fitter than any of *these* birds. I take a few pictures now and again myself."'

Shirley said nothing, merely rolled her eyes and sneered in one well-practised, fluid motion as she continued to assemble kit components.

'I didn't think he'd seen me but then he turns around and goes, "Oh, hello gorgeous, we can make it a threesome if you like." Ooh, I nearly slapped him! Then he said he was going to come in here for – listen to this – a *luurve* kit. He actually said *luurve*,' she emphasised with a shudder.

Shirley affected a look of exaggerated nausea.

'Is he still sleeping with Maggie whatsername?' Christine wanted to know.

'And the rest,' Shirley sneered archly. 'I don't know how, he's such a pig. And they're getting younger as well.'

'It's his wife I feel sorry for,' opined Christine with genuine feeling. 'She hardly shows her face these days 'cause everybody knows what he's like; I mean, he's so blatant about it, like he enjoys the reputation. Anyway....' she summed up with a sniff, subject exhausted, and eyed Shirley's mug, perilously below half-full. 'Fancy a top up?'

Shirley beamed at that. 'That would be *lovely*, Chris. I'll just finish off these kits.'

The following week was the busiest either of them could ever recall. On Monday Christine met with a web designer who promised he could provide the Koven with something called a 'state-of-the-art e-commerce platform', on Tuesday she was interviewed for a feature on local businesswomen in the *Brimley Argus* and on Thursday she spoke to the bank regarding the possibility of expansion into the supply of coffee and cakes. All the while Shirley proved remarkably adept at running the shop alone and even more skilled at affecting interest in Christine's protracted reports of the day's events. Between putting up the increasing number of mail orders and their evening shifts building up stock at the kitchen table, they rarely saw their beds before midnight.

The night Eddie Brunson's cottage burned to the ground both sisters slept soundly, only Christine stirring briefly at the wail of passing sirens before slipping back into her comforting world of exciting plans and unlimited possibilities.

Naturally enough, the blaze was the talk of the town for weeks and when police found a substantial quantity of heroin in the stables and the horses badly neglected, local opinion sighed with enormous relief at the back of Brunson, who escaped unharmed but facing serious charges.

The view of officialdom was that he had finally trodden on one toe too many or that some latent enmity had followed him up the M1. Nevertheless, the preliminary report of fire investigators could find no evidence whatsoever of foul play.

Shirley sat and seethed all afternoon. She hated rowing with Christine, which was odd because she was really very good at it. The issue had been the forthcoming County Show at which Christine wanted to have a table, Shirley refusing on the grounds that she'd been there before and it 'stank of shit'. Christine had accused her of not pulling her weight and she had told Christine to do it her bloody self if she was so keen on the idea, at which point Christine had stormed out.

It was the day of Christine's big meeting with a buyer from a department store in Coventry who was interested in stocking the kits on a trial basis. It was a big deal, she knew, and now felt guilty for not being more supportive, angry at herself as well as her sister, and not a little taken aback at how forcefully Christine had argued her case.

And on top of that was the vexing question of her magazine supply; she'd read them all from cover to cover and was now beginning to feel the cold fingers of withdrawal clawing at her soul. For at least the past hour she'd been considering sticking up a "Back in five minutes" note and popping out to the Mini Mart; instead, she sourly observed the movements of the townsfolk through the window, hoping for hints of scandal.

Then, in a flurry of jangling, Christine was back. In her smart coat and clutching her leather briefcase she looked every bit the modern businesswoman, or at least she would have, were it not for the way she clattered through the door to stand wide-eyed and open-mouthed, gawping at Shirley like a child in a toy shop. She was bordering on breathlessness.

'Oh. My. God. You will not *believe* this!'

At least the morning's contretemps appeared to be forgotten. Shirley raised an eyebrow. 'Don't tell me, the FTSE's up six points?'

But Christine just stood there, shaking her head in disbelief.

'I've just seen Joanne Long in the High Street. You know, the nurse? She says they brought Dave Slinney into A&E last night. You know, the carpet guy?'

Shirley looked up sharply.

'She said Maggie whatsername drove him in at two o'clock this morning,' Christine explained. She bit her lip, stifling a laugh, then glanced over both shoulders to confirm that they were completely alone.

'His *thing* dropped off,' she said finally.

The smile on Shirley's face was a sight to behold, broad and of seemingly limitless joy. 'You what?' she somehow managed to ask through it.

'Just dropped off. In bed, apparently,' Christine clarified.

'Maybe he's finally worn it out.'

'Can that happen?' gasped Christine from behind her hand. Shirley chuckled at her sister's innocence and was just about to suggest hearing all the gory details over a nice cup of coffee.

The chimes made a most curious noise on their way to being flattened against the wall by the flung door.

There was something of the Western about the scene as Dave Slinney stood framed menacingly in the open doorway. Certainly, he moved like a recently-dismounted cowboy as he limped his way towards Shirley.

No longer the Man in the Beige Suit of Brimley legend, now just a shambling figure in an old blue track suit and body warmer, scruffy and unshaven. The hair, finally freed from its unctuous restraint, flopped lifelessly while the face, for the first time without a trace of its trademark predatory leer, was home only to a cold, dark fury.

'*You* are a nasty, evil, conniving *bitch*!' He jabbed a menacing finger in Shirley's face. Shirley merely stared back calmly, the picture of outraged innocence.

Then Christine slipped her slight frame between them. 'Excuse me!' she stated with unexpected assertiveness, 'I don't know what's wrong but you can't talk to her like that or I'll have to ask you to leave!'

Dave turned his gaze on Christine and for a moment it was like he'd never laid eyes on her before.

'Leave?' He gave a slightly hysterical laugh. 'I haven't even *started* yet! I want compensation. I've been injured by your defective products!'

'Faulty equipment?' asked Shirley helpfully.

Dave's face flushed. 'You two are responsible, with those bags of shite you've been flogging.'

'The kits?' Christine frowned. 'But you've never been in here before. Have you bought one?'

'No, *she* turns up at the office with an envelope,' he jabbed another finger in Shirley's face. '"With compliments", it said. I should have known something was up.'

Christine shot her sister a quizzical look.

'That's right,' Shirley explained sweetly. 'A free sample. Word of mouth and all that, you know?' And then for Dave's sole benefit, 'I just dropped off a small package.'

Further confused, and now prey to the nagging suspicion that Shirley was somehow enjoying herself, Christine still didn't give up. 'OK then,' she said appeasingly, 'if you think something's wrong with it, bring it back and we'll have a look.'

'Ha! I can't though, can I?' His fury now seemed to have descended into a kind of mania; he wasn't blinking nearly as much as he should be and now he'd taken to waving his hands in unnecessary flourishes as he spoke. 'Because you're devious bitches, aren't you? Everything gets used up. Very clever! Even the instructions are on the little red card that gets burned. There's nothing left to bring back, is there?'

Christine was beyond confusion now. 'Erm... I'm sorry, but the cards in the love spells are green...'

'Perhaps he's colour blind?' Shirley ventured.

'No, I'm bloody not!' Dave barked back.

Christine calmly retrieved a 'Love Potion' kit and held it out carefully like a placatory bone to a mad dog. 'Was it one of these?'

'No, that's completely different,' he snapped. 'And the candle was black. I thought that was odd.'

Christine stiffened.

Shirley's eyes narrowed. 'Right, I've had enough. *Get out!*' Casting off the butter-wouldn't-melt facade, she rounded the till and appeared on the end of Dave's arm in a heartbeat, dragging him towards the still-open door, as he squealed and struggled to keep his legs apart. With a final, firm, almost comical shove, he was ejected from the shop. Shirley slammed the door, slid the bolt and threw her weight against it while she regained her breath.

For an age neither of them spoke. Christine stared blankly, desperately combing her feelings for anything that might make sense. Shirley scowled at her shoes as if awaiting a headmaster's wrath.

Eventually Christine willed herself to speak. 'He's right, isn't he? You did it.'

Shirley's petulant flick of the head served only to further enflame her sister.

'Shirley, he's going to sue us!'

'Get real, Chris, of course he's not,' Shirley laughed awkwardly, finally peeling herself away from the door and coming closer. 'Who's going to believe him? And they don't do *those* sort of trials any more, in case you hadn't noticed.'

'We were doing so well and you've ruined it all!' Christine was on the verge of tears. 'What gives you the right to spoil my dreams?'

That set her off. Rounding furiously on her sister, dark eyes blazing, Shirley erupted. 'Oh, why don't you just *shut up*? Shut up and *listen* for once in your bloody life!'

Christine recoiled visibly. In all of their arguments across the years, Shirley had never once yelled at her like that.

'*We* haven't built this, *you* have! I couldn't do any of this, I don't know the first thing about business but you've got a real feel for it, you're a natural. You always had more about you than I did. You might be my little sis but when we were kids, I thought you were *brilliant* – really looked up to you – and guess what? I still do. You've got talents I couldn't dream of – you're a hell of a lot cleverer for a start – and you've got a real knack with people. I couldn't do that even if I wanted to.'

Shirley was breathing hard. 'But I'm not completely useless either – the one thing I could always do was look out for *you*!' She paused for a moment, then gritted her teeth and went on. 'How do you think you got on that business course, anyway? They don't just invite people at random, you know. You have to be proposed. And who sat up all bloody night listening to you, like a nodding dog, as you went *on and on and on* about how you didn't think you were up to it until *eventually* you somehow decided you'd go after all?'

Christine was speechless but the way Shirley spoke was just as shocking. She'd seen her incensed, yes. Abusive, certainly, and downright hateful on countless occasions; but never before had she spoken with such passion. Never with such... *feeling*?

'Your only flaw is your lack of confidence; you're delicate, Chris. All your life you've been the clever one but you've also been the gentle one. And that lot *out there*,' she swept her hand viciously across the darkening window, '*they* don't like that! They sense vulnerability; it draws them like flies to anyone who's different. They're jealous. They only want to snuff you out and given the chance they would – just like *that*!' and she snapped her fingers in Christine's stunned face.

Once again Shirley paused, hesitating, as if on some terrible threshold.

'People like Hannah Taylor,' she finally spoke, as softly as she could.

What little colour there remained in Christine's complexion fled in the face of a twenty-year-old horror. For a moment it looked like she might collapse – and time was, she would have – but not today, not now. She just stood, shakily perhaps, but she stood.

Shirley was in no hurry, thought it best to let her sister connect the pieces for herself. That was always the best way with this sort of thing, so she waited in respectful silence for as long as it took.

'You?' Christine whispered.

'Tell the truth. Would you have finished school if she'd still been there?'

Christine shook her head.

'But... they said it was a riding accident.'

Shirley shrugged casually. 'It doesn't matter. What matters is that *you're* here.'

Despite herself, Christine nodded.

'Remember the trouble we had getting you to eat? And everything else...' Shirley trailed off, taking up Christine's hand and gently, very gently, squeezing the forearm under its long sleeve. *Always under the long sleeves.* 'Hannah Taylor would have snuffed you out.'

Christine licked her lips thoughtfully. 'But isn't it dangerous? I mean, isn't there some rule about... well, about *that* sort of thing?'

Shirley laughed dismissively. 'That's just something we tell kids and people who can't cope with the real world. Not big, strong, successful, intelligent women like Christine Madeley.' Another squeeze; this one stronger, supportive.

Now it was Christine's turn to laugh, nervously, and in spite of herself. 'If you say so.'

'There's only one kind of magic, Chris, Gran must have told you that; and its only purpose is to restore balance or... justice... or whatever you want to call it. We *never* - we *couldn't* - work against the will of the cosmos.'

Christine said nothing. Remembering, reflecting, accepting.

'These people came into *our* lives, not the other way round. And what brings them is that they know they're doing wrong and so they seek – they *crave* – self-destruction. We just ease things along. Deep down, you know that.'

Christine nodded, still a little uncertain. 'OK, but no more. Please?'

'I can't promise that. Because what if one day someone else decides to threaten my baby sis? I reserve the right to deal with them. Listen, Chris, no one – not Hannah Taylor, not Dave Slinney, not me – is going to take this away from you because it's yours and you deserve it and because I won't let them.'

She leaned forward and kissed Christine softly on the forehead. 'Because I love you,' she said and smiled brightly for the briefest of moments and then it was gone. 'But – we never, *ever*, talk of this again, right?' It wasn't intended as a question and was delivered with a formidable look and a final squeeze, this time much firmer.

'Right,' Christine whispered.

Shirley nodded once and swept away to the living quarters.

Alone again, Christine gave her surroundings a lingering, affectionate appraisal. It was her empire and she stood at the centre of it. Shirley was right, she deserved all this. It was her hard work, and her ideas. Why should all that be threatened by anyone?

She glanced at her watch; there seemed little point in opening up again for the last fifteen minutes and there really was a lot of work to be done for tomorrow. With a satisfied smile she flicked off the lights.

And besides, she could hear the kettle boiling.

MUD

L.C. GIBSON

The German Countryside
April 1945

The rain blew straight at me over the hood of the jeep, stinging my face. My GI raincoat leaked like a sieve. I hunched down as low as I could behind the dashboard, pulled the rim of my helmet lower and tried to keep my map dry. I had no idea how Bennie could see to drive.

It had been sunny and almost spring-like when we moved out two hours ago, but then the clouds had rolled in, the temperature had dropped, and the rain had started. Again.

I had trouble remembering a completely dry day since our battalion crossed the Rhine, and that had been ... what? A week? Ten days ago? They all blurred together now that it seemed that the war was winding down and the Kraut resistance was collapsing like a dry rotted tree. One hard push and it would fall over. Like everybody else, most of the Germans included, I just wanted it to end, and to still be alive when it finally did.

Up ahead perhaps a half mile, the muddy farm road made a wide turn that skirted around a small tree-covered hill. I took a quick glance at the map. The hill was maybe 5 miles this side of the village where we were going to hold up for the night.

Bob Allison, standing braced behind the pedestal-mounted .30 caliber Browning, kicked the back of the driver's seat.

"Hold up a minute, Bennie!" he yelled over the engine noise. Bennie Goldstein slowed and edged over toward the verge, careful not to get a wheel too close to the bordering drainage ditch. As slick as the road was, it would be too easy to slide right into the ditch, and we would be stuck until someone happened by to tow us out.

"See something?" I asked as I retrieved my musette bag and fished out a dry pack of cigarettes.

"I ain't sure." Bob squinted through the rain, which seemed to be slackening for the moment. "I think I seen a flash up there in them trees, maybe light reflecting from a window. Then again could be field glasses."

Bob was suspicious of everything, which is a good trait to have for a soldier, especially one with a wife and a baby daughter that he had never seen, waiting for him to get back home. I hadn't seen anything on the hill, but I had been concentrating on keeping myself and the map dry.

"A flash?" said Bennie. "You saw a flash? Don't you need sunlight to see a flash?" He wiped his wet face with a dirty bandanna. "Well, while you two hillbillies decide whether or not to notify General Eisenhower personally about this ominous development, I gotta take a leak."

He switched off the ignition and climbed out of the jeep, picked up the M3 grease gun he insisted on carrying everywhere, and slung it over his shoulder.

"Back in a flash, troops," he said, unbuttoning his fly as he sloshed into the field, the mud sucking at his boots.

Bob and I grinned at each other. Bennie Goldstein had absolutely nothing in common with Bob or me. But the three of us – Bob, a big silent man from a West Virginia coal town, me, son of an Alabama cotton farmer, and Bennie, a brash, mouthy kid from Brooklyn - had grown inseparable since we joined the battalion as replacements in Belgium four months ago. It seemed like we'd been together a lifetime now. I reckon we knew each other's life stories as well as we knew our own.

Carefully, so as not to tear it, I laid the damp map on the hood and we bent over it. "It appears like one or two buildings up there, and maybe a church or something. Not even big enough to be a village, even though it's got a name." I said.

"Good place to dig in an 88," said Bob. "They can sight right down the road and take out a whole damned column if the gunners know what they're doing." Bob looked dourly in the direction of the hill. "Or maybe they have an MG42 in the church tower. Or maybe just some crazy-ass Hitler Youth with a scoped rifle and a death wish."

"Or maybe nothing," I said.

"Yeah," he said doubtfully. "Maybe nothing."

A dotted line on the map indicated a secondary road branching off up ahead. It was probably more like a cow trail, if what we'd been driving on was a primary road in these parts. It wound up toward the crest of the hill on the side opposite us before it appeared to peter out near the buildings.

Bennie finished up his business and wandered back over to us. He peered at the map, bummed a cigarette from my pack, then looked up at the hill.

"The map says it's called *Schwartzekirche*. What's that mean?" Bob and I shrugged.

"Whaddya say we go up and take a look?"

Bob frowned. "We'll be sitting ducks if we just drive up to it."

"Hell, we're already in range. If they wanted to shoot us, they'd have done it by now," said Bennie. "If they're up there, they're waiting for a better target than a lousy jeep. Like the battalion main body. Whaddaya think, Red?" They both looked at me.

"Bennie's right," I said. "We can go right on past to the other side of the hill like we didn't see nothing, and then work up the little trail and come up behind them. If we're lucky, anybody watching us will just figure we stopped so Bennie could take a pee."

I wasn't crazy about it, but we couldn't just sit here all day waiting for the main body to catch up. We were the reconnaissance element, so we had better start reconning. Sometimes those three stripes on my sleeve felt pretty heavy.

We mounted back up and Bennie fired up the jeep. "OK, Bennie," I said, "Fast as you can without getting us into a ditch!" Bennie grinned and popped the clutch.

The run past the hill and then up the trail turned out to be uneventful, except that Bennie's hell-for-leather driving, throwing up big rooster tails of mud while sliding in and out of slick curves, scared the crap out of Bob and me. He stopped the jeep just below the crest of the hill. Bennie and I dismounted and eased up the path while Bob stayed on the gun to cover us.

The trees on top of the hill were black in the gray of the afternoon. They overhung the muddy path, choking off what little light managed to filter through the clouds and rain. It was dead quiet, except for the sound of water dripping from the dark leaves. I shivered, not entirely from the cold.

Ahead to the left were two small buildings that might have held livestock once long ago. I covered the entrance of the first one while Bennie ducked inside and took a quick look. He emerged shaking his head. Nothing.

We repeated the process on the other building, but this time it was my turn to step inside while Bennie covered me. As my eyes adjusted to the semi-darkness, I saw that the interior was almost bare except for a couple of empty pens, their wooden rails broken and lying in heaps. Near the far wall a rickety table and solitary chair sat forlornly. Old bits of harness, pieces of farm tools, and moldy trash lay in haphazard piles on the stone floor. I swept the muzzle of my carbine carefully from right to left across the room, pausing on anything that could possibly conceal a person, and confirmed my initial impression. Nobody had been here for a long time. I backed out of the door and gave Bennie the thumbs up.

Ahead through the trees we could just make out the third building. As we slopped up the path toward it, it became clear that this was indeed a church, or maybe a chapel. It was not large, although it was topped by a cupola—or belfry, or whatever you called those things. Granite steps led up to two heavy wooden entrance doors that hung ajar on shattered iron hinges. The outside of the church was covered in vines, some thick as my forearm, except where they had been blasted and burned leaving bare patches on the stone that looked like black scabs. The doors themselves were scorched and pockmarked with shrapnel holes. The broken remains of two big windows flanked the entryway on either side, and bits of stained glass glittered in the mud below their frames. The whole place stank of burned wood and high explosives. Although the damage was recent, I had the impression that this was a place of great age. This building, or maybe something else, had been here for a very long time.

Taking a deep breath, I craned my neck around one of the doors and peered inside through the gap. No movement. I withdrew my head quickly and looked at Bennie.

"Go back and bring the jeep up. I don't like not having it in sight."

Bennie turned and slogged hastily back down the path. In just a few minutes, although somehow standing there alone it seemed to me much longer, Bennie and Bob pulled up, Bob scanning the area from behind the .30 caliber. Bennie dismounted, grabbing his grease gun, and we pushed open the doors to the chapel.

If anything, the dark interior stank even more of smoke and destruction. The central area of the large room was shattered and blackened. The wreckage of charred pews lay scattered among fallen masonry and fragments of broken statues. We spread out, stepping carefully through the debris, aware that a chunk of the vaulted ceiling could break loose and flatten us at any moment.

We worked through the gloom toward a raised platform at the far end. An intricately carved altar stood in the center of the platform, a large ragged hole blown straight through it.

"Panzerfaust," mouthed Bennie. I nodded. Somebody had fought hard in this place. But who? And why?

Bennie pointed to a circular staircase that wound up to the tower. He gestured for me to cover him and cautiously ascended the stairs. He disappeared through an open trap door at the top of the steps.

A few minutes later Bennie's head appeared in the opening and he grinned down at me.

"It's clear, Red. Come on up and take a look."

Scooting up through the trap door, I barely avoided banging my helmet on an iron bell suspended from a beam across the ceiling. Bennie was crouched low, looking out of the open tower window at the road we had traveled. There was no sign of movement anywhere.

I moved around to the other side and looked down at Bob. "Nothing here," I yelled down to him. "See if you can raise Battalion and give 'em a report." He waved acknowledgement, and I motioned for Bennie to follow me back downstairs.

We got outside just as Bob was taking off the radio headset. "Lt. Harper says they've been held up. Be another thirty minutes or so before they get here. He wants us to wait until they join up."

"Suits me," said Bennie. "Let's get out of the rain for a while and have some chow." I nodded.

"That's a right good idea. But let's go into one of them other buildings. For some reason I just don't like the way this here church feels."

I expected a wisecrack from Bennie, but he nodded grimly. Something was just not right about the place.

Bennie and Bob grabbed a box of ten-in-one rations and the squad stove from the jeep while I headed into the building that I had checked earlier. I ducked through the low doorway and stopped short. A man was seated behind the rickety table, his face obscured in the dimness. Swearing, I scrabbled to unsling my carbine.

"Nein! Nein! Kamerad!" The man spread his hands wide and half rose from the chair.

"Where the hell did *you* come from?" I shouted, my hands shaking and my heart pounding as I leveled my weapon at him.

"Sie sind Amerikaner?" The man's teeth showed white in a broad smile. *"Wilkomen.* Welcome! I am to finally see you so pleased!"

Bob and Bennie crowded into the doorway behind me.

"What the hell! I thought you cleared this place, Red!" Bennie had his grease gun pointed over my shoulder at the man.

"I did, dammit! There was nobody here!"

The man smiled again and sat back down behind the table, and I started to make him out clearly in the gloom. He was tall and thin, with side-whiskers framing a face that could have belonged to a man of forty, or just as easily of seventy. He wore a high-crowned, flat brimmed hat. A ragged, old-fashioned black suit over a dingy white collarless shirt draped his skinny frame.

He looked benignly through his round, horn-rimmed spectacles at Bennie.

"Don't blame your officer, *Junge.* I am very good at hiding." He turned his smile at me and winked as if we shared a secret joke.

"I ain't no officer," I scowled. "Who are you, and where'd you come from?" As we spoke, the three of us had moved further into the room and were spread out in a line facing our intruder.

"Ah. I am called Lev. I am a... how do you say? A peddler. Yes, that is the word. A peddler. I wander from place to place. Sometimes I buy, sometimes I sell."

Bennie's mouth dropped open. "You're Jewish! How? I thought the damn Krauts had rounded everyone up!" Then his eyes narrowed. "Wait. You been playing ball with those Nazi bastards? Informing?" A muscle in his jaw twitched. "Is that why they let you roam around, you son of a bitch?" Bennie pointed his grease gun at the man's head.

Bob and I knew about Bennie's mother's family. She and his grandmother had emigrated to the States years ago, but the rest of them, aunts, uncles, cousins, had all still been in Europe when Hitler took over. No one had heard from any of them since the war began; but there had been rumors about what happened to them. Bad rumors.

Lev the Peddler smiled again and spread his hands palms out.

"I said before, *Yingel*, I am very good at hiding. I am an old man. I have been wandering the countryside, my own business minding, for a long time. Practice, *Ja*? And the Germans can be stupid. They see only what they want to see."

"OK, Mr. Peddler, so you're right good at hiding," I said. "Anybody else hiding that we should know about?"

"No. Just me. I am alone. Always."

"What happened at that church?" Bob asked. "It looks like there was a helluva fight in there."

"*Ach*. The *Deutschen Soldaten* came. *Waffen* SS. *Zeyer shlekht*—very bad. They wanted what was kept there. The ones who guarded this place didn't let them have it."

"Guarded it? Were they soldiers too?"

"In a way." Lev shrugged. "But not how you mean. E*s tut nisht enin*. They are all gone, and the thing they guarded also."

This was getting too deep for me. "Make sense, dammit! What happened to the Kraut soldiers? And what was it they wanted so bad?"

Lev shrugged and smiled again. "So many questions! The Germans are gone. It is here safe now. *Alles gut, ja*?" He eyed the box of rations that Bob had dropped. "*Bistu hungerig*? I have not food had today, and you hungry must be also."

"Ah, the hell with it," I said. "I don't think we're going to get much from this old bird that we can make heads nor tails of. We'll turn him over to Lt. Harper when the battalion gets here and see what he makes of him. In the meantime, we might as well get some chow."

Bob fired up the stove and we dumped the contents of the rations into an old pot that we'd picked up in Belgium and carried with us ever since. When the mess was heated up we gave the old man more than an equal share, which disappeared into his mouth at an amazing speed. As coffee boiled in a canteen cup, he sniffed the aroma and sighed contentedly.

"So much good food! And *kaffee*! You Americans are very rich!" He stared meaningfully at me as I fished out my pack of Luckies and pulled out a smoke. Sighing, I handed over the pack and he shook out a cigarette that I lit for him. He nodded in thanks as the remainder of the pack disappeared into the breast pocket of his ragged black coat.

He leaned back in his chair and seemed to consider for a moment as he blew a perfect smoke ring.

"You are good boys. So generous to a poor old man. I must something give you in return."

"Like what?" said Bennie, for once sounding as suspicious as Bob.

"First, I tell you a story. A good *Yidel* like you maybe knows it already, but the *goyim* maybe not." He settled more comfortably in his chair, removed the canteen cup from the stove and took a sip of coffee. The hot rim of the cup scorched his lip and he grimaced.

Then Lev began. "Have you ever heard the story of Judah Ben Belzalel Loew, the Rabbi of Prague, and his Golem?"

"Yeah." Bennie nodded. "A fairy tale. My grandma came from Prague. She used to tell it to me when I was a little kid. Tried to scare me with the Golem to make me go to bed."

"Ah, but a fairy tale it was not. It is true, *Yingel*. In the year 1608 the Prague Ghetto was by the Christian peoples there besieged. They had heard many terrible stories about the Jews and they were angry and frightened. Using blood of Christian babies for dark ceremonies, witchcraft, all kinds of crazy talk. It was *unsinn*, nonsense, of course, but the Christians believed them, and they wanted to slaughter the *Yiddische tzibur*."

"Yeah, yeah, I know the story," said Bennie. "So, this Rabbi Loew guy goes down to the riverbank and makes a giant monster out of mud to protect the Jews. And the monster kicks the mob's ass and they all run away."

"And do you know what happened then?" Lev's eyes seemed to glitter behind his spectacles.

Bennie squinted in thought. "I think the Rabbi decided that the Golem thing was dangerous, since it didn't have a soul. He was afraid it might turn on the Jews in the Ghetto and so he destroyed it."

"Very good! Such a smart boy! Always listen to your grandmother! And do you know how the Rabbi gave the Golem life, and how he took it away?"

"No. I don't think she ever said. Maybe nobody knew."

Lev leaned close to Bennie, his voice almost too low to hear. "But *I* know."

He drew back in his chair. "The Rabbi a was very learned man. All his life he studied the *Kabala*, the secret tradition. The *Sefer HaYitzirah*, the Book of Formation. He knew that to make such a creature is not a task possible for an ordinary man. To wield such power, to make that which does not live alive, takes someone very special. A mystic. Almost what the *goyim* would call a saint. Even for such a man, to cast such great magic takes weeks and weeks of strict preparation. He must be purified. Ritual must be followed exactly without error. The Rabbi was such a man to do this. He had the knowledge. More important he had the . . . the spirit. The soul, *Ja*? After many trials and much time, he succeeded. Just in time to save the Ghetto from destruction, he was able to breathe life into the Golem. And when the time came, he was able to banish that life with his power."

Lev studied Bennie's face. "I see maybe some of that spirit in you, *Yingel*. I think maybe you would do anything to save your people, *nein*?"

Bennie snorted. "Save 'em? Yeah, I got that spirit, alright." He patted his grease gun like he was Edward G. Robinson in a gangster movie. "Kill every damned Nazi that I can any time that I can. Help finish this friggin' war as quick as possible so's we can hang any of the murderous bastards that are left."

He gave a shrug. "But a Golem? Naw. Hell, I barely graduated high school. Scholar material I ain't, even if I had a Golem-making manual, which I don't happen to have. And if it wasn't all a fairy tale, anyway."

Lev smiled. "But you have not heard the rest of the story, the fairy tale, *Ja*?

"The great Rabbi in his studies discovered that there was another way, a simpler way to make a Golem that was maybe how do you say, cruder. A living mud man, maybe not quite so powerful, but still with great strength.

"It was said that the great Patriarch himself, Abraham, had crafted a gem of great beauty and great power. With this gem anyone, *anyone*, who knows certain words to speak could call a Golem to life when he places the gem in the creature's head. And when the Golem destroyed must be, the jewel is removed and other words spoken. After years of searching, the Rabbi found this gem and learned the words that were to be spoken. And *these* are the words."

Lev leaned forward again, his mouth nearly touching Bennie's ear, and whispered to him for what seemed like a long time. He drew back, grasped Bennie's head in his hands, and stared into his eyes.

"Remember," he said softly, his eyes burning like coals. "Remember."

Bennie stared, his eyes wide, his face pale. Then he shook himself and laughed.

"Damn, old man, you had me going for a minute!"

Despite ourselves, Lev's story had transfixed me and Bob, too. We joined Bennie's laughter, but in my case at least the laughter was a little forced.

Lev studied us all for a moment, then bent over and rummaged around in an old pack on the floor that I had somehow not noticed before. He murmured in satisfaction and withdrew a small object that he placed on the table. It was a wooden box about the size of a paperback book, inlaid with gold leaf and carved with strange symbols.

"Rabbi Loew's cedarwood box, made from fragments of the Temple."

It was just a box, but somehow it filled me with a sense of unease. Looking at Bob, I saw he felt the same way. But Bennie had an expression almost of awe on his face. I'd never known him to be superstitious or even religious, but it seemed like the old Jew had struck a chord.

The peddler slid back the cover of the box. Inside, nestled in velvet cloth, lay a large stone that glittered in the reflected flames of the stove. I don't know much about jewels, but the oval red gem might have been a ruby.

"The jewel of Patriarch Abraham," said Lev as he handed the open box to Bennie.

"You're giving it to me?" Bennie asked breathlessly.

Lev indignantly snatched the box back out of Bennie's hands and slid the cover closed with a snap. "Give? Oy! Of course not!"

"But you said you were giving us a gift!"

"The story was free. The gem? It's for sale, *dummkopf*!"

"How much?" Bennie asked eagerly. I had a very bad feeling about this.

The peddler thought for a moment, took another swig of coffee, and held out another one of my cigarettes for me to light. "The box and the gem, they are very valuable. Precious. But I cannot spend money in this place where there is nothing to buy." He studied the glowing end of his Lucky Strike.

"For you, here is my gift. I will give you the Rabbi's box and the jewel for almost nothing. A carton of these American cigarettes, a pound of coffee, only. And that." He pointed to my prized Zippo.

"Now, wait just a danged minute," I started, but Bennie dashed outside to the jeep and returned at a run with our last precious can of coffee and a carton of Chesterfields from his musette bag. The rat – he'd been bumming cigarettes off me for two days!

"Not a chance," I said. "Who knows when we can get more coffee, and you owe me about half that carton, Bennie. And I'm damned sure not giving this old bullshitter my lighter for some fake ruby!"

"Please, Red!" Bennie pleaded. "My Uncle Max is in the business back in Brooklyn. I worked for him one summer. I know prime stuff when I see it! This stone is definitely worth hundreds, maybe thousands. And the box – a real antique. With the monster story, even better! We can get coffee and smokes when the battalion shows up. And I'll get you another lighter. A better one! Engraved, even!"

I shook my head. "Please, Red," said Bennie. "Remember back in Bochheim, when you almost stepped on that mine? How you said you owed me? Please."

He had me. I sighed and tossed my Zippo to the skinny old man, who caught it deftly and pocketed it like he was performing a magic trick. The coffee and cigarettes changed hands and disappeared into the peddler's pack just as quickly. Lev presented the box to Bennie with a grave bow. He looked seriously at Bennie, and then his gaze took us all in.

"Be careful, *Jungerman*. There is power here. Do not use it without wisdom."

Bennie still had that strange look on his face. "You don't believe any of this old peckerwood's line, do you?" I asked.

He forced a laugh. "Of course not, Red! This is strictly business. We can sell this and have a helluva party when we get to Berlin!" But his expression still bothered me.

The sound of engines reverberated outside. We grabbed our weapons and rushed to the door. A jeep followed by three tank destroyers labored up the muddy hillside. The TDs spread out between the buildings as Lt. Harper, our recon platoon commander, unshaved, wet, and looking pissed, climbed out of the jeep and came towards us, cursing as the mud covered his boots to the ankles.

I walked to meet him but didn't salute. He hated being saluted in the field. "This place is secure, Sir, but it looks like there was a pretty big firefight here not too long ago. No sign of any Krauts, but we do have a civilian, uh, detainee with kind of a strange story."

"Detainee? What the hell have you been up to, Red? Where is he?"

"In here, Sir." I showed the lieutenant to the door as Bennie and Bob moved aside.

The room was empty.

The lieutenant gave me one of those looks. "Well?"

"He was just here, Sir, I swear! Bennie! Bob! Where'd he go?"

"I dunno," stammered Bennie. "He couldn't have gotten past us." Bob just shook his head.

"Well, never mind that now," said the lieutenant. "If he's around he'll turn up. We'll talk about that later, *Sergeant*." He spat the word out like he was cussing.

"Right now, I need you clowns to grab your gear and get on the road. The Krauts are trying to mass on the other side of the river for an all-out defense. If we don't get across before they can consolidate, they will make us pay, and pay dearly, to force a crossing. The infantry is getting slowed down by spoiling attacks, so we need to push armor up now. The rest of our battalion will be here soon."

He stabbed a dirty finger at the folded map in his hand. "We need to find a way to get our TDs and the 825th's tanks across the river. We've got every recon element that we can muster looking for an intact bridge."

He looked at each of us square in the eye for a moment. "If we move fast we just might be able to end this thing for good. We could finish it. I want you to get your asses down to the river and find me a bridge. Now."

As officers go, Lt. Harper was normally a good man to work for; but when his blood was up, like it was now, it was best to get moving.

The village that we were to have stopped in for the night over-looked the river. According to the map, not far below it was a combination railroad and highway bridge. If we were very lucky, the bridge might still be usable. So that's where we headed, as fast as Bennie could drive while still looking out for ambushes and roadblocks.

Daylight was fading fast. When we finally came to the crest of the bluff that edged the abandoned village I figured we had maybe another hour until full dark. We stopped behind the cover of a ruined wall and looked down. There below us was the river, not very wide, but rain-swollen and swift. Railroad tracks and a parallel road followed the contour of the river for several hundred yards down-stream to a double bridge that spanned it. The bridge looked rickety, but intact.

Something caught my eye and I looked more closely at the approach to the bridge. Partially hidden by trees on the bank, men were moving around a low boxy camouflaged shape that I recognized right off. It was a Stug III – a German self-propelled assault gun. It was thinly armored and would be no match for the TDs when they got here, but it was way out of our league, with us having nothing bigger than .30 caliber. Around it and on the opposite bank their infantry was setting up firing positions with what looked like a lot of machine guns while other men, probably engineers, moved back and forth on the bridge itself.

"Get on the radio, Bob, and tell the lieutenant that we got him a bridge. But they need to get here in a hurry. I think the Krauts are rigging it for demolition."

"Hey, Red! Look!" Bennie pointed upstream.

Puffing smoke, a small locomotive pulled half a dozen closed cars, each with an armed man sitting on top, in the direction of the bridge. A couple of infantrymen stepped out onto the tracks and began waving wildly. The slow-moving train halted fifty yards short of the bridge approach. An officer, obviously pissed, dismounted from the locomotive along with a couple of enlisted men and strode toward the infantry.

Unlike the regular soldiers in their filthy camouflage and field gray, the officer's tunic was spotless, his boots gleaming. Through the field glasses I saw black collar tabs with the double lightning bolt insignia, and on his peaked cap the Death's Head skull badge. I handed the glasses to Bennie.

"SS!" hissed Bennie.

There was a heated argument, and the SS officer suddenly drew a pistol and began waving it in the air. The infantrymen leveled their weapons at the officer and several machine guns traversed onto him from the bridge positions. We couldn't hear the conversation, of course, but it was clear to us what was going on. The SS man wanted the train to continue across the bridge, and the infantry wasn't going to let it go, probably because they were preparing to blow it.

The SS man turned on his heel in disgust and shouted something to the men atop the box cars. They clambered down and began unlocking the doors and shoving them open. Hurried along by shouts and blows from the guards, the occupants of the cars started disembarking. They looked like scarecrows. Some wore baggy striped uniforms that looked like pajamas, and others wore ragged civilian clothes. On most of their coats was a yellow patch.

"Holy shit!" Bennie stared at the motley line forming up in the rain under the furious direction of the guards. "They're Jews!"

The ragged line of prisoners, hands on their heads, was marched down into the ditch that separated the road from the tracks. The guards took positions spread out along the road, looking down at them. A shouted command from the officer, and we heard the rattle of weapons being readied.

"They're gonna shoot 'em." Bennie said dully, his face white as a sheet. "We gotta do something."

"Bennie, there's nothing we can do. They see us and we're dead." I felt like I was about to throw up. We were going to witness a massacre and were helpless to stop it.

Bennie turned on me with a snarl. "Do what you want! Do nothing, you damn coward! I ain't gonna let them be slaughtered like animals!"

He tore his musette bag from the jeep and stuffed it with extra magazines for his grease gun. Before I could grab him, he vaulted the wall and began half running, half sliding down the steep bluff toward the river.

He was almost down to the road before the Krauts even noticed him. One or two of the SS guards turned to gape, and a couple of the infantrymen by the bridge pointed at him in surprise. Bennie, still running and sliding down the bluff, leveled his grease gun and fired from the hip without aiming, the bullets spraying all over the place. Even so, it was enough to cause most of the guards to seek cover, and their return fire was slow and sporadic. The Krauts still weren't exactly sure what was going on.

"Sweet Jesus have mercy," I said, and aimed my weapon. "Cover him, Bob!"

The big .30 roared into life, nearly deafening me. Bob was an artist with that machine gun, and his short, well-aimed bursts were slapping into the Germans on the road, knocking them over and making the ground around them erupt in gouts of mud. The empty train began backing up the tracks as fast as the engineer could make it go.

I popped away with my carbine, wishing I had a machine gun too, while I watched Bennie in amazement. He had not only made it to the road, but he had crossed both it and the railroad tracks to take cover behind the slope of the river bank. He was crouched there, half exposed, emptying magazine after magazine into the guards. We had them in a crossfire.

Just then the wall in front of the jeep dissolved in a deafening explosion. Bob was knocked head over heels, and I felt as though I had just been hit in the face with a Louisville Slugger. The assault gun crew had seen us and nearly turned us into ground beef with their first shot. A hail of machine gun fire from the bridge followed, and we scrabbled for shelter behind the remains of the ruined wall.

Bob examined his mangled left arm and then looked back mournfully at the jeep. "The gun is gone, Red. Smashed to pieces. Don't think I could work it no more anyways."

I tore open Bob's first aid kit and bandaged his arm as best I could. Another round ripped the air overhead and impacted a few yards away with a tremendous noise. Mud and gravel sprayed over us.

I rolled to the gap in the wall and looked down toward the river. The train was out of sight up the tracks. Bodies of SS men were scattered along the road. There was no sign of the prisoners. They must either be all dead or sheltering on their bellies in the ditch. The assault gun at the bridge had fired up its engine and was maneuvering to get a better shot at us. I looked for a sign of Bennie.

I couldn't spot him at first, but then I made out a slight figure prone on the riverbank. He was alive, but he was moving slowly. It looked like he was trying to crawl down to the water. Machine gun rounds plowed the mud around him as he painfully inched down the bank.

At last he reached the water's edge. He paused as if gathering his strength for a moment, then pulled off his helmet and began feverishly scooping up mud.

Bob, pale from blood loss, joined me at the gap and stared down at Bennie as another round from the assault gun tore through the air and hit a building behind us.

"What the hell is he doing? Digging a foxhole?" Bob said, puzzled.

I didn't reply. I had another real bad feeling.

By now, Bennie had dug up a good-sized mound of the sticky river mud. He flung away his helmet and began shaping the mud with his hands as the German machine guns continued to blaze away at him. How he wasn't hit was damned near a miracle. As Bennie kept working the mud with his hands a rough form took shape. I could make out arms, legs, a head on a neckless body.

As he worked, the wind began to howl, driving the rain in horizontal sheets. Lightning played through the clouds. The hair rose on the back of my neck.

Bennie reached into his musette bag and withdrew something I couldn't make out. Rising to his feet, he spread his arms wide and lifted his head to the sky. He shouted in a voice that wasn't his, competing to be heard above the wind and thunder and chatter of machine guns.

A massive bolt of lightning crashed into the riverbank, illuminating the object in Bennie's outstretched fist. It was the cedarwood box. I could swear that it was enveloped in a crimson glow, as if the lightning had set it ablaze. Bennie tore open the box, pulled out the big red stone, and flung the box aside. Turning to the mud mound at his feet, he shouted strange words again and jammed the stone into the mound. Lightning struck once more, blinding me.

For a long moment nothing happened. Then, as my vision cleared, I saw the mud *move*.

Slowly, ponderously, a figure rose on stumpy legs, straightening, seeming to expand. At first only the size of a child, it stood erect, sucking more mud into its body as it enlarged and transformed into a hideously human shape. Three feet tall, then five, then ten, it grew as more mud was pulled into its grotesque form. At last, nearly the height of a two-story building, it turned its massive, featureless head toward Bennie, waiting.

Bennie stretched his arms out to the creature as if in benediction, then shouted words lost in the wind and rain. He dropped his arms, then pointed toward the Germans around the bridge. The monster turned as if in slow motion and waded out into the water toward them.

I saw the assault gun steer on its tracks to aim its cannon at the approaching thing. It fired nearly point blank and a massive hole opened in the creature's chest. In an instant mud closed the hole as if it had never been. The creature reached down against the side of the heavy vehicle and pushed it like a toy. It tumbled down the bank into the river and sank out of sight.

Men began running in panic from the German positions. The monster used its arms to swat and its feet to crush, like a bear smashing a nest of field mice. Bodies and weapons flew through the air. Bloody smears marked the path where its huge feet had ground human beings into the mud.

In minutes not a living man remained on the bridge or either bank. Every German still alive was fleeing in terror away from the river as fast as they could run. The creature turned slowly, then paused for a moment, as if pondering. Then in two strides it was at the bridge itself, half its massive body submerged in the river. It began to tear at the support girders.

"Oh shit! It's destroying the bridge!" I wiped blood from my face as I gazed in horror.

Bennie, still on the bank, yelled and began running, waving his arms. The creature shook a girder with its huge hands. The metal groaned, audible even above the wind and thunder. Bennie reached the bridge, shouting and gesturing at the creature to stop. The monster ignored him, intent on its task of destruction.

Bennie, frantic, climbed out on the support, almost level with the creature's head. With a desperate cry, Bennie leaped from the support beam and grabbed at the monster's forehead. The mud gave him no purchase and he slid screaming down the body of the creature into the water below. Clutched in his fist was a gleaming red stone. Both Bennie and the stone sank without a trace.

The monster froze. In moments, the current began to wash away its legs and lower torso. Support for its giant form lost, the upper body and head of the creature crashed into the water and were gone.

Some time later I helped Bob to his feet and we staggered down the slope, clutching each other for support. After a long while, pausing every few yards to rest, we reached the ditch by the road and looked down. Most of the prisoners, dazed and confused, were slowly getting to their feet, some praying, some crying, some merely staring.

The SS officer, hatless, covered in mud, stared up at us from the crowd of prisoners where he had been cowering and raised his hands. Bob drew his .45 and shot him in the head.

As Bob holstered his pistol we heard engine noises from the direction of the village. The battalion had arrived. Better late than never, I reckon.

"What do we tell the lieutenant?" Bob asked me wearily.

It took me a good while to reply.

"The truth," I said finally. "Bennie died securing the bridge. His body was lost in the river."

∼

Lev the Peddler sat by the river, smoking a cigarette and enjoying the morning sunshine. The water sparkled in the light as the current danced along. From upriver he could hear the sound of vehicles crossing the bridge below the little village. "Ah, the *Amerikanen*," he smiled, a little sadly. "So eager. So many marvelous machines. But they do not understand true power. They are *nur kinder*. Only children."

Something glittered in the sunlight at the water's edge and caught Lev's sharp eye. He bent closer to examine it and gave a murmur of satisfaction as he recognized what it was. He thrust his arm into the shallow water and withdrew a small wooden box. He slid open the lid to reveal a large red stone nestled in velvet cloth.

Lev closed the lid and stuffed the strangely dry box into his pack. Slinging it over his shoulder, he straightened and glanced back upstream for a moment. Smiling, he turned and began to walk along the path by the river, humming a half-forgotten tune.

ALTERNATIVE (VETERINARY) MEDICINE

J.S. ROGERS

D r. London Daniels—veterinarian, alchemist, over-worked recent graduate—found a unicorn problem waiting when she arrived at the Willamette Clinic for Magical Animals. The shimmering creature stood in the parking lot beside a beat-up trailer painted to tell the world it belonged to the West Coast Magical Creature Sanctuary and Conservation Society. The unicorn seemed to be passing the time by making additional smaller, smellier problems.

A tall, solidly built, red-headed woman wearing a shirt from the conservation society stood beside the unicorn. The embroidery over her shirt pocket proclaimed her to be Sheila McMilloun, Director of Large Creatures. Sheila walked over to London's Jeep and asked, as soon as London opened the door, "Do you work here?"

"I do." London shivered. Winter refused to give way to spring and the bite in the air promised another snow storm in the near future. She'd shoved a knitted cap down over the mess of her dark curls, but it barely helped. "We're not going to be open for another half-hour or so, but—"

Sheila shook her head, motioning London towards the unicorn. "We don't have time to wait," she said. "Look at Fred. You see his eyes? They're not supposed to be dull like that. And he hasn't touched his feed in a day. And...." Sheila grimaced and gestured to the unicorn's horn. The grayish discoloration of it was hard to miss. "Can you help?" Sheila asked. "Please."

London stroked a hand down Fred the unicorn's neck—he felt unusually warm—and frowned. The discolored horn was a bad sign. Technically, the clinic didn't open for a half hour, but... "I'll need to run some tests," London said, shaking her head. She herded Fred and Sheila around to the back of the clinic, in through the large-animal entrance, and across to an assessment room. She went to find some over-the-elbow gloves while Mathilda, the clinic's early-morning receptionist, brought over a mountain of paperwork.

Magical creatures were, in many ways, difficult patients. Traditional medicine did little for them and their conditions were challenging to address with the assessments used for non-magical animals. Each creature's ailment presented a unique problem, a puzzle that London had always enjoyed solving when no one else could.

Fred the unicorn submitted to the tests she conducted with no more than an occasional baleful look of protest. She drew his blood into several small bowls that she could mix with different chemicals and brews of her own creation. She'd spent months developing her processes while in school, ignoring invitations from friends and classmates in order to complete her work. The long hours of work and the papers she'd written about her discoveries had earned her this job, be it ever so far from home, but left her phone silent most nights.

It seemed a fair enough trade to London. The quiet stung, sometimes, but the medical options for magical creatures were so slim. Many of them died from illnesses that could be cured, if only they were understood and treated properly. Someone had to work to improve the magical veterinary field. Sometimes London felt like the only one willing to make the effort.

London shook her thoughts aside and took clippings of Fred's mane and tail, swabbed the inside of his mouth, wiped a cloth across his horn, and plucked a single eyelash from his right eye. He whickered at her and leaned his head against her shoulder. His behavior earned him knowing looks from Sheila, who only occasionally surfaced from the paperwork. There were so many release forms to sign for a creature of Fred's stature. But signed they eventually were, allowing London to guide Sheila to the door, with a promise to call as soon as they had some clue about his condition and how he might be treated.

Fred's test results took hours, but London had developed a hunch about his ailment in the parking lot; there weren't many illnesses that could discolor the horn of a unicorn. Magical wasting was the only condition she could think of that would also lead to a loss of appetite.

It was a rare disease for a unicorn to contract, with only a handful of cases ever recorded, but it made sense.

She started researching treatments immediately. By the time the test results confirmed London's hunch, she'd already identified the main obstacle. "What do you mean?" Sheila demanded, when London called and delivered the news. "How can you not have the medicine on hand to treat Fred?"

London shrugged, sitting in the clinic's little break room and punching another search into her laptop, trying to figure out how to treat Fred most effectively. "Reagents don't store well, generally. They lose magical potency over time. Most of the items I need to make the potion that will treat the magical wasting are easy to get. I'm only looking for elf's-ear mushrooms. If you've heard of any in the area, I'd appreciate knowing about it."

"We'll see what we can find," said Sheila, her voice grim, and soon hung up. London held out little hope that the conservation group would come up with anything. Elf's-ear mushrooms were uncommon, growing only during the winter months, which was a rare bit of luck for them all. The fungus grew only at a thousand feet above sea level or more, in what London's texts described as 'the deep old woods in troll caves.' Deep old woods London had aplenty; mountainous central Oregon offered trees for days. But human incursions into the area in the past few centuries had driven out all but a few trolls. No one thought to note the coordinates of their caves afterwards.

London tore through legitimate sources to look for known troll-cave locations and then, as the day passed, through increasingly illegitimate sources. Message boards for hobbyist alchemists contained a lot of exclamation points, some wildly false claims about methods for turning straw into gold, and thorough listings regarding where reagents had been found in years past. London found word of a troll cave in a post by AlcheMama1043, grimaced, and wrote down her findings.

AlcheMama1043 claimed that she'd found the mushrooms deep in the Willamette National Forest, with the help of a woodsman who stayed in a cabin up in the woods. She neglected to include coordinates for either the cave or the cabin, but she did list directions to the cabin. The information was years old and written with only the barest hint of coherency, but it was something. More than London had before.

Everyone else had left the clinic long ago. The sun sat low on the horizon and snow clouds, heavy with potential, smothered most of the light anyway. They threatened about twelve inches of snow, should the prognosticators at the local news channel be believed. London went back to check on Fred, who had folded up his legs and leaned against the wall in his pen. He blinked his rheumy eyes at London and barely stirred when she knelt and stroked his long neck.

London called Richard, Bernice, and Hannah, the other three veterinarians for the practice, but it was a Friday night and she was the only one on call. They didn't answer. London hadn't been working long enough to know them well, and, anyway, they were all legitimate mages. London didn't have their magical power. According to Richard she was only a glorified cook. She was used to their condescension. London left brief messages saying she'd be off hunting troll caves, a plan building in her mind, and then turned her phone back and forth in her hands.

The storm would likely hit soon. The prognosticators were rarely wrong. That amount of snow would make the mountain dangerous, and she knew it. Fred rested his head against London's thigh, his horn already darkening to a terrible gray. Magical wasting could move quickly. London doubted Fred had more than a day, *maybe* two, before he would be too far gone to get back, and she would need time to brew a potion....

London looked at the directions again—they led out of town, deep into the Willamette National Forest—sighed, and patted Fred. "I'll be back," she told him. "Don't worry, sweetheart." She walked from the pen and started pulling on layers. She loaded her beat-up Jeep with some water and a container to carry the mushrooms.

It started snowing shortly after she pulled out. By the time she reached the unmarked path inside the state park noted on AlcheMama1043's directions the world had gone gray and cottony. Heavy flakes landed on her dark hair as she wrestled with her coat, turning her gaze towards the surrounding trees. AlcheMama1043 claimed that the cabin was less than two miles into the woods. London could go two miles before the snow got too deep. She had to. The snow continued falling as she trekked up paths that disappeared under a carpet of white.

London's cell phone lost service somewhere between one tree and another, leaving her with only a vague idea of where to find the cabin. She shook the phone, walked in a circle, and swore, but none of those rituals brought back service. Movement in the woods caught her eyes, over and over, but it always turned out to be falling snow. Her jeans soaked through. Her toes went numb. She stamped her feet, tucked her hands under her arms, and forged onward in the direction that seemed right. The snow got thick enough that she bumped into trees and some of the trunks started to look very familiar. She sniffled, worry for Fred building in her gut, and looked up when the scent of a wood fire caught her attention. She felt warmer immediately.

The smell of the smoke led her through a frozen stream, directly into two logs fallen at shin height, and to the cabin. London breathed on her frozen fingers and looked at the ugly little building. Smoke curled up from a squat chimney. No light escaped from the windows. Shutters covered them. An old truck sat off to one side under a snow drift. London stopped half-way to the door.

She didn't get out much, but even she knew it wasn't a great idea to approach a strange cabin in the middle of the night. If not for Fred, she would have turned around. As it was, she reached into her sodden pocket, grabbed a canister full of a liquid she'd personally brewed to burn eyes and choke a person's breath, and continued on. Not for the first time, she wished she'd been born with more destructive magical talents. No one treated alchemists as serious threats, mostly for good reason.

No one answered the first time London knocked on the door. Or the second time. Her knuckles stung. The smell of wood smoke taunted her. She glanced at the creepy truck and scowled. "Hey," she yelled, banging on the door with renewed vigor. "I know you're in there! Let me in! I need your help!" She continued banging until the door cracked open, releasing a wash of heat and warm golden light. A man stood on the other side of the door, tall and rangy, with a scruffy reddish beard and tired eyes. London shoved the toe of her sodden boot into the crack between door and frame.

"You can't be here," the man said, frowning at her.

"I need your help."

The man's scowl deepened. "This isn't a good night." His eyes flicked upward, and London took advantage of his distraction, shoving hard on the door. They could continue their discussion when she wasn't standing out in the snow, freezing. She managed to push the door open just enough to slip through the crack, into the warm space beyond.

Empty walls greeted her. No furniture except a ragged sleeping bag waited in the room. Black-out curtains covered the windows. An axe leaned up against the roaring fireplace. Ice melted off the handle into a puddle.

The only other thing in the room was a cage easily large enough to hold a person, made with thick metal bars. Stained, torn scraps of fabric covered the bare floor. The room stank. London backed into the doorframe, bounced off the wood, and turned to gape at the man. He held his hands up. He seemed a lot bigger than he had a moment before. "Hold on," he said, his mouth pulled up into a terrible rictus and panic in the corners of his eyes. "I can explain, it's—"

London splashed him full in the face with her caustic elixir, shoved him as he cried out, yanked the door open, and fled. A terrible growling sound followed her out into the night. London charged forward with no destination in mind, the snow sucking at her ankles, branches whipping at her face until she ran full on into a tree. Her face ached and she stumbled in a circle, completely lost. Cold cut through her, and something crashed through the trees nearby, spurring her back to motion. She made it a grand total of three steps before an arm seized her around the waist and lifted her. She screamed.

"Quiet," the man said, panting. London screamed again. "Stop! You're going to die!"

London thrashed and beat at everything she could reach, but he bore her along like she weighed nothing, cursing all the way. They stepped over the threshold to the run-down cabin—London missed her chance to grab the doorframe—and he dumped her onto the floor, beside the messy sleeping bag. London kicked out at his legs, raising her arms defensively against... nothing. A second later the cage slammed shut with a metal bang. The man cried out. Clothing tore. London caught her breath on the floor while the fire crackled merrily behind her.

Eventually she dared open her eyes, all full of adrenaline that had nowhere to go. The front door hung open, blowing cold air and snow into the cabin. Strange, fleshy sounds filled the room. Inside the cage, she found the... man. After a fashion. His clothes lay shredded on the floor, joining the other rags. His body had turned into something huge and hairy, standing nearly nine-foot tall, with glinting eyes and a jaw full of dagger-like teeth. He growled and tried to turn, but the cage didn't leave him enough room to move easily. London closed her eyes and opened them again. The beast remained. It gummed absently at one of the metal bars. "Well," she said, "alright then." She sniffed in disapproval. "You could have just said. I've treated lycan-thropes before, you know."

After reassuring herself that he couldn't get out, she closed the cabin door and then sat, staring at the wall. Going back out in the snow seemed beyond foolish. She'd have to wait until morning to resume her search. That was only a few hours away. She didn't *like* the idea, but her guide was currently indisposed.

A pack, filled to bursting, sat in one corner of the cabin. She dug through it, finding some unopened bottles of water, food, clothes, and a wallet. "Henry Harris" waited in the metal cage, according to the driver's license she squinted at. London took one of Henry's trail bars and munched on it while wandering around the rest of the cabin. There wasn't much to find, though she did locate a hidden bottle of whiskey. She sloshed the amber fluid back and forth and smiled grimly.

Alchemy, when taken simply, merely involved mixing together reagents with specific characteristics to get a desired result. And alcohol was, when you got right down to it, a poison. London went back to Henry's pack and withdrew a water bottle. She poured most of it out, dumped some whiskey in, added the remnants of her disappointingly ineffective defense elixir, and twisted the lid back on.

Typically, alchemy involved careful measurements, but London could eye amounts when necessary. It was one of her more useful abilities. She took a drink of the remaining liquor and shook the concoction while chanting under her breath to make the spells work. Without heat, or proper tools, it took a lot of time, but finally the mixture glowed faintly and bubbled, indicating completion. London shoved it under her coat and, feeling more secure and very tired, she hunkered down against the wall and slept.

The metal cage woke London when it creaked open. The failing fire barely lit the cabin. London wiped at the drool dried to her chin as Henry crept out of the cage. He had his shoulders hunched up, and his hair lay plastered around his ears. He held scraps of tattered fabric in front of his waist and blushed a brilliantly red color halfway down his surprisingly hairless chest. "Listen," he started, sounding miserable, and then he slipped on the snow that had melted across the floor and landed so hard that the cabin shook.

"You should really keep some aspirin here," London said, after she helped Henry to his feet and checked his eyes to make sure they still focused. He stayed very still when she touched him, watching her out of the corners of his eyes. She was not certified to provide medical assistance to humans, but, well. Henry seemed like he fell under her actual purview, at least a few nights a month, and old habits died hard.

Henry paused in the middle of pulling on a new shirt from his pack and scowled, "I never needed them before. What are you even doing here?"

London sniffed. Her mouth tasted terrible. She wasn't used to patients talking back, except in very rare cases, and she'd never been very good at talking to other people. Conversation felt easier with Henry, possibly because he wasn't exactly always other people. "Hey, I tried to leave last night, remember?"

Henry colored across his cheeks and down his neck, which was nice to look at as well. She'd never spent much time with under-dressed men. "You would have frozen to death out there. You can't go hiking in weather like this. You shouldn't even be in the park."

"Neither should you," London shot back. "Lycanthropes can seek medical aid now, when it's their time. Not...." She waved a hand back towards the cage. "Lock themselves up and hope for the best. This isn't the middle ages."

"Yeah, well, I don't like hospitals, and it's a free country. I rent this cabin from the state. It works well enough for me."

She knew that lycanthropes had a difficult time of it. Alchemists might have been mocked by serious magic users, but they'd never been hunted down. She frowned, dark considerations of why he might be hiding up here in the mountains in a cage creeping into her mind. "I could help you work up a treatment plan that wouldn't require... this. Or hospitals."

He stopped digging through his pack. "That's... kind of you to offer. But I've been coming up here for years with no problems. I think I'll stick with what I know. Besides." He abandoned the bag and frowned at her. "You're lucky I was here. There's no one else around for miles."

"I know." London sighed and gave up trying to untangle her dark hair. "That's why I came to find you."

He stiffened across his shoulders. "You came to find me?"

"Yes. I heard that you knew where I could find an old troll cave, up in the mountains."

Henry pivoted on his heels to stare at her, his head cocked to the side. "Who told you that? No, you know, I don't want to know. Yeah, I know where there used to be a troll, but I won't take you there now. I mean, there's two feet of snow out there. I think it's best if I dig us out and drive you down to your car. You parked down by the road, right? Most people do."

London's stomach sank. Fred's condition would have progressed through the night that she wasted. Time ran away, moving far too quickly. She gathered up her coat and shoved her feet into her soaking boots. Her toes squished into the bottoms. She pushed open the front door and looked at the expanse of white and buried trees.

"Hey, just come back inside." Henry followed her out the door. "I'll get the truck started and we'll get you out of here before tonight's full moon." She wished he'd stop offering help she didn't need. She was used to finding solutions on her own; his input only worked at cross-purposes to her needs.

"I'm not leaving." London squinted. "If you won't help me, I'll just have to... find the cave on my own. Just tell me which way it is." Her legs already felt like lead, but her only other option was to go back to town to watch Fred waste away.

"Well." Henry leaned against the doorway beside her and snorted. "That's not going to happen."

London turned and met his gaze, setting her jaw. "Then a unicorn is going to die."

"So you're telling me that nothing besides this fungus will work? Really? You guys don't have medicine, or something?" Henry wrinkled his nose in disbelief.

London shrugged. "It's a rare disease. And most magical disorders can't be treated by mass-produced medications. Look, I'm not even sure the fungus will be there. But I have to at least try." She stamped her feet, trying to work a little more heat into them. "I'm so close and I'm the only person who can help. So."

Henry stared at her for a moment and then reached up and dragged his hand across his face. "You're not that close," he said, before waving a hand. "Come back in and get warm. I'll get dressed."

"You don't have to come along," London said, even as she shuffled closer to the fireplace.

"I know the way up," Henry said. "And I can't very well stand by and let a *unicorn* die." He sounded only slightly mocking.

"I really hoped you'd have snow shoes, or something," London panted, later, trailing behind Henry as he forged a path upward through the trees. He broke some of the snow as he went, but that seemed to make moving through it more difficult. "A four-wheeler, maybe." She eyed his back. "You know, last night you carried me really easily."

"Last night I wanted to eat you," Henry said over his shoulder.

"So is that a no, or...?" London trailed off when Henry came to a stop, sniffing at the air. "Are we here?"

"We're close." London stepped forward, and Henry stretched his arm out, blocking the path. "But something smells weird."

"Maybe it's the mushrooms?"

Henry took another deep breath. "Maybe. It smells... musty. It's a big smell." He sighed and looked at her. "Look, stay here. I'll go see what it is, and then—" London raised an eyebrow and he stopped. "Fine," he said. "Just, go carefully, okay?"

They found the cave opening a half-mile further up the path, mostly buried in snow. "Finally," London said, blinking when Henry cut in front of her to enter the cave first, his eyes wide and his shoulders up. "Watch your step," she said, scrambling after him, "my notes say the mushrooms grow close to the ground." He grunted in reply.

They found no mushrooms in the cave's mouth, but it stretched back into the mountain, the depths hidden by a sucking kind of darkness. London fished out the tiny flashlight on her key ring and shined it towards the back of the cave. "I don't know if we should go down there," Henry said.

"I don't have a choice," London said simply. She crept forward, focused on the floor; Henry scowled, but followed after her anyway.

They went around a bend and the light from the cave's mouth all but disappeared, leaving them only a pinprick of light to guide the way. London's keys swung and clattered until she grabbed them tight. Henry walked too close in the dark, bumping into her, but London didn't complain. She reached out and took his hand, instead. He took a sharp breath in the dark and she started to draw back—she never knew when she was overstepping a social boundary—and then he tightened his grip, threading his fingers with hers.

She felt her cheeks flush, grateful for the dark, even as she dreaded it. The back of her neck itched terribly, but they had to keep going. They needed those mushrooms.

And they found them, finally. The ghost-white fungus grew along base of a wall, round at the bottom and growing to a tapered point that *did* kind of resemble an elf's ear. London cheered, far too loudly in the quiet of the cave, and knelt to gather some of the mushrooms just as something large moved in the darkness and growled, low and angry.

Sweat broke out across London's skin and she swung the flashlight around, unthinking, to illuminate a lumpy creature, with shoulders like two boulders and a head like a malformed turnip sunk down between them. Large, dark eyes glared out above a mouth full of a tremendous amount of teeth. A troll. It really did smell kind of musty.

London grabbed a handful of mushrooms, shoved them into the container she'd brought, and scrambled to her feet as the troll stood and shook, its shaggy hair rustling back and forth. Henry squared off against it. One or both of them growled. Damn lycanthropes, anyway. London dug her fingers into Henry's arm and snapped, "Don't! We have to run!"

Henry argued, "It'll follow us. You go, I'll—"

The troll lunged towards them. They barely managed to dodge, and the creature pivoted immediately to follow. London fumbled in her pocket, knowing he was right. It *would* follow them, given the opportunity. Trolls were territorial that way. "I can douse it! I just need a minute—"

Henry pushed her against a wall in the dark, hard enough to jolt her teeth together. The scant light showed her Henry's back and waving arms as he moved sideways. The troll turned to track the moving figure, its snarl revealing a broken tooth and purple tongue. It shook its head, lowered its shoulders, and Henry leaned forward and roared at it.

The sound echoed terribly in the cave, speeding London's pulse. She grabbed her potion, shaking it quickly back and forth, hoping it would activate properly. It began to glow, slightly. London watched the troll turn to focus on the light source, narrowing its eyes. She cursed, fumbling at the cap as it charged her, and Henry slammed into its side, shoving it just enough off course that it hit the wall, instead of London.

She reached out and grabbed him as he stumbled, yanking him away from the troll's sweeping blow. "We need to go!" he yelled, dragging her bodily backwards. London could only nod. She wished they'd put some distance between them, but that couldn't be helped.

The cap finally gave, unscrewing with a soft hiss of sound. London yelled, "Don't breathe!" She threw the new repellant at the troll as they hurried up the passage. She kept her grip on Henry's arm, and he stumbled alongside her. Behind them, the troll roared. A meaty sound, like a beast weighing a couple of hundred pounds running into a stone wall, echoed.

London's eyes and throat burned terribly and tears streamed down her cheeks just from the mixture's fumes. The light swung wildly, as though attached to a drunken moth. The mouth of the cave yawned blindingly white, and they burst out into the snow, followed by the sound of wracking coughs. London folded in half, grabbing her knees and sucking at the sweet, cold air. Henry leaned against a tree and wheezed.

"You pushed me out of the way," she said, when her throat stopped burning enough for her to speak. He'd argued, again, as well, but it had taken both of their ideas to get out successfully. "And then you roared. I didn't think you could do that outside of a full moon."

He grimaced before turning away. "We don't tell outsiders every-thing," he said. "But you don't have to be afraid, I—"

"I'm not," she interrupted, and laughed. It seemed a strange thing to say, but she *wasn't*. She'd just fought a troll with a lycanthrope. She had no more of her defensive tonic. She was lost on a mountain. But she didn't feel afraid, even when he turned and stared at her, his eyes wide and his cheeks gone pale. It was... nice, to have his company. She shifted and brushed her hands on her pants. "Thank you. For your help. I don't think I could have done it without you."

"You're not afraid?" he asked and took a step closer.

The troll roared, then, before Henry could reach her. London straightened. "Maybe a little afraid of him. We should keep going," she suggested.

Henry managed to lead London directly to her car, given only the barest hint of where she'd left it. The noises of the troll's distress faded behind them. "You want to come along?" London asked. "See if this works?" She gestured with the mushrooms.

Henry eyed the position of the sun over the mountains and shook his head. "Nah. I better head back. I like to stay close to the cabin during the full moon."

"Right," London said. Right, he was going to turn into a giant beast again. He hadn't wanted her around in the first place. She'd almost forgotten. "Well, thanks." She fumbled at her door handle.

"Hey, wait. Uh. I could give you my number." Henry flushed red over all the visible skin that London could make out. He wetted his lips and shifted his weight from foot to foot, all while she stared at him, wide-eyed. "You could let me know what happens."

London's heart gave a little jerk in her chest. "Alright," she said and smiled.

Exhaustion made the world fuzzy as London pulled back into the clinic. Her phone blinked at her from the passenger seat with dozens of missed messages, all destined to be ignored a little longer. Fred the unicorn looked worse when she checked on him, though he nuzzled at her enthusiastically. "I missed you too," London said, before walking back to her lab.

It took most of the night to properly extract every ingredient and to mix them in a tincture that London finally injected into a bag of saline solution. Fred leaned against her when she started his I.V., breathing damply against her cheek and nibbling at her hair. "There," she said, patting Fred's neck. "Let's see if that works." She yawned. "I'm going to sleep."

Morning proper broke with a cacophony of cheers as the Sheila arrived and found Fred bright eyed and faintly glowing. The noise woke London from a dead sleep. "Bring him back in two weeks so we can check on him," London told Sheila on the way out the door, trying to guide Fred's wet nose away from her face.

It took hours to get caught up on all the work she'd missed. London collapsed, finally, with her cellphone. Henry's number beckoned. She stared at it for a moment, wondering when she'd last texted anyone outside of work or school. It could have been another lifetime. She shrugged. *Unicorn made it*, she finally typed and sent.

Great, Henry replied, seconds later. *You want to grab some dinner and tell me about it?*

IN PURSUIT OF MEMORY

STEVE COOK

M arc looked at the woman who had sat down opposite. She was holding two glasses of wine, one of which she placed in front of him.

He moved it gingerly to one side. "Thank you?"

"You're welcome." She drained half of hers in one gulp, tipping her head back. Her white hair drifted away from her ear-tips, and Marc felt something lurch inside him – a queasiness that put him off balance. He squashed the sensation and flashed her what he hoped was a cocky grin.

"So, ah. What's a nice elf like you doing in a place like this?"

She held his stare as she took another deep draught and placed the glass down. "Really? That's your opener? It's like something out of a bad romance. Look around," she said, leaning closer. He followed her gaze around the room as it took in the plush leather seats and the wood-panelled walls with their ornate elven carvings. Orbs of fae light danced around, their ever-shifting shadows lending everything an organic feel. "If anything, I should be wondering what a scrappy country boy like you is doing in a place like this."

"Country boy? How do you—"

"You're dressed better and smell better than the city humans, but not well enough to be someone's servant. I don't know if you've noticed, but the clientele here are..." She gestured around. In one corner, the enchanted piano tinkled away, and the few other customers were mostly well-dressed elves casting him glances across their drinks. A human was waiting tables, dressed in an elfmake robe.

"Yeah, well, my silver's as good as anyone's," he mumbled, tugging at the worn sleeves of his sweater. He dropped his voice to a murmur. "I'm looking for... gear. Tommen said this was the place to come."

She raised an eyebrow. "Tommen? What exactly did that reprobate say?"

"He said that I should come here, sit at this table, and when a smart-ass woman comes over and smart-mouths me, I should give her this." Marc reached for his jacket pocket and drew a little square of metal out of his pocket, laying it on the table with a click.

She slapped a hand down on it as soon as he let go, and when she lifted the hand back up the coin was gone. "I'm Maerrican," she said.

"Is Mae ok?"

The look she gave him was odd, old and sad, but it was fleeting, dead as soon as it was born.

"Mae, then. Drink your wine and let's go."

"Uh, I shouldn't," Marc said, pushing the glass back towards her. Some of the amber liquid splashed onto the table. "Mum's always told me never to accept food or drinks from fae."

"Your mother has some very old-fashioned ideas," Mae said, "if healthy ones. Drink up, or no shopping."

Marc scowled and reached for the glass. He brought it to his nose and sniffed, but there was only the faintly sour-sweet wine smell.

"Do you think you could smell poison or a magic spell?" Mae shook her head sadly. "Always so much to re-learn."

He drained the glass, gasping slightly as the alcohol hit the back of his throat, then set the glass back down. "What now?"

"Follow me."

She got up and began to gracefully weave through the crowd, her long leather jacket almost dragging along the floor. More than a few eyes turned to follow them as they went through the door and out onto the misty night-time street.

It was one of the nicer neighbourhoods, far from the slum, and peaceful with it. Marc's gaze flicked around the quiet street; only the occasional human met his eyes, exchanging nods. A carriage was waiting there, a horse harnessed to it, and without pause Mae pulled the door open and stepped into it. She slid into one of the seats and gestured to the one opposite her. "Quickly now."

Marc looked around, but none of the passers-by were paying them any attention. He climbed into the carriage. "There's no driver," he said.

"No need for one," Mae said, leaning forward and knocking on the front wall of the carriage. "The shop, Harris, thank you."

"Aye miss," a gruff voice replied, and the carriage moved off.

· · ·

Mae pursed her lips as she considered the young man sitting across from her. His heavy-knit sweater was torn and repatched a dozen times over, and his scruff of beard was uneven. She repressed a frown as he tapped his boots idly together, leaving crumbs of mud on the polished wood.

"Magical horse?"

She frowned and shook her head. "Of course not. Why would anyone waste magic on that? Harris is a citizen; he and I go a long way back." She folded her hands on her knee and narrowed her eyes at him as the carriage bounced over the cobbles. His outline blurred slightly, and she blinked rapidly to avoid the headache that inevitably followed this piece of subtle magic. "Now then. The wine did have a spell on it – or more specifically, it contained a magical reagent designed to make the cells of your body resonate in a slightly different frequency. You won't notice it, but it will enable you to pass through the various barriers that lead to my shop. I should point out, at this juncture, that any attempt by anyone who isn't me to try and enter the shop would otherwise end in failure. Quite... *painful* failure at that."

"Got it," Marc said.

"Good, because we're here," Mae said. The carriage clattered to a halt, and she got up to open the door.

"We only just left! We can't have gone further than..."

Marc tailed off as the door swung open to reveal countryside, lit only by the moon. The carriage had come to a stop at the top of a grassy hill, a single tree the only thing that marked its crown. The faint glow of the city, graceful towers and flickering star-beacons, danced behind tall walls, dozens of miles down into the valley. Closer, the smoke of the tattered human shanty town, pressed as close to the walls as possible, hung in the air.

"Not *my* magic," Mae said, stepping lightly down, "but a magical horse after all, perhaps." She pulled a small pouch of coins out of her jacket pocket and slipped it under the horse's saddle. "Ok to wait?"

"Sure thing," the horse said, and began to crop at the grass.

"Thanks, Harris."

She walked up to the tree and touched one slender hand to the tree's bark, sending a little power into the wards hidden amongst the knotted bark. Almost immediately, a crack opened up in the tree, parting it vertically, and she held a hand up her eyes to shade them from the dazzling light that poured out.

She looked back at Marc. "Walk into the light."

"I swear, you're just saying things that you know sound creepy now," Marc said. She laughed, an almost liquid sound, and walked into the tree.

The room the other side came to life as she entered, light-globes warming with an almost-imperceptible hum.

"Goddamn it," she heard Marc say through the interface. One of his hands came through, fingers waggling, and she sighed.

"Every time..."

Bracing herself, she grabbed the hand and yanked, pulling him through. The crack snapped closed behind him and she released his hand, letting him stagger to a stop in the middle of the room.

"What is your *problem?*" he shouted, voice echoing around the metal walls. "I mean, seriously. It's like you lot exist to keep us off-balance or something."

"Not 'our lot'," Mae muttered, walking past him. "Just me." Her boots rang out on the floor as she moved around, taking her jacket off and swapping it for a long silken house-robe that hung on a hook. The robe was deliciously cool as she slid it on over her short-sleeved shirt and tied the cord.

"Right then. What are you looking for?"

"Oh, a couple of bits. Maybe more. What've you got?"

She rolled her eyes and reached over to touch a small wooden sigil attached to the wall. More lights came on in the next room revealing it to be very long and filled with racks that bulged with equipment.

"On your left, we've got the stuff most people are interested in. Personal alarm systems, a few guns – no, none of them are loaded, so don't try anything. There're a couple of tablets that have limited functionality, and I've got an absolute shedload of cables for all of them.

Pretty much, if you want a cable for something, I've got it." Mae moved down the row, gesturing to the left and right. "House alarm there, some speakers, a few laptops – though most of those will need a lot of work to get going again." She plucked a small white cylinder off a shelf and waved it at him. "This is what used to be called a personal assistant – like a servant, but without a body. So, useless, these days. None of the other systems that supported it exist." She dropped it back into the rack with a clang and walked on. "Then we're on to the mundane; digital clocks; a lamp, got a few bulbs for that; box of fuses. Batteries."

She reached down and pulled a tray out from under the shelves. It was full of colourful wood and plastic shapes, some small enough to be handheld. "These are the toys. Couple of gaming systems in there, a few board games that had electronic components, that kind of thing."

Marc followed in her wake, staring from left to right in amazement. "I had no idea there was still this much left," he whispered. "When they purged the tech from the world... I thought they got it all."

"Eh, there's plenty out there – if you know where to look," Mae said.

"And where's that?"

She tutted. "Here and there. So. See anything that takes your fancy?"

Slowly, Marc walked down the racks, fingers gently teasing over some of the items on display. Sleek metal casings brushed shoulders with scuffed and dented plastic, some of the tech clearly older than he was. "How do you keep it from being detected?"

In answer, Mae stamped her foot on the floor. "Cold iron. Whole structure's made of it."

"Doesn't that hurt you?"

"It's uncomfortably warm in here for me, and I'd be in trouble if I lay down on it, but no. The discomfort's worth putting up with for being undetectable. And the tree was very accommodating – the promise of long life will do that for you." She leaned her back against the wall and thrust her hands into the pockets of her robe. "Oh, everything with a plug comes with an adapter – Tommen makes them for me. You'll be able to hook it up to a fae power source like a ball of dreams or a moonlight well with little problem. Otherwise what would be the point?"

"Quite." He held up a thin black shaft of plastic, several buttons missing from its surface. "What's this, some kind of gun?"

"That's a remote control. Would you believe? Once upon a time, it was considered a great power to be able to do things from a distance instead of having to get up and cross the room." She smiled sadly. "Times change, I guess."

"Huh." He put the remote down and began to poke through the rack.

Mae sighed. "Look, I'm going to go and make a cup of tea while you browse. Do you want one?"

"Sure," he said absently, tugging at a cable. Something shifted, sending several rectangular boxes sliding to the ground, and as he tried desperately to catch them all she turned away.

Marc poked around in the contraband tech for a few minutes. He pulled out several items that seemed useful, but more and more he found his gaze returning to the doorway through which Mae had gone.

He wandered closer, trying to feign interest in the tech, and was finally rewarded by the sight of her bending over a table with a ceramic bowl of water. She sprinkled a few leaves into the bowl, then covered it with both her hands. The bowl glowed for a moment, white-hot, and when she took her hands away the water was steaming.

She picked the bowl up and began to pour the water into two cups, then paused. "Do you intend to watch everything I do?"

"It's interesting," he said, abandoning all pretence. "We don't get much opportunity to see magic out in the sticks."

Her lips quirked in what might have been a frown, and she

gestured to the little table. "Come and pull up a cushion. Take the weight off your feet for a few minutes."

He dropped what he was holding into the nearest rack and moved into her living quarters. Red drapes embroidered with gold runes covered most of the walls, held back against the wall by tables and cabinets. Most of them were filled with more artefacts from before the Purge, metal and plastic, more decorative than practical. A silvery vase sat on one pedestal, a single white rose blooming in it. He blew the steam from his cup as he considered the room.

"Roses, huh. Mum's favourite."

She was watching him over her own cup. "So, what's it like where you're from?"

"Yapsley? It's... dark. They don't let us have any of the magical globelights, and there's no electric lights, nothing like that. Candles and fires. Smells better than the city districts though, out in the countryside. I live in a cabin with my mother..."

"How is she?"

He frowned. "Do you know each other?"

Mae dismissed the question with a wave of her hand. "No. I just... phrased it poorly. Your mother, is she well?"

"She's had some sort of cough. Pretty horrible to listen to, sort of rattles on her lungs. The doctor we spoke to said he didn't have any medicine that could do much for it, but recommended fresh air and exercise."

She was on her feet in an instant, pulling a large wooden crate out from under a side table. It was filled with small coloured globes that clinked like glass as she sorted through them. The one she drew out and held up to the light glowed with a greenish hue.

"Here." She tossed it to him and took her seat again. "If she swallows this, she'll feel better."

"That's... surprisingly generous of you," Marc said, holding the globe delicately. It was no bigger than his thumbnail. "What is it?"

"It's a crystallised memory. The memory of health, you could say," Mae said. She sipped her tea. "Keep it safe. So... have you seen anything you particularly fancy?"

"There was a kettle," he said. "I mean, we've got one, and it was a good one, but it broke."

"You had an electric one before," she said softly. "The glamour on it broke when it stopped working."

"I..." He looked at the greenish liquid in the cup and frowned. "I suppose I did. It doesn't boil any more, though."

"Any of your other things broken, Marc?"

"No..." The bottom dropped out of his stomach and he held his breath, carefully setting the cup down on the table with a click. "You know, I don't think you ever actually asked me for my name."

She closed her eyes, lips moving in something that might have been a curse.. "No... no, I suppose I didn't."

"What's going on here?"

Small wrinkles developed between her eyebrows as she stared him straight in the eye. "Nothing bad, I can promise you that. You're safe here."

"I don't feel safe," Marc said, "and I'm not some child to be protected. You elves, fae, you're all the same. You came here, you took over, you took our tech, and now we're second-class citizens."

"It's not like that for everyone—"

"You all sit in the cities with your magic to keep the lights on and the water boiling, and meanwhile we're stuck out in the wild, back to cooking over an open fire and hunting for meat..." He trailed off when he realised her expression held nothing but compassion.

"Once upon a time, that was considered a luxury, to camp, to cook over an open fire," Mae said.

"There you go again," Marc snapped, the anger finally bubbling over. "'Once upon a time', like it's some sort of fairy story. It's our lives we're talking about, and none of you care to notice. Even you, charging us to get ahold of our own stuff, like you genuinely feel sorry for the way your lot treated us. You pity us, but not enough to actually help."

"Not enough to help. If you had any idea..." Mae rose smoothly to her feet, her tone sharp. "When you get back to your cabin, take a look around. Don't you think maybe your candles are bright and never seem to get shorter? Your oven cooks things thoroughly and never seems to need more fuel? Maybe have a look at the clock you never have to wind."

"What are you talking about?"

His voice rang oddly in the chamber, rattling around the iron walls, and he teetered on the balls of his feet as she stared at him. With an effort of will, he unclenched his fists and folded his arms. "What is going on here?"

"Every time," she muttered. "It would be wonderful to get through one of these without some sort of argument." Mae sighed. "Sit down. You're hurting my neck, looming over me like that."

Slowly, he lowered himself back into his seat, hands ready in his lap.

Mae tried not to notice his hunched shoulders, his beetling eyebrows. She turned her teacup in her hands. That was easier than meeting those angry eyes. "What do you remember from the Purge?"

"Remember it? I wasn't even born," Marc said.

"From your lessons, I mean. When I was young, my father taught me that we came among you all of a sudden. It wasn't a question of conquest," Mae said. "We were so far ahead of you socially, magically... it was like saying that someone who runs a zoo has conquered the animals there. That was the way he told it."

"And that's not true?"

"Not in the slightest. In reality it was a much closer-run thing. We're uniquely weak to the electrical fields generated by human tech; it messes with our magic, makes us sick. As soon as that was identified, it resulted in the Purge. A lightning strike; homes turned inside-out, mountains of technology taken away and destroyed, and an enchantment placed across you all that made sure you'd never want to use anything electrical." She gave a tiny smirk. "Most of us, anyway. There are a few who can put up with it, people born from the union of a fae and a human."

Marc winced, one hand half-going to his temple, but the pain seemed to clear almost as soon as it had come.

"You ok?"

"It's nothing." He shook his head. "You're talking about half elves, right? They're outlawed."

She chuckled, making air-quotes. "'Outlawed', heh. Such children would be killed, according to the law. But there's no such thing as a 'half-elf,' Marc. It happens, of course, despite everything, but when a human and a fae have a child it's either fully fae or fully human. If it's twins, it's guaranteed to be one of each. And in that union, there's some crossover of genetic traits; whatever quality makes me immune to the interference is one of the things that are inherited."

"So you're the child of a human... But that means you'd have to be younger than the Purge, too."

"That's right. And by accident of birth, I'm fae. So that's what's going on, or most of it. I owe my existence in part to humans, and this is my way of giving back. My thanks."

Like it had so many times in the past, understanding tinged with panic chased the anger away. "So who is it? Who's your human parent?"

"I think you know," Mae said. "But try to understand-"

"No. You tell me now."

She sighed, gently shaking her head. "Someone who I'm unwilling to put in danger. She... and my brother, both. But I help in little ways. Little things that make your lives easier."

Marc stared at her, then clutched at his head, wincing in sudden pain.

"What-"

"The headache is a product of the conditioning given to humans who've had their memories tampered with. I've tried, Marc, tried to remove the block Father put there, so many times." She across to try and place a hand on his shoulder. "He thought he was doing the right thing, hiding his infidelity. I argued with him when I found out, trust me. I just want us to know each other, live together again—"

He slapped her hand away.

"Don't touch me!" His fingers became claws as though he could dig the memory out. Mae rose and came to stand behind him.

"This was his compromise. Bury your memory, hide you in plain sight. If you knew, you'd be at risk from my kind – and so would I. Elves that could live side-by-side with humans, that could wield human technology? There could be an uprising – there's enough of us that sympathise. You and I, we represent something those in power would rather didn't exist... I'm sorry, Marc, it has to be this way, for now."

She placed her hands on his temples and he crashed into sleep, whole body spasming slightly. One leg kicked out, cluttering into the table and knocking the teacup off. It smashed wetly on the floor, and she sighed, letting him slide down onto the cushion.

"Every damned time. Every time. You'd think by now I'd have worked this out. And even before he knew, so argumentative. Sometimes I wonder what Father saw in humans."

Quickly, she moved around the shop. Into a canvas sack she threw a new kettle, glamoured to look like it was made of ornate copper. Next to it, a couple of new candle bulbs, and a small stack of leaf-wrapped elfbread from the cupboard. Then she dropped it by the portal that led back to the real world and went back for Marc.

He was snoring, sleep barely disturbed as she grabbed his collar and dragged him through the workshop, grunting with exertion. "I'm making life too easy on you," she muttered. "You need to lose some weight."

He made a noise, something approaching words, and she froze. He turned over, smacked his lips once, then lapsed back into sleep.

She knelt by him and placed her hands on the sides of his head again, fingers arched. With a faint sound of wire being drawn over metal, she began to tease his memory out, fingers weaving a complicated web that resolved into a small glowing ball. Images flickered across the ball; Marc meeting Tommen, their time at the inn, the carriage ride. Their argument. The memories played back, over and over, trapped inside the orb. She stowed the orb in a pocket and began again. This time, the images flowed from her into him, not perfect or complete but close enough. He went to a shop, got a good deal on a kettle and some candles, and came home. In the back of his mind she planted the idea that Tommen might be a good person to know, and refreshed the shields that she had placed around the empty areas in his memory. She paused, then added in the suggestion that white-haired elves were inherently trustworthy. "Maybe that'll help next time," she muttered. She released him and wiped her hands on her robe, blotting the sweat that had appeared there.

She slapped the exit sigil and, grabbing him under his arms, walked backwards through the light.

Back out on the hillside, Harris was still waiting. He trotted closer so that she could wrangle Marc's sleeping body into the back of the carriage,

"Any better luck this time, Mae?"

She leaned against the carriage to catch her breath. "No. The distrust is systemic, and the spell residue from the Purge is just too tightly wound up in his human physiology. And whatever Father did made it worse, destabilised the enchantment." She sighed, straightening her shirt and robe. There's just no easy way to tell him... or at least in a way that wouldn't send him mad, or worse."

"You'll get there in the end. I have faith," the horse said.

"The irony is, the very thing that keeps him safe from observation would kill him if he knew too much. No-one can read his mind and find out about our past, but he doesn't know about it either." She closed the carriage door and summoned the ghost of a smile. "Back to his home, please. He'll wake up in about twenty minutes thinking he had a couple of drinks on the way back from the shop and somehow had the presence of mind to order a carriage."

"Of course, Mae," Harris said, and set off down the hill.

She passed back across the threshold into the tingling heat of her cold iron home. As she passed them, she stroked each light-globe in turn, dimming them. Odd shadows, thrown up by the junk that filled the racks, seemed to move of their own accord as she darkened the room and retreated to her quarters.

From her pocket, Mae pulled the small memory orb, rolling it around in her fingers. Kneeling she pulled the chest of memories out again and opened it, placing the newest one atop the pile. From the box, hundreds of crystallised moments flickered over the tiny balls; two children, playing together in a forest; a woman, love in her eyes; hiding in a cupboard as their remote house was ransacked by cruel-eyed elven warriors. She held this one up to her face, peering deep within. As the elves rampaged through the house, their leader came in; his eyes widened as he saw their mother, and he ordered the soldiers out. The memory was flooded with light as the cupboard door was opened, and through Marc's eyes she saw her own face as a child, shouting defiance as his hands reached out, and abruptly the memory went dark. Some were more recent; the many visits to this hideaway, each one ending with the same sudden darkness as she worked her magic. Over and over she saw her own face, seen through Marc's eyes, the anger, sorrow, the pain. The dozens of attempts to reach him through the magic wound into his very being.

"One day," she whispered. "For you. For all of us. I'll find a way to give these back to you."

Slowly she closed the box and, in the dimness of her shop, began to pick up the broken fragments of Marc's cup.

THE EXTRA

MAX SPARBER

There I was, onscreen, standing in the background of a movie I had never made. I paused the DVD.

There was, briefly, a store down the street from my Minneapolis apartment, and this is where I had bought the DVD. The store opened rather suddenly. One day it wasn't there, the next it was, and I didn't expect it would last long, as the storefront had been home to dozens of businesses in the past few years, none lasting more than a few months.

This store was a junk shop. It was crowded with merchandise, as these places always are, and everything they sold looked like it was rummaged from an abandoned apartment or pulled out of an over-stuffed Dumpster. There were books with their covers torn off, clothes with visible moth holes, badly battered furniture made of pressed wood and laminate, that sort of thing.

The store was run by an odd man. He was small and bald, and it was almost impossible to guess his age by looking at him. He might have been in his early 20s, but if you told me he was 50 I would have found that credible.

He sat behind a monstrous metal desk, the sort you found in offices in the 1940s and were so heavy that they had to be moved by gangs of workers. He watched me as I looked around the store. He wore a grimy t-shirt that said "ask me anything," and he whistled constantly, a melody I did not recognize.

As I moved around the store, his whistle seemed to respond to my movements. As I went one direction, the whistle went lower, and when I went the other, his whistle rose. I finally ended up in front of a shoebox full of DVDs, and his whistle canted upward to a steam kettle-like whine. I glanced over at him.

"Ten cents a movie," he said, then started to whistle again.

I leafed through the films. They were mostly popular and uninteresting. Then I looked at one, and the salesman's whistle piped up to teakettle levels again.

The DVD was a Western starring Harrison Ford, one I had never heard of before. I held the DVD up. "When was this made?" I asked.

The salesman shrugged. "Ten cents," he said.

I brought the DVD to him and fished a dime out of my pocket. He took the money, slipped it into his pants pocket, and then produced a brown paper bag and slid the DVD in. He patted it and gave it to me.

"Ten cents is pretty cheap," I said. "Do you make enough to stay open?"

He shrugged again. "I don't worry about money," he said. "I just want people to find exactly what they need."

He leaned in close to me, grinning. "Junk is always a little adventure," he said conspiratorially.

He held up the bag and handed it to me. As I took it, he held onto it for a moment, resisting the tug of my hand.

"Watch the chase scene," he said. "Watch it a few times. I think you'll be surprised."

I don't know when the store closed. It was soon afterward. The next time I passed that corner, it was gone.

It took me a few weeks to watch the film. It wasn't an especially good one, and I let it play without paying much attention. But there is a foot chase through a Western backlot that is rather comical, with Harrison Ford chasing a young pickpocket through various western homes and through humorous scenes of western life, including a brothel where an embarrassed mayor leaps into a rain barrel. Moments later the chase continues through a blacksmith's workshop and so startles the blacksmith that he presses a red-hot horseshoe against his apprentice, who joins the mayor in the rain barrel to cool his burned backside.

Then, just as Harrison Ford passes a livery stable, he passes a man in a cap. I failed to notice this man on the first viewing, but the chase scene was enjoyable enough that I watched it again. On the second viewing, I paused the video.

It was me.

At least, the man in the cap looked like me. His face was an oval, just like mine, and had puffy eyes and a slightly startled look, like I do.

I don't know if I would have recognized the man from just that. I am often told people look like me, and I don't see it; it's possible I wouldn't see it even if someone looked exactly like me, as this man did.

No, there was more. He was wearing thick glasses. My glasses. He had a gray newsboy cap on his head, and it was my cap.

But it wasn't me. Of course not. I had never been an extra in a Harrison Ford movie.

The only explanation that made sense was one of coincidence: There must be another man out there who looks very much like me and happens to have a newsboy cap and thick glasses. It seemed like an improbable coincidence, but aren't coincidences always improbable? And that should have been that.

That wasn't that.

Since I first saw the man who looks like me in the Harrison Ford movie, three years ago, I have seen him 135 times.

He has appeared in low-budget horror movies, big-budget special effects spectaculars, foreign art house films, and three documentaries.

He is never anything more than an extra, and rarely appears for more than a moment. He is always in the same outfit of cap and glasses.

He also appears on television shows with alarming frequency. I see him at least once per week, and sometimes daily, appearing in crowd scenes in sitcoms, in the background of news footage, on made-for-television movies, and occasionally in music videos.

At least, I think I see him. I will see glasses for a moment, or a cap. Just for an instant, mind you, a subliminal blip that I think I recognize.

I can't help but be curious about the man. I presume he is a professional extra. I have heard about such people — apparently, it is possible to make a living in New York and Los Angeles by working regularly as background talent in films and on television.

This man must be particularly good at it, as I have seen him in productions that were not just filmed in New York or LA, but in Chicago and San Francisco and New Orleans and Florida, among other places.

He's a curiosity, all right. I don't think I have ever seen another extra wear the same clothes from film to film. He does. And generally extras don't appear in documentaries. He has.

I have done some digging. His name isn't listed on any credits, but, I learned, they wouldn't be. Only actors with speaking roles are given credits. Extras are essentially set dressing, and you wouldn't credit them any more than you would a chair or a table.

But full-time professional extras are only represented by a few agencies, and I have called them to see what I can learn. They have not been helpful, even when I lied and claimed to be a film producer looking for that extra to offer him a more substantial film role. I claimed I had seen him in a Ben Affleck film and thought he looked right for a part. I was desperate to learn more about him, desperate enough to make up a story.

It worked, in that the agencies genuinely tried to help me locate the man. They simply couldn't. They handle so many extras, and, in crowd scenes, there may be 200 or more people, most of whom are not under contract and simply respond to a call that goes out on a mailing list.

He's just a guy in a crowd, and they don't know who he is. Except he's a guy in almost every crowd scene filmed, it seems. And he looks just like me.

I was adopted as a baby. Sometimes I wonder if this man might be a relative, even a sibling. I have heard stories of twins who have been separated and discovered each other through unlikely circumstances. Perhaps that is my story.

I think about him a lot. So many questions remain unanswered.

Why does he appear in documentaries? I can't make sense of it. I saw him once standing behind the president during a televised speech, and how did that happen?

Some nights, all I do is think about him.

I won't be satisfied until I track this man down. And I think I know how.

I have some vacation time coming, and I have friends in Los Angeles. Perhaps it is time I was in a few crowd scenes of my own.

Over the course of a week, I appeared as an extra three times.

In the first, I stood in the doorway of a Hollywood souvenir shop as a martial artist scampered up a wall near me, fleeing black-suited killers from the mob.

In the second, I cheered a baseball team to victory. In the third, I pretended to be terrified as an unseen dinosaur, represented by two volleyballs on the end of a long stick, attacked the La Brea Tar Pits.

It was not hard to get these roles — they were low-paying, non-union jobs on low-budget films, and you can sign up for them online.

I spent most of the time on the set in a large holding area for extras, snacking on crackers and Tootsie Rolls they left out for us. Every so often a productions assistant would grab a few of us and we would go to the set for a half hour or so, stare at volleyballs, and then return to the holding area. It was not hard work. I enjoyed it.

I discovered how the man in the cap managed to wear the same clothes in every shoot. Because I did too. I wore my chunky glasses and my newsboy cap, and nobody said anything about it or seemed to care much.

Most of the extras had brought books and small collapsible chairs, like you might buy to take to the beach or a parade. Many were retirees who did this all the time as a sort of hobby. I talked to some of them. None had ever seen a man who looks and dresses like me, although they listened to my story with amusement.

The man in the cap, the one who looked like me, did not show up for these crowd scenes, and so I never met him and did not find out what his story is. This was disappointing.

When I returned to Minneapolis, I continued to get emails telling me about opportunities to appear as an extra in the Los Angeles area.

I have decided to move to Los Angeles.

I found work entering calendar listings for a newsweekly. The pay wasn't good, but I also found regular work as an extra, signing on with several agencies and call services, which alert you to background jobs. These supplemented my income. It wasn't really what you might call a living, but it was enough.

I continued to dress in my cap and glasses in the hopes of meeting my phantom double, but never did. Because I exclusively appeared in crowd shots, the film crew never cared what I wore. They scarcely noticed me, in fact.

There were a few days when, walking down Hollywood Boulevard, I would pass a news crew doing an interview, and I always made a point of walking into the shot, in the background, just to pass through. I guess I hoped my double might see me on television and try to seek me out.

It takes about a year for a film to appear in theaters once it has been shot. So a year after my first job as an extra, I went to a screening of the martial-arts film.

Other extras had warned me not to expect too much when I watched a film I had been in. The scenes go by quickly, and there are usually so many people on the screen that the chance of seeing yourself is remote. If you're lucky, you'll catch just a little blur of yourself, just for an instant.

But this scene, the first I had ever filmed, went on for more than a minute as the martial artist battled a black-clad ninja in a Hollywood souvenir shop. I was clearly visible in the shot for most of it, idly looking at a map to the homes of stars as the martial artist did some astounding acrobatics behind me.

And there, to my right, in cap and glasses, was my double.

He doesn't appear in the scene for long — he walks up to a register, wallet in hand, across the store from me, apparently preparing to buy something.

It's maddening, but I think know what happened.

We were both on the set, but never in the same place at the same moment. We were dressed the same. And, because we were never seen side-by-side, people assumed there was just one of us.

I don't know how I missed him. I can only assume that because it was my first film appearance and I was a bit overwhelmed, and because there was so much going on, I just didn't notice. Besides, he only appears for a moment. So, strange though it may seem, the fact that we were in the film together and did not know it makes a kind of sense.

A frustrating kind of sense.

There's just one problem with that theory, though.

The extra appeared in the next film I was in as well. The baseball film.

Worse, we're in the same box, cheering the same team, maybe seven feet from each other. We never seem aware of each other, but I can't believe I would have been in the same scene with this man, and be so close, and not notice him. Additionally, what director would put us both in the same shot?

I struggle to explain this. I suppose the director might have thought we were twins, and might have thought it would be funny to have us together, as identical twins are always a source of onscreen humor or cheap surrealism. Still, it seems unlikely.

The third film I was in eventually came out, and I went to see it, dreading what I might see. It was the dinosaur movie, and the volley-balls on sticks had been replaced by a surprisingly unrealistic example of computer animation.

In the film, this dinosaur creates havoc in Los Angeles, eventually sinking into the tar pits, while a group watches him die.

I am in the crowd. So is my double.

We are standing side by side.

As the dinosaur dies, my double looks at the camera and winks.

I have decided not to worry about it.

I continue to appear in the background of movies, and my double continues to appear next to me, neither of us aware of each other.

But something has occurred to me, and I keep thinking about it, because I can't help myself.

I keep wondering if somewhere out there, in another town, there might be another me. Maybe a junk shop opened near him. Maybe a strangely ageless shopkeeper whistled as he neared a box of DVDs. Maybe he bought one, maybe a dinosaur film.

Maybe right now he is watching it and seeing two men who look exactly like him.

Why not? It's no stranger than what is going on now. In fact, thinking about this gives me a little thrill, and an unexpected bit of comfort.

Because it would mean I am not alone in being confused. Somewhere in the world, right at this moment, another person who is just like me might be watching a movie and puzzling at what he sees.

Perhaps he will make some phone calls. Perhaps one day he might even wind up in Hollywood, dressed in his cap and glasses, and make his way onto a film set to appear as an extra in a crowd scene.

Tomorrow, when I head to another set to do another day of work, if I can get away with it, I'll look directly at the camera and give it a wink.

It's a wink for him. And for however many more of us there might be out there.

HIGHWAYMEN

AARON C. SMITH

The headlights grew larger in the rearview mirror. The riders were getting closer.

The half-dozen motorcycles had blinked into existence about ten miles back, when the clock read midnight. The witching hour.

Had to give them credit for appreciating the classics.

"C'mon, baby," I muttered. But the motor home wasn't a horse. Sweet words or an apple core couldn't get more out of it.

"They're coming, aren't they?" Paloma asked from the passenger cabin. Her wheelchair didn't fit up here. Besides, she had work on her laptop.

She was calm, for a thirteen-year-old being hunted by bikers. I'm three years older and keeping my nerves down took work.

"Yep," I replied, one eye on the road, the other on the mirror.

"And it's them?"

"You got info on another gang riding this stretch of road?"

I knew the answer was no. And that was saying something; the Temple sucked information from the alphabet-soup agencies that sucked information from damn near every American. The best thing the Poor Fellow-Soldiers of Christ and of the Temple of Solomon ever did was letting people think old King Phillip and Pope Clement V destroyed us. Being tinfoil-hat stuff made our jobs easier. Others usually did the heavy lifting.

This time was different; the Temple's own sources had dick-all on vicious supernatural bikers. Instead, we were stuck relying on a source who should have told the truth—but who we didn't quite trust.

They closed the distance.

The bikers could catch us – hell, pass us – any time they wanted. They were cats playing with mice.

Being mice sucked.

I needed a smoke; but even if I had one, smoking in the coach was against the rules. Wrath of God level.

God damn McVeigh, his plan and his rules.

෴

It hit as soon as we entered Crossroad Pawn. Magic slammed against the glyphs inked onto our chests. My half-abusive, total-asshole foster-father McVeigh and his coal-black mastiff Titan had to have felt it too, but they didn't break stride.

The tattoos protected against whatever spell we'd stepped into. We'd have headaches later. How long and how bad depended on what hit us. Magic always came with a price.

"Anubis charm," McVeigh said under his breath, taking the time to instruct me and Paloma. She provided overwatch from the RV we called home and recorded our activity for the Temple. "Weighs your soul, see if you mean harm or not."

So, we were meeting a player. And it was good he didn't get too close a look at my soul.

"He live here?"

"Paloma's research shows he owns a house outside town," McVeigh said. "You should know that, boy."

He has power, or access to it, then, since there's no threshold.

That was Titan. His kind has been upgraded from normal dogs. He was McVeigh's Companion, humanlike intelligence in a dog's body. He could beam his thoughts directly into our heads. He also slung some mean spells. Shave him down, he's more inked than a dead-tree newspaper.

He'd been partnered with McVeigh for years, even before Paloma and I went to live with him. Titan's magics also made him damn hard to kill, so long as McVeigh stayed breathing. After that, Titan got to retire with another couple decades on his clock.

I liked Titan a hell of a lot more than McVeigh.

But even McVeigh couldn't make this store boring. My boots clacked on the hardwood floor. Real wood, from the sound of it. And old, darkened in spots where liquid had pooled and sat. I'd seen those kind of stains in pictures of old crime scenes.

The display cases weren't the chrome and glass stores normally used. Instead, the antique cases were made of an old, yellowish material some folks might think was wood. My lessons with McVeigh let me recognize human bone when I saw it. But hell if the smooth, glossy bone hadn't been worked by a master. The bone supported thick old glass that hadn't been tempered by any modern method.

I walked around the room, looking in the cases. One held all kinds of blades. Buck knives, combat blades from around the world. A few straight razors had been displayed. Hell, there was even a ninja star. None of the weapons had been cleaned and all of them carried dark stains.

In the next case, guns were laid out. There was one automatic pistol, the rest revolvers. The newest of them must've been old when McVeigh'd been born sometime, like, last century. The rest looked like they'd seen action at Normandy or the Western Front.

Don't get me started on the jewelry. I mean, was that a frigging Super Bowl ring in the case over there?

"Dreams," McVeigh muttered.

"Huh?"

"Nobody comes into this place flush, boy. People come here when life's gone to shit. That ring? You think someone who played in that game wanted to give it up? That wedding band? Did they break up? She died? A guitar? Music's a soul's language. You sell that, what've you got left? The dreams are gone in this place."

McVeigh hadn't even started drinking today.

Behind us, someone let out a humorless chuckle. "That was poetic."

We turned and saw an anorexic version of the Night King wearing a cheap black suit. Greasy black hair fell over grub white skin. His jade-green eyes watched us like frogs he was getting ready to dissect. Two twins who could've been Brock Lesnar's big, bald brothers stood behind him in larger versions of the cheap suit. Instead of his button-down white shirt, they wore black T-shirts under their jackets.

"Am I to assume you disapprove of my business?" the pale man asked.

"Dreams die," McVeigh said with a shrug. "At least you give people a few bucks to make it feel better."

During McVeigh's depressing philosophy lesson, I checked out the three men. They didn't show any signs of carrying weapons; but in our world, that didn't mean much. For example, McVeigh and I had aces up our sleeves.

Literally up our sleeves. We each wore a highly detailed tattoo of a knife on our right forearms. McVeigh's a Ka-Bar and mine a Fairbairn-Sykes. When triggered, the tattoos became blades. It hurt like hell, but they beat pat-downs and metal detectors.

Our blades weren't just nice for pointy-stabby business either. When they'd been forged, the Blessed Blades – yes, the Temple talks about them in capital letters – were engraved with glyphs. They cut through most enchantments like butter. The cold-iron blades with inlaid silver also put the hurt on most monsters.

Aside from the blades, there was me. I'm not scrawny but most folks wouldn't bet on me bench-pressing McVeigh.

We ate for free a lot that way.

Being Nephil had its advantages.

"You're Graves?" McVeigh asked. The man nodded and reached a hand out.

Do not touch him, Titan warned. He cocked his head and took several sniffs. **Something's** *wrong* **here.**

McVeigh just stared at the offered hand. Luckily, the Knight's enough of an asshole that being rude looks natural on him. "Dylan McVeigh. This is my associate, Alejandro Guerra." I tipped my Stetson.

"A pleasure to meet you... gentlemen." Graves looked at me. "You responded to my advertisement quite quickly."

Normal people find work on Craigslist. The powers-that-be don't think people deserve to know about the things that go bump in the night. Folks in the know used Dark Web sites that made Silk Road look like Amazon.

Paloma watched them like a hawk.

Theoretically, we didn't actually need jobs. King Phillip didn't get near as much of the Temple's wealth as he thought. That fortune grew. The economy had its cycles, but our tentacles reached out far enough that calling it "insider trading" was a cute understatement.

But people would notice Knights if they were always flush. Questions would be asked. And folks thinking we were Temple would be bad. Monsters hated us like El Chapo hated the three *federales* he didn't have in his pocket.

Thanks to my grandpa, a lot of hunters carried a hate for the Temple that made the monsters' hatred look trivial. I felt their pain. He left Paloma a life without using her legs and left us both without parents.

So even Knights had to work for their cash, some of it anyway. Plus, getting gigs gave us a good excuse to contact men like Graves. A good way to keep tabs on the bad guys; maybe I'm judging a book by his cover, but I seriously doubted he walked the right-hand path. Paloma had opened a file on him, and now the Temple would watch and see who else came here.

"I did not expect a high-schooler to respond to my advertisement. That is troubling."

He wasn't even condescending. You couldn't tell my strength looking at me. But if being strong and more durable than the average human were benefits of being Nephil, the downside was the angel riding shotgun with my soul. It had anger issues that could bleed over to me.

It had taken me years to control the Celestial. And by control, I mean building a solitary-confinement cell inside a supermax in my mind. A glyph for the word "prison" had been etched over my liver – the real source of passion according to a lot of dead people – to help maintain my balance.

My lip curled. "I dropped out, if that makes you feel better."

"You apparently left before they taught you manners." Graves chuckled again, revealing two rows of bone-colored teeth.

I'd be pissed even without the Celestial. My mom'd worked damn hard to drill common courtesy into me and Paloma. My fingers curled into fists. Graves's meatheads shifted their positions, just enough to send a message. Ignoring them, I shot back, "This is America. We never learn."

"I'm training him," McVeigh said, putting a hand on my forearm. "He knows his business." They were probably the most honest words he'd utter in the meeting.

Graves nodded, narrowing his eyes. "One man barely out of retirement? And a boy?"

"If you know about me, you know I retired by choice, at the top of my game. I took a break to raise Alejandro here, train him up. He may be missing school but not to sit on his ass. I trust him to watch my back. That should be enough for you."

That was the closest thing to a compliment McVeigh had paid me. If I thought he actually meant it, I might've teared up.

"Besides, if we screw up, you can just send others."

Graves shook his head. "This matter is time-sensitive, and my property would be difficult to replace."

"And yet you posted an ad and didn't hire operators, like, say, Viktwa Security or the Band."

Graves spread his hands and shook his head at the mention of the mercenary groups. "I am a simple merchant. I do not have such resources."

"Why not send your friends?" McVeigh asked, nodding at the sides of beef.

"They are hammers, not scalpels."

"Well, we can make nice clean cuts. So, let's either get down to business or stop wasting each other's time."

Graves nodded. "A group of thugs on motorcycles calling themselves 'The Wild Hunt' hijacked a shipment carrying my property. A precious jewel."

"Better than a Super Bowl ring?"

"Vastly," Graves said, eyes narrowing in annoyance. "They ran the driver and his partner off the road. Their vehicle was found abandoned. Whether they knew if it was carrying my property or not, I do not know. However, they contacted me and offered to sell back what belonged to me." His voice rose as he finished his explanation.

"What happened to your people?" I asked.

The merchant gave a dismissive wave of his hand.

"So, this 'Wild Hunt.' They're trying to bend you over?" McVeigh asked.

"They ask for a trifle, compared to the value of what they hold. But I do not deal well with thieves."

"Understandable policy. Now, you mentioned a special fee."

Graves nodded and stood, opening the box and leaning it towards us.

A shriveled, wax-covered object. However, not enough wax had been poured over it to hide that it was a human hand.

"A Hand of Glory," Graves said. "The donor for this particular specimen was quite a talented computer programmer in his native China, until he fell afoul of the Communist Party. It will open electronic as well as more mundane locks. Upon retrieval of my property, it is yours."

McVeigh smiled, and his eyes gleamed. He didn't have to pretend much; I practically drooled at the thought of what that Hand could do for us. "We have a deal. Now tell us everything you know."

Turns out he knew a lot about the Wild Hunt.

According to legend, a bunch of fairies would get together and decide to go for some fun. The thing is, everything you've learned from Shakespeare or cartoons about fairies is bullshit. They're not helpful. They're not tiny fashion-models with wings.

Read the Brothers Grimm. There's a reason they warned kids to stay the hell out of the woods and not trust strangers on the road.

The Fae were Hell's original inhabitants from before Lucifer and his band of malcontents got kicked out of Heaven. They feed off the nastier human emotions. A bunch of them getting together for a hunt isn't good news. Especially when they're hunting *us*.

From her perch in the passenger cabin, Paloma asked, "How many?"

"Same as before."

"And their motorcycles?"

I didn't know much about bikes but I these weren't just weekend-warrior crotch rockets. "Harleys, I think. Like Graves said."

"He has excellent information," she muttered while typing. "Why didn't we hear of them?"

The two bikes at the front of the pack gunned their engines, popped wheelies and then shot ahead, pulling alongside our motorhome. They slammed their fists against the side of the vehicle.

Bang! Bang! Bang!

My hands tightened on the steering wheel. The Celestial roared inside my head. It would be easy to turn the wheel, force a biker to spill out. It might not kill the bastard but would sure as hell hurt.

If I had my gun, I could have some shots at the riders. Hunter's rounds – hollow tips loaded with silver and iron in a suspension of holy water – would end a Fae.

We didn't have anything more dangerous than a butter knife. Well, I could be dangerous, but McVeigh insisted we play the role of prey.

Prey didn't have weapons or fight back. We were just supposed to run until we couldn't run any more.

The riders sped maybe three, four football fields down the road and stopped.

I slammed the brakes. Metal squealed on metal.

The riders stood still as we flew towards them. They didn't even flinch, even though the motorhome stopped just a foot away from them.

A pair of bikers flanked the motorhome and the last two stayed behind us.

One of the Wild Hunt bikers swung off his bike and walked towards, stopping next to my door. A gloved hand tapped on the window.

Prey wouldn't do anything. Rabbits pinned in the headlights.

It tapped again. Harder.

I sat still.

Another knock. The glass rattled. Another hit and it would shatter.

Finally, I rolled the window down and heard a chuckle.

"A kid." Barely a whisper from under the helmet. The voice carried a Southern twang. "Where're your parents, cowboy?"

Son. Boy. Why the hell did everyone over the age of twenty-one treat me like a child?

"It's just me and my sister."

He snorted and looked past me. "Howdy there, sister. Do you have a name?"

"Paloma." Although the tone made the word sound like *screw you.* "What's *your* name, dickhead?"

"You've got some fire there, Miss Paloma. I'm Jenkins and you're on my patch of road. Now are you going to tell me what y'all are *really* doing on my road? Or am I going to come in there and teach you some manners?"

Why was everyone so obsessed with manners?

I'd have laid money that she was recording the conversation to the cloud. Whatever happened to us, the Temple would get information about the Hunt.

"Alejandro told you the truth. It's just us. They were assholes and we didn't have to put up with it. My brother's got his license, so we just took off."

Jenkins turned to the other bikers. "Looks like we got us a couple of strays. What do y'all say about that?" They laughed, an ugly sound. "Well, kiddoes," Jenkins said, turning back to us, "My boys have decided you'll get to be our guests."

Jenkins reached for the door handle and opened the door. He reached for me.

And then his hand jerked backward, like he had touched a hot stove.

We *lived* in here. It had a threshold.

There's a reason that a lot of monsters liked getting an invitation. Crossing a threshold without an invitation put a straightjacket on magic powers. Vampires were so dependent on those magics that they'd generally die – again – without it. The Fae, not so much. It was an inconvenience but not fatal.

I wondered if Graves had been wrong about them being Fae. Even if I could see its face, that wouldn't tell me anything. It could be a glamour or skin suit, covering up the monster underneath.

His voice was no longer cheerful. "Invite me in, kids."

"I'm not really feeling that," I said, making a show of shrinking away from him.

Damn McVeigh and his plan. If I had my Colt, I wouldn't have to put up with this.

"Invite. Me. In."

Maybe it *was* a vampire.

"Invite me in or I'll tell my boy Deeks back there to walk over to your gas tank. We'll stuff a rag in and you'll come out in a damn hurry.

For a moment, I thought about opening the door to the Celestial's cell, just a little. Even without a gun, the Wild Hunt would be a grease stain.

Focus on the mission.

"Come in."

"Asshole," Paloma added.

Jenkins nodded and entered. As the thing entered the motorhome, the temperature dropped, like we were back on the ranch in New Mexico, before my mother and father died. The coach seemed darker, too.

Not a vampire.

Fae. House of Shadows. They fed off fear. The ward over my heart was not triggered because its magic was manipulating the world around the Fae, not me.

My mind began working the glyph to call my Blessed Blade. My arm tingled as it began forming.

Paloma reached out, grabbed my hand and squeezed.

"No," she whispered, though her hand was ice cold.

I squeezed back. She was right. I might be able to fight Jenkins and win; but the others outside?

Only if I let out the Celestial. I don't know if I could get him back.

Besides, there was McVeigh's plan.

Paloma liked watching this show about pirates. The chase and battle, a ship being taken and becoming the pirates' prize.

I guess the Hunt should've run a Jolly Roger on our roof.

They surrounded us and led us down the highway for a few miles and then turned onto a faint path in the dirt, which led on for even more miles.

The glamorous life of a monster hunter.

We ended up outside a farmhouse. It wasn't falling, or the set of a horror movie, but it had seen better days. A barn sat a few yards from the house and *that* could've been in a slasher flick. Its door might be locked but that didn't matter when you considered the gaping hole in the structure's side.

Jenkins pointed at it. "Go. You try anything cute, cowboy, we'll have you right here and now."

I hesitated. He grabbed Paloma's wheelchair and yanked. My little sister fell to the ground.

"Asshole!" she screamed. If she'd been armed, there'd be dead bikers.

They'd touched my little sister.

Anger – my own without any juice from the Celestial – flashed. The Blessed Blade started to wake again, and I reached for the 1911 that should have been holstered on me.

Jenkins cocked his head. "Think, cowboy."

Gritting my teeth, I lifted Paloma over my shoulders in a fireman's carry as a trio of Fae surrounded me.

Just outside the structure, they stopped me in front of a trapdoor in the ground, held in place by a wooden crossbar. Maybe it had started out as a root cellar. I didn't want to think of what the Fae used it for. A rider opened the trapdoor.

"In," it ordered. I carried Paloma down rickety stairs into darkness, as the door above me slammed shut and the crossbar ground back in place.

I set my sister on the ground and tried to let my eyes adjust to the darkness.

Tried. The problem was that there just wasn't any light. The wood trapping us down here was solid.

Darkness didn't bother me. McVeigh had forced me to make friends with the pitch-black. Lots of monsters hunted in the dark.

I listened in the darkness.

Paloma breathed hard but steadily. Knowing her, she'd be more worried about distracting me than our living nightmare.

I wanted to hug her and hold her close. The sound of movement brought me up short. It wasn't just Paloma breathing.

We weren't alone.

Was there a Fae down here with us? The darkness would suit it. They're called the House of Shadows for a reason.

I rolled up my sleeves.

We'd played our part in McVeigh's plan. The time for being a victim was over. Focusing on the tattoo of my Blessed Blade, I bit down on my lip to avoid letting out a scream.

I couldn't see in the dark, but I knew what was happening. My skin boiled from the inside. Energies coalesced, gathered and tore from my flesh.

It hurt like hell, but I'd trained for that. Before I'd been inked, McVeigh trained me to endure the pain of the blade manifesting. His methods included smashing a Louisville Slugger into my forearm. Repeatedly.

My teeth ground into my lip hard enough to draw blood; but I didn't make a sound as the blade fell into my hand.

Now I was armed. But McVeigh's lessons about fighting in darkness hadn't turned me into a ninja. If there was a fear demon down here, the darkness was its home. I was just visiting.

There was a way to even things up.

It wasn't something I wanted to do.

Paloma was laying at my feet, trembling. It wasn't that cold.

We were all facing things we didn't want to do.

I closed my eyes and envisioned the Celestial's spiritual prison. My hand reached out, sliding open the window to its cell.

The Celestial stood with its back turned to me, wearing a sackcloth robe.

"Hey!" I yelled, banging the door with my mind. "Look at me."

It did, translucent skin covering cobalt veins on a face dominated by two huge golden eyes.

I focused on those eyes and fought not to gasp as a trickle of ice-cold power flowed into me, like a tiny leak in the hull of a boat. It was a promise – maybe a threat – of an ocean of power surging behind it.

There was a reason I kept the Celestial contained. Any more freedom, it would drown me.

But opening my eyes, I Saw. It was like night vision goggles but with a golden light instead of green.

Paloma sat, her back against the wall, looking towards the corner of the basement where we heard the noises coming from.

I didn't make it that far.

Because I saw them first.

A man and woman. They reminded me of my parents. Tall, lines on their faces and streaks of gray through their hair. They'd worked the land surrounding the home.

And they were dead.

Ghosts. I'd guess buried here; but I'd bet they were so closely tied to all their land that even as new spirits they could roam free. I wouldn't have been able to see them without my augmented vision.

They'd died harder than my parents, at least in a physical sense. My parents' bodies hadn't been broken, not like these two. The Fae fed on fear—and they made sure these two felt plenty of that before they died.

This was another reason the Celestial stayed in its prison. The things I experienced with its power would stay with me until my dying day.

I forced myself to ignore the dead. They didn't breathe and didn't make noise either. "Stay here," I ordered Paloma. She nodded. I crept towards the thick support beam in the middle of the cellar, watching the shadows for any more surprises.

I walked towards the beam and heard noises shifting away from me. "Come on out now," I said, hoping that some of the Celestial's strength bled into my voice.

Nothing.

"Come out, where I can see you."

I heard the breathing become more labored. Then, a faint whisper: "It's too dark."

You couldn't even call the voice a whisper. Was there another ghost I hadn't seen?

"I can see you and I need you to come out."

More movement.

I tensed, knife ready in case I needed to stab—

— a teenage girl?

In the golden light of the Celestial's vision, her dark hair flowed over a pale, oval face. The girl's jeans and t-shirt weren't much protection down here in the dark.

I looked hard at her, searching for any tricks.

She was human and terrified.

"Please. Please don't hurt me."

I lowered the knife but kept it ready. She might be human, but humans could be dangerous, especially teenage girls.

After all, I knew Paloma.

"I'm Alejandro," I said. I didn't reach out and kept the blade close to me.

"I... I'm Jewel."

Son of a bitch.

Jewel. *Graves'* jewel.

The asshole had been playing us or thought it would be a funny joke. Most hunters didn't cotton to human-trafficking. The thing about fighting the forces of evil is that it let you recognize evil. We fought monsters. We didn't feed them.

I took Jewel's hand and led her towards where Paloma waited. "Paloma, this is Jewel."

Paloma gasped in realization; then, more calmly, she said, "It's good to meet you." She held a hand up to shake. "You'll have to excuse me for not standing. My legs are sort of just for looks."

Jewel took her hand and smiled nervously. "Pleased to meet you?"

"Great," Paloma said. "Now what's so special about you?"

"What?" Jewel blinked, trying to understand the question.

"Isidore Graves thinks you're special. Why?"

Jewel began crying, deep heaving sobs.

"I w-was running on the trails, when th-they showed up. Two men in suits. I thought they might, might be cops but how many cops are twins?"

I asked her to describe the men and damn if she didn't describe Graves' bodyguards. He'd said the men transporting Jewel had been killed.

That had to be a lie, right? Or were they quadruplets?

"Did they say why they took you?" Paloma asked, wheels moving behind her eyes.

"No. They just said their master needed me. Then they did this."

Jewel lifted her arm. Her wrist was red and inflamed, like my forearm would be from the blade.

He said we'd know his property.

The son of a bitch had branded her.

"What's your birthday?" Paloma demanded. Dates and numbers meant things in the metaphysical world that normal people wouldn't consider. Magic works to its own logic. It has costs and the more powerful the spell, the rarer the ingredients. Ripping natural laws apart took special balance. And sometimes, special *people*.

When Jewel answered, my sister shook her head. Paloma then peppered Jewel with a list of questions about herself and her parents, trying to find out exactly what caused Graves to take her.

Pretty soon she's going to ask about Jewel's pets and her pets' Zodiac signs, I grumbled to myself. But then I heard McVeigh's plan unfolding. The *pop-pop-pop* of gunshots told me that he had begun his assault on the bikers.

While the Hunt had taken our home, McVeigh and Titan had been hiding in the luggage compartment. The Trojan RV.

The next part of the plan was up to me.

Of course, that had been less a plan and more what I called wishful thinking. We assumed they wouldn't just kill me and Paloma straight off. McVeigh said there was always a market for kids out there and if they were monsters, well, they had to eat.

Then we assumed that they would put us somewhere I could escape. I'm not Superman. I can't bend steel. However, I'd learned lots of tricks, by necessity. "Escape room" was a fun game for McVeigh before they became a thing.

We hadn't assumed a root cellar. The rickety wood stairs didn't look like they'd let me build up enough momentum to break through the trapdoor.

If McVeigh'd let me learn some basic spells, I'd've been able to blast the doors off their hinges or something.

I stared, trying to game the possibilities; then the wood creaked and I heard the crossbar being removed.

McVeigh was good. But there was no way he had taken out the Hunt and figured out where we were being held.

After a decade of watching – and sometimes living – horror movies, I knew there was only one possibility. I took a position under the stairs.

Our visitor was a rider, without a helmet. Through the Celestial's eyes, I saw walking shadow hidden under the flesh suit. Smoke with no fire.

"Move back!" The Fae ordered as he took a step down.

Then I became the horror movie. My blade slashed through the back of his legs, severing its Achilles tendon. Gravity pulled the creature down and I was on top of it.

I pistoned the knife through its neck, damn near decapitating it.

The kill only took a few seconds. I looked up and, through the Celestial's eyes, saw the horror on Jewel's face.

And ignored it, searching the Fae's body for anything useful. I found a Bowie knife, turning my eyes from it. The Celestial's eyes didn't need to see that blade and the things it had done. I needed to sleep at night.

Light spilled into the cellar and I no longer needed the Celestial's vision to see. It took a lot of effort to force the Celestial back into its cage, however. I'd be distracted. This was not the time for that fight. I needed focus.

I handed Paloma the knife. It probably did great work on scared motorists but would do dick-all against Fae. I'd hoped for a gun – even without hunter's rounds, physics still applied, and a well-placed shot could temporarily hobble a Fae – but monsters tended to avoid firearms. They'd spent millennia coasting off their strength advantage. Modern firearms had tilted the balance to the good guys.

Still, I was leaving her, and it wouldn't be unarmed.

"You have to go." She wasn't stating the situation. It was an order.

More gunshots.

I sprinted up the stairs and entered a warzone. Fire blazed, dry grass going up like tinder. But the motorhome and house were in no danger.

McVeigh had taken cover behind a series of large rocks, shooting at a rider. It loosed crackling bolts of electricity back at the Knight.

The great black dog Titan stared at a Fae running towards McVeigh. The monster burst into flame.

I began moving towards them.

And a rider sprinted towards me.

Or, more accurately, towards the barn. I recognized the horns on the biker's helmet. *Jenkins.* The bastard was going for Jewel.

Jewel *and* Paloma. He had to know that McVeigh had come with us. Jewel was valuable, and Paloma was his shield.

I wanted to yell to McVeigh to take a shot. But he was in his own duel and, with the shooting, he might not be able to hear me.

Besides, this was my asshole to deal with.

"Jenkins!" I shouted. The creature turned, and I launched into a tackle, dragging us both to the ground.

Its helmet hit, the visor popping up.

I damned myself for letting the Celestial continue riding shotgun, as I stared into living shadow.

Then the darkness flowed over me and I saw nothing.

Literally nothing. A blackness so deep it didn't just swallow light. It killed light, buried it. The root cellar was nothing.

Ice crystallized around my heart, trying to encase it.

I saw my parents' dead bodies. The shredded corpse of the first girl I loved. The knowledge that I brought the creatures that killed her into our lives. My failure to protect her.

All of that in a second. The weight of a misery in my life, short as it had been.

It should've crippled me.

But McVeigh, he'd taught me about pain. I didn't live with it.

I owned it.

My pain burned, a different fire than the Celestial.

There are some antidotes to the despair the Shadow inspired.

My love for Paloma.

The righteous anger at the things that had been done to Jewel, the couple in the cellar.

The Shadow touched me, and I wrapped my hands around its nonexistent smoky throat.

It screamed, just before I shoved the Blessed Blade until its tip buried itself in the back of the helmet. The riding leathers collapsed under me.

After a few seconds of catching my breath, I stood.

McVeigh's rifle barked. The last Fae fell.

I walked over to the Knight.

"Good to see you, boy. I thought you might want to sit this out," and his voice took on a sardonic bite, "after being put out there as bait and all."

"I'm not good at sitting."

He nodded and withdrew a flask from his pocket, knocking back a taste. A better man than him would've had a smoke for me.

"You'll want more of that," I warned, and told him about Jewel.

He did take another swig.

"And what're you wanting to do about it, boy?"

I smiled. "Graves owes us some answers. And we've earned that Hand of Glory."

Dodgy meetings always seem to end up in the same sort of place. Outside of town, away from prying eyes and the surveillance systems that had sprouted up like weeds after September 11. Abandoned offices, that sort of thing.

That's how we ended up in a concrete box, four walls without a roof. A sign said that it was going to be a burger joint. If the owners were smart, they could've charged rent for these kinds of deals.

Hell, Paloma could put together a website, a directory for shady meet-ups.

She could make a killing.

We arrived at the site for two hours before the meeting. One thing that McVeigh had in common with my father was the belief that being early was on time and on time was late. When you're meeting a creepy asshole, that's even more true.

"How's everything look?" I asked into my Bluetooth headset.

"Good. I've got a car approaching from the east."

Paloma didn't need any magic for her overwatch duties. She piloted a drone from the motorhome, watching for any sort of trick. Titan stayed with her, as backup. But he'd been drained in the fight. She was watching over him as much as she was us.

We'd used the drone to scout the location and make sure Graves hadn't decided to get here two-hours-and-one-minute early. Now we made sure that he was playing by the rules we set up for the exchange.

They were simple. Me and McVeigh, Graves and a bodyguard. No guns but McVeigh and I wore Blessed Blades sheathed on our waists.

Graves would show us that the Hand of Glory worked on the electronic safe we had brought. We'd hand over Jewel. Everyone walked away.

That was the plan.

But when the hell did anything go according to plan?

"He's out. Two bodyguards. Repeat two. They look like the ones you and McVeigh described from the store."

Like the ones that Jewel described.

Jewel looked over at me, as if she heard Paloma.

Two was more than one. Things going wrong already.

McVeigh wasn't breaking a sweat and I couldn't either.

Graves walked into building, flanked by the two guards from his office.

"You can't count?" McVeigh asked.

Graves spread his hands out in mock apology. "You are two trained and skilled killers. You defeated the Wild Hunt. Can you truly blame me for being careful?"

"You sent us to bring you a person," McVeigh said, words flat and clipped. Calm and professional.

You had to know McVeigh to know just how deep you were in the manure to hear him talk like that. I glanced at my blade.

"Yes?"

"She's human. We're hunters." Graves should understand the code.

"You brought her here. You must have found the price... enticing." I swear Graves' eyes glowed for a moment.

"The boy," McVeigh said. "He wants assurances. About the girl."

The merchant's mouth curled in a smirk. "Of course. However, if you are unwilling to teach him such lessons, I will. The truth? I am a simple middleman. An individual came to me, needing someone with certain attributes. My searches led me to the Jewel."

"That's enough for you?" I blurted out.

Graves turned towards me. "I have my ledger, its names and my numbers, boy. It is all I need. Talk to your teacher. It will be for your own good to understand how the world works."

"And how the world works is there's going to be an issue if *that* doesn't work," McVeigh said, pointing at the wooden box Graves carried.

"Quite right." Graves said as he opened the box, with slow and deliberate movements. He lifted the Hand, pointed it at the safe and spoke the activation words.

The artifact glowed, its index finger straightening to point at the safe. The light from inside the hand pulsed, orange and then white.

The safe's keypad squealed and then clicked, the door opening. Graves nodded to the bodyguard to his right. The man knelt, opening the safe.

If Graves had been paying attention, he'd have seen us letting our jaws hang slightly open and looking away from the safe. That meant when the flash-bang grenade in it exploded, we weren't completely incapacitated by the effect. That gave us a precious few seconds to draw our pistols and fire two rounds into each of the bodyguards' foreheads.

That's why I couldn't bring myself to be so upset with Graves bringing more than one bodyguard. We'd always been planning to cheat.

Graves was not getting Jewel.

The next step of the plan included putting a few rounds in Graves, collecting the Hand of Glory and getting Jewel back to her family.

Plans always change.

Our rounds blew into the bodyguards' foreheads and exited through the back of their skulls. At that point, physics demanded that the men would be carried back by the force and fall. Biology demanded that the ground behind them would be sprayed with blood and gray matter.

These assholes must've never been to school because they just stood statue still as black sand leaked from their wounds.

The bodyguard closest to me swung a haymaker, connecting with a hit that would've knocked a normal person's head off. I staggered back.

"Sand men," Paloma said, watching the fight from above as I

dodged more blows. "Like golems but not. Make a model from sand, pop in a spirit. Even if their bodies are destroyed, if you have sand from the same source, the spirits can be popped back in. That's how Graves knew so much about the Hunt attacking his drivers."

"That's great, sis," I said through gritted teeth, narrowly avoiding a shot to my face. "How do we take them out?"

Before she could answer, Graves stepped forward and grabbed Jewel. He began dragging her away as McVeigh ducked the other bodyguard's punch. McVeigh kicked at the thing's knee. It should have snapped like kindling, but the Knight actually bounced back as if he'd kicked a wall.

That's all I had time to see because my dance partner locked its hand around my throat, squeezing and lifting me off the ground, knocking the Bluetooth from my ear.

The Celestial screamed from inside its cell. If I died, it died.

Before I went nuclear, I'd try something old-school. I flipped my legs up, planting a kick into its chest. It had the same effect as McVeigh's kicking the partner's knee, except for one thing. It put me in position to grab the Blessed Blade from my sheath.

I slammed the blade into the thing's forearm.

It didn't flinch as my knife impaled it.

However, smoke poured from the wound. Score one for the Blessed Blade, cutting through the magic that made the sand man. I pulled the blade back towards me. I've cut flesh before. This was different. The sound of butcher paper ripping filled my ears as the blade worked itself free through the creature's hand.

The hand holding me crumbled and sand poured out of the wound at a faster and faster rate.

I fell to the ground. Still pouring sand, the creature stepped towards me. I shoved my knife into its thigh and pulled towards me.

More smoke and sand poured out. The bodyguard stumbled as its leg lost the structural integrity to keep it standing. Unable to maintain its own weight on that leg, its damaged hand didn't let the bodyguard catch itself. The creature stumbled and lashed out with its uninjured hand.

A vise grip locked on my ankle. I tried to shake it off without any luck.

Graves was using our distraction to drag Jewel back toward the exit.

"*Hijo de puta!*" I screamed, shoving the blade into my attacker's skull.

More sand poured out and the head deflated like a balloon, but the hand held tight. I sawed at the wrist until the monster's hand finally couldn't hold me.

I turned towards McVeigh. He was on the ground, being choked and unable to reach his blade.

I threw my knife, the blade burying itself in the sand man's side.

McVeigh grabbed the hilt and pulled towards him. Sand spilled out, but it wasn't going to be fast enough for him to be any help.

Graves was almost across the room.

He was fast. I had to give him that.

My bullet was faster.

This time, physics worked as normal. It carried Graves forward and his brains splattered across the ground. Thinking of his glowing eyes, I emptied my magazine into Graves' body at strategic spots.

I dropped the magazine, loaded another and repeated.

"You done?" McVeigh asked.

"We do reloads. It's not a waste."

He grunted. "No. Are you done?"

It was a test. I thought for a moment.

"His ledgers. His shop?"

I looked at the box, the Hand of Glory inside. Suddenly McVeigh's plan – the real, big-picture plan – clicked.

Son of a bitch. McVeigh saw something like this happening from the very beginning.

Bastard.

He smiled and looked at the box. "Good. Let's go back to the pawnshop. That ledger he talked about, with all of his customers? I think we'll be working off it for a while."

BANISHMENT FOR A
HOMESICK DEMON

WONDRA VANIAN

It was the kind of day poets wrote heavy, existential poems about. The sky was dark as evening, although it was only just past noon. A thick mist hung low on the mountains like a wispy shawl of gloom. The cold and damp sank into Maisie's bones as she trudged up the tallest hill in her decaying little town.

If she had been so inclined, Maisie might have penned a poem herself; one that captured the way the sun struggled half-heartedly to break free from the clouds that obstructed it – and failing so miserably in the attempt that the day seemed more dismal for the effort. She might have immortalized the broken set to the shoulders of the grim-faced people she passed. Or, she might have tried to capture the crunch of dried leaves between boots and the pavement.

If she had been so inclined, Maisie might have written a few lines that made that one November day live in the hearts of readers for all of time.

She was *not* so inclined.

Mostly, Maisie just wanted to punch something. Or, someone.

Preferably someone.

Like the someone who'd dragged her all the way across town without any explanation other than "It's urgent!" She stomped up the looming hill, ignoring the locals who took one look at her thunderous expression and scuttled out of the way.

A small, surprisingly busy gift shop sat at the pinnacle of the hill. The cheerful window display was full of grinning sheep and the wooden sign outside, hand-painted with a dragon, bore the words, "Cymru Crafts." It was, most visitors agreed, quite charming.

Maisie was not charmed. She threw open the shop's door and stormed inside. A jangling bell over the door announced her arrival.

"Hiya, Mais," the young woman behind the counter said without looking up from her phone.

"How did you know it was me?" Maisie asked the young woman, whose nametag read "Fred" even though her name was Abigail.

There was probably a story behind the nametag, but Maisie wasn't in the mood for stories. She'd been in the middle of a dozen different things when she got the text message. The poppets would wait but the potions had been ruined beyond repair when she abandoned them to answer the summons of the shop's owner.

Abigail's fingers were a blur. She tapped the screen a couple of times before dropping the phone into the pocket of her green apron. Nodding toward the bell above the door, she answered. "It only rings that angrily for you."

That was nearly enough to make Maisie laugh. Nearly.

"Where is she?" Maisie demanded.

Before Abigail-Not-Fred could answer, an old woman bustled through an open door at the rear of the shop. Her wispy silver hair must have started the day piled high on her head but mostly hung loose around her lined face. The thin-rimmed glasses perched on the end of the old woman's nose appeared to be mostly decoration; her sharp gaze cut right over them to fix on Maisie.

"There you are!" the old woman said by way of greeting as she rounded the counter to pull Maisie into a hug. "Where have you been? We've been waiting for you!"

Maisie patted the old woman's back affectionately, rolling her eyes. She was impossible to stay mad at. "Hi, Beryl. Nice to see you, too."

Beryl released Maisie and waved away the sarcasm. "Of course it's nice to see you, lovely, but-"

"What a minute," Maisie interrupted, "did you say 'we'?"

The old woman nodded excitedly. "Yes," she said, "yes, we've been waiting."

Maisie nearly groaned aloud. Beryl meant well but had been trying to set Maisie up since she'd moved to town, nearly five years before. Without a lick of success. No matter how many times Maisie told Beryl she wasn't interested in "settling down" anytime soon, the old woman saw it as her life's mission to find Maisie "a nice young man."

And they didn't exactly share similar tastes in men.

"Nope," Maisie said, backing away. "Not interested. It doesn't matter who is he, or what he does, I'm not interested." This *is what was so urgent that I had to drop everything? I can't believe her!*

"Now, now," Beryl said, looking chagrined and patting her flyaway locks nervously, "there's no need to be like that."

Maisie stared open-mouthed at her. "I'll give you three reasons," she said. "One, lived at home with his mother but didn't believe in feminism."

"Oh, well, you see..."

"Two, worked as an accountant, collected stamps, and insisted on taking *my* leftovers home to his cat."

Beryl blushed. "Yes, but..."

"Three, complimented my shoes and insisted on trying them on. During dinner!"

A snort came from behind the counter. Maisie shot Abigail a look but the girl appeared to be very interested in her phone. Too interested to eavesdrop, though her shoulders shook with repressed laughter.

"I don't care who you've dug up this time, Beryl, the answer is no!"

"Well, now," a silken voice said from the back of the shop, "isn't that a shame?"

Maisie turned to face the speaker – and froze. Her mouth fell open in astonishment.

Now you're talking...

The man who stood in the entrance to the backroom was *exactly* the kind of guy Maisie wished Beryl would have set her up with. He looked to be about Maisie's age or older. His dark hair was cut short, his eyes were like cold sapphires, and – icing on the cupcake – he wore straight-legged jeans with a faded tee-shirt. Maisie could forgive a lot of things, but skinny jeans weren't among them.

"I must apologize," the man told Maisie, coming closer with a dancer's grace. "If you have been inconvenienced, the fault is entirely mine. I asked Ms. Gordon to send for you."

Gorgeous *and* articulate? Damn. Maisie took back every bad thought she'd ever had about her elderly friend.

Thank you, Beryl.

"No," Maisie lied, "no trouble at all. I'm Maisie Owens."

"A pleasure," the man said. He reached for her hand.

Zap.

When their palms touched, Maisie felt a rush of electricity pass between them. She was too experienced to mistake it for anything as ordinary as attraction. Her suspicions were confirmed when the man's face shifted. His features contorted, became too sharp, too angular to be human and he smiled to reveal a mouthful frighteningly sharp teeth. His eyes flashed – blue one moment, red the next, then back again – as Maisie recoiled from his touch.

"A DEM-" She broke off and looked around the shop for any ordinary customers that might be lurking. There were none in earshot, but Maisie lowered her voice anyway. "A *demon*? You're trying to set me up with a *demon*?"

"While the thought does appeal," the demon said, giving Maisie a once-over that earned him a glare, "I'm here on business."

Ah. It was Craft, then. Maisie was both relieved and, surprisingly, a little disappointed. She was a freelance witch who performed certain... services for those with magical leanings but no talent of their own. She created charms, mixed potions, performed summonings, and dabbled in healing.

For *human* clients. "I don't work for demons," she snapped immediately.

Beryl inserted herself between them. "Give him a chance," she urged. "Tozrach is just trying to get home. You know what that's like, don't you?"

She had to go there.

Maisie was something of a refugee. There were mitigating circumstances that kept her from returning to America. Mitigating circumstances like an order to stand before the High Coven on charges of the wrongful deaths of seven ordinaries, which weren't exactly Maisie's fault. Well, not *entirely* her fault. Sure, she may have cut a few corners in her hurry to be done with the job, but she couldn't have known the ring had already been hexed by another witch. If the clients had warned her, she never would have added her own hex to it and they would still be alive.

The American Council didn't see it that way, though, so she had appealed to the British Council for sanctuary – which they had given, provided she kept her nose clean. Dabbling with demons didn't fit under that category.

"I'm from another *country*," Maisie said, "not another plane of existence!"

"Home is home," Beryl reasoned. Her voice was gentle, persuasive. Beryl was what Americans would have called a "bleeding heart"; she believed that everyone – and, apparently, *everything* – deserved a second chance.

Dammit. Maisie had never won an argument against the old woman. Beryl was a master of the guilt trip; she always said it was a magic Maisie wouldn't master until she had children of her own.

Maisie always replied that she'd stick with real magic, thanks, but now she wondered if maybe Beryl wasn't more powerful than she was.

"What are you doing here, anyway?" she asked the demon, defeated.

"I was looking for you," Tozrach explained. "Well, not *you*, exactly. Any witch will do. You were simply the closest."

"I'm honoured," Maisie replied sarcastically.

Beryl stared at her, giving Maisie a look that threatened weeks of not-angry-just-very-disappointed talks if she refused. It would be easier to give in. But Maisie had a rule about working with demons. Goddess only knew where she could go if she had to vacate Britain in a hurry, too.

"No," she said finally, "find yourself another witch."

"I can make it worth your while..."

Maisie rolled her eyes. "Oh, gee. I've *never* heard that one before! Let me just compromise my ethics for—"

"A kiss."

That shut her up.

Kissing a demon stole a fraction of their power. The more powerful the demon, the greater the power that was stolen. Tozrach must be a very weak demon, she decided, to consider offering *any* of his power as payment.

Or, very desperate.

"How did you manage to get yourself stuck in the human world?" Maisie asked, curious. If he'd been summoned, Tozrach wouldn't be wandering around, looking for a way home. He must have gotten himself into the human world under his own power, without making plans for return. Stupid, rookie mistake for a demon.

Tozrach coughed uncomfortably, which did intrigue Maisie a little. She'd never seen an embarrassed demon before.

"Ah, well," he said, "I made a mistake."

"Me too," she said dryly. "I made the mistake of answering a text that said, 'Come quick! It's urgent!'" She shot a look at Beryl, who became preoccupied with re-arranging a display.

"Does it matter how I got stuck here?" Tozrach asked irritably. "I just want to get *back*. The human world is... difficult."

True, that.

Maisie considered his offer. She was relatively powerful, but nothing compared to some of the other witches she knew. More power could never be a bad thing, could it? And she'd be doing the world a favour by ridding it of a demon. Something about the situation made her uneasy, though. Demons were usually trying to get *into* their world, not *out* of it. Why was this one in such a hurry to leave? Surely there was mischief somewhere he would be missing out on...

Beryl and her young assistant were pointedly *not* watching the exchange. No help there.

"Okay," Maisie said finally. "I'll send you back to Hell, in exchange for a kiss – from you, paid before the banishment is completed."

She made sure the terms were very clear. Demons could be trickier than leprechauns.

"Deal," Tozrach said without hesitation.

Maisie looked down at the hand he long-fingered proffered but didn't take it. "Your word will do just fine," she said.

"Oh, good," Beryl said, bustling over. She smiled at them. "Now that all that's sorted, how about a nice cuppa?"

∽

By the time Beryl allowed Maisie to leave (three cups of weak tea later and with a demon in tow), the weather had improved just enough to be miserable, rather than oppressive. A damp wind blew across the valley. It churned up the thick pea soup of clouds above and allowed a few thin rays of tired sunlight to fall through the cracks. The afternoon sun warmed the mountains enough for them to shake off their misty mantles. Another cuppa and Maisie might have emerged into a rather nice day.

Not that she noticed the weather. Her attention was... otherwise engaged.

The walk across town from Beryl's shop to Maisie's semi-detached felt like the longest of her life. Probably had something to do with the ravishingly handsome demon who walked beside her, earning open looks of lust from many of the women (and often men) they passed. The demon who had *zero* concept of personal space.

"If you touch me again," Maisie warned the second time Tozrach casually draped an arm across her shoulders, "I'm going to stab you."

He laughed but removed the arm. "You know that won't kill me."

"No," she conceded. "But it will make me feel better."

They walked in silence a few minutes before Tozrach said, "Why do you hate my kind?"

Maisie stopped so suddenly that Tozrach took a few steps before stopping to look back.

"You're joking, right?" she asked incredulously. "You demons come into my world, wreak havoc, then head back to Hell, leaving us to clean up after you – and you want to know why I hate you?"

Tozrach sighed. He gestured for Maisie to continue walking before he spoke again.

"Demons are usually *dragged* into this world, remember," he said. "Against our will. To do *your* bidding."

Maisie said nothing, scowling.

"Is it fair to blame us for the evils perpetrated by *your* people?"

They stopped to allow an old woman to pass by. She held the hand of a little girl in a school uniform. The old woman smiled at them gratefully while the girl, apparently in a mischievous mood, pulled a face at them. Tozrach waited until the old woman's back was turned, then pulled a face back – his true face. The little girl screamed, practically climbing her grandmother's leg to get away from Tozrach.

"Don't do that," Maisie blurted. Mostly because seeing him reveal his true face in the middle of the day unnerved her. It didn't matter how many unglamoured demons she saw; they always managed to chill her blood.

He laughed. "She started it."

Maisie decided that she couldn't banish Tozrach fast enough.

Once at her snug, cluttered cottage, the demon wandered around with a familiarity Maisie found infuriating. He was worse than a toddler; while Maisie was busy gathering components for the banishing spell, Tozrach touched *everything* and put nothing back in its original place. She considered stabbing him after all, just to make up for the hours of cleaning she'd have to do after he was gone. There weren't enough smudge sticks in the world to get his essence off her belongings.

"Would you stop that?" she snapped when Tozrach picked up a tiny ceramic replica of Stonehenge. For the third time.

Tozrach did exactly what Maisie expected him to do. He ignored her. "I find your... what is this?" The demon held up a cheap, stuffed bear an old boyfriend had won her.

"That's a teddy bear," Maisie said impatiently. She juggled an armful of candles and chalk to snatch back the bear. "Wait a minute... where did you find that?"

The demon shrugged. "Your closet."

"What were you doing in my—" Maisie forced herself to take a deep breath. "Sit," she barked.

He obeyed. Tozrach plopped himself down in one of the armchairs Maisie had pushed aside, to make room for the banishment sigil that would send the demon back to his home—in this case, Hell. It didn't seem like much of a home to Maisie but, hey, Tozrach probably wouldn't enjoy hanging out in her hometown, either. She shook off the wave of homesickness that came over her at the thought of the town she'd never see again, and got to work.

Maisie began by drawing a large circle on the wooden floor with chalk, then lining it with candles. Banishments were tricky business; their energy needed to be carefully contained, or else Maisie risked letting something in from the other side, or even being caught in the banishment herself. She started to draw another circle, inside the first, when she realized how quiet it was – never a good sign when a demon was about.

Sneaking a peek at Tozrach, Maisie found him staring into space, arms crossed across his chest, a sullen expression on his borrowed face. If she didn't know better...

"Oh, my god," she said. "You're sulking."

"Am not," Tozrach argued in the sulkiest voice she'd ever heard.

Maisie shook her head with a laugh. Human or demon, men were all the same.

"What's the deal, anyway? Don't you have knickknacks in Hell?"

"Not exactly," Tozrach said evasively. "Less knickknacks, more..." he waved a hand, "entrails."

Well, *that* was a delightful mental image.

"If Hell is so awful, why are you in such a hurry to get back?"

He didn't answer immediately. Maisie looked up from the symbol she was drawing.

"Home is home," Tozrach said when their eyes met. His words held a sense of longing Maisie could identify with. What wouldn't she give to be able to go back to her crappy little town in the middle of Nowhere, USA?

Nope, she thought. She was *not* taking a ride on the Self-Pity Express. Not today. Though it took more effort than she cared to admit, Maisie shook off the homesickness that threatened to overcome her.

"Any place can be home," she told the demon.

He studied her. "You mean that, don't you?"

Maisie got back to work on the sigil, uncomfortable with

Tozrach's scrutiny. "Sure," she said as dismissively as possible. She didn't like the morose place the conversation was taking her.

Tozrach let Maisie work in silence. As she drew curving symbols on the floorboards inside the circles, she could almost forget he was there, watching as she made her way around the circle and back again. Almost.

It wasn't until Maisie set her chalk against the wood, to draw the final symbol, that Tozrach spoke again – right next to her. His hand came to rest on her wrist.

"Would you like to collect your payment now?"

Surprise made Maisie's pulse race. Surprise and...

She knew that the human mask he wore wasn't what Tozrach really looked like but damned if it wasn't a pretty mask.

"Now?" Maisie asked, rather breathlessly.

He smiled. "Now."

"Okay."

Tozrach drew Maisie close, wrapping an arm around her waist as she lifted her face to his. He leaned forward, touching his lips to hers and—

Her world exploded.

Tozrach was no low-level demon, willing to forfeit a tiny fraction of his power to get home. He was more powerful than any demon Maisie had ever encountered. The slice of power his kiss gave her rocked through Maisie, almost too strong to be contained by her puny human form. The chalk fell unnoticed from her fingers as she brought her hands up. Grabbing Tozrach's shoulders, she held on for dear life.

He slid a hand behind her head, deepening the kiss as his fingers tangled in her hair. Her legs came up of their own accord to wrap around his waist. His teeth nipped at her lips and Tozrach growled his pleasure. Goosebumps rose along Maisie's flesh.

Was it one kiss? A thousand kisses? Maisie felt like lightning, stuffed inside a human body. She buzzed with barely leashed power. Power, and attraction. Humans rarely survived sexual encounters with demons but, if Tozrach had tried take her then, Maisie would have done nothing to stop him, even knowing the consequences. Hell, she was about two seconds away from shoving him down herself and riding him to oblivion.

"Do you find the payment acceptable?" he asked, heavy-lidded, as he pulled away.

"Hm?"

English, Maisie. Use English.

"Is the payment acceptable to you, witch?"

She had to shake herself to bring the world back in focus. Tozrach watched her with an amused look on his face.

"Acceptable?"

"Yes," he said. "If not, I can provide another—"

"No!" Maisie scrambled backward. Gods knew what she would lose if she let the demon kiss her again.

"Just... just stand in the circle," she told him.

Still grinning, Tozrach took his spot in the centre of the circles.

Maisie turned her back on the demon, so he couldn't watch her struggle to catch her breath. It was dangerous to perform magick in an agitated state, but she wanted Tozrach out of her house as quickly as possible. Rather than light the candles by hand – and reveal just how badly they shook – Maisie lit them with a flick of her wrist.

"Careful, witch!" Tozrach exclaimed as the candles flared a foot high.

"Sorry, sorry!" The flames died down to a normal level. Maisie's cheeks burned hotter than the ring of candles. She had forgotten about the new power coursing through her. It was going to take some time to get used to her enhanced abilities. Probably best if she didn't play with fire until then.

"Are you ready?" she asked.

"Are you?"

No. Maisie hadn't been prepared for a single thing that had happened that day. If she could live it a thousand times, she doubted she'd ever be prepared.

She nodded to cover her unease, then began.

The banishment ritual was simple. Maisie had done it so many times that she could do it in her sleep if she had to. Everything went exactly to plan. The air hummed as power was drawn into the circle, forming a ring around the demon. It shimmered an iridescent purple that glittered like starlight. Tozrach's feet left the ground as Hell called him home.

Everything went exactly to plan.

Until it didn't.

In the space between the moment Hell reached for Tozrach and the moment it dragged him across the dimensions, the demon's hand closed around Maisie's wrist. She stared in shock and horror at the spot where their flesh met.

"What?" she gasped. "How?"

With a wicked grin, Tozrach looked pointedly down at the sigil between them and Maisie saw her error. The demon had stopped her from drawing the final symbol. She'd been so distracted by Tozrach's kiss that she'd forgotten to go back to it. A stupid, rookie mistake. One she could never take back.

Tozrach pulled Maisie into the circle. One impossibly strong arm clamped around her waist. His lips found her ear and spoke the words that had sealed her fate.

"Any place can be home."

Then, the ritual finished its work and, with a *pop*, demon and witch left the human world.

MIND THE STORE

VANESSA WELLS

Clair Pendergrass, my boss, mentor, and local witch repacked her briefcase for the third time, pushing sweaty red hair out of her face in irritation as she tried to force the latches to hold back more paper than their design limitation. She eventually muttered a spell, then sat on the case and snapped it shut.

I didn't bother to hide my grin. "You know I could e-mail you those files when you get there, right?"

She gave me a scathing look. "I don't trust computers with spells, Gwen. You don't want these to fall into the wrong hands." She swished at her hair with a hand and it fastened itself in a knot at the back of her head, silver streaks decorating the bright red strands like a candy cane. "I won't be gone long. Two or three nights, maximum."

"If you don't want the papers to fall into the wrong hands, you'd better not check the baggage. And it's fine. I'll get the sales tax done while you are out. I need to work on the 01-339 form, and if I have time I'll get the latest shipment categorized and out on the floor." I glanced at the teetering pile of boxes with a small sigh.

Clair nodded. "I made the deliveries yesterday, so we're good for a month with the funeral home. There's extra in potions locker if they run out."

'Making deliveries' was code for taking a batch of unguent down to the funeral home in old margarine tubs to slather on the newly dead so they didn't accidentally rise as zombies.

Because that kind of thing happened in Topeka, Texas; and it wasn't pleasant. It was one of the many pitfalls of being the single largest reservoir of magic in North America.

I turned to my boss and mentor. "You aren't going to have time to get through security at the airport if you don't hurry."

She raised a brow and I rolled my eyes, knowing very well that she'd *nudge* the TSA agent with enough magic to fell a rhino if they got in her way. Maybe I should feel bad about that deliberate undermining of important airport security, but honestly, witches with Clair's power didn't need a bomb to take down an airplane if they were feeling particularly murderous, so the whole idea of security was a bit moot.

"I know you can handle the business part for the antique shop..."

I rolled my eyes affectionately. Despite still being in high school, I could and *did* handle the "business part." Clair was a great teacher, a good boss, and a powerful witch. But she was pretty lackadaisical about restocking new antiques.

And she was a really lousy bookkeeper. She hated doing the day-to-day taxes and accounts and couldn't hire someone to do it for her —explaining this particular antique business to a normal CPA would be nearly impossible. The assets were sold online, and then customers returned the antiques to a hub in Florida, and they made their way back to the store to get a refill. And that didn't even begin to cover the disparity between potions ingredients and the products she made and gave away.

It wasn't like she could just say, "Oh well, I spent a thousand dollars to make this mystical potpourri, but I sold it at three dollars a bag because I wanted to make sure that no one gotten eaten over Halloween." A real CPA would probably ease out of the room before calling men with white jackets to take us to a nice padded room where we couldn't hurt ourselves or others.

Because our business wasn't really antiques. Our business was keeping the results of magic away from normal folks—and shipping magical energy out via E-bay so that magic-users in dry areas would have power to work with. The antiques were both an absolute necessity (objects that were around magic for decades could be used to make a canteen to hold magic) and as a front for the so-called "normal" people around town (because no matter how many times they saw evidence of real magic, their brains kept explaining it away.)

"Call Kit if there's anything magical that comes up," Clair went on as she selected several ugly rings that were brimming with magic and adding a truly atrocious necklace that clashed with her shirt. "Don't let any dragons into the shop."

"Not likely." I wasn't a fan of dragons, at least not the few I'd met. They were pushy, self-absorbed, and had a nasty habit of eating magical beings... and kidnapping others for brides. They really needed to find their way into the proper century, but I suppose that was difficult when most of them were older than the Edo era.

"I know Kit isn't the most..."

I raised a brow at her pregnant pause. "Responsible?"

Her lips quirked. "That's one way to put it. But if there is magical trouble, call that shape-shifting furball to cover your six."

I grabbed her duffle as we headed out to her Cadillac. "You should make the shape-shifting furball drop you at the airport."

"Nonsense. Then I'd just have to get him to pick me up again. No one wants to take time out of their day to do that."

I privately thought that Kit would happily take time out of his day to get an hour alone with Clair, but I kept that observation to myself.

It's always better to avoid annoying a witch.

I opened up the store the next morning with the ease of having worked in the shop for half a year. Saturday mornings were usually just for orders, filling canteens of magical energy and getting them ready to ship out when the mail-lady came by to pick them up. She thought we were just selling antiques on the internet, which honestly was probably as impressive in a small town as actual magic. It took a little over an hour to get the canteens filled and carefully boxed to go out in the mail.

I began working on the taxes, since they required more attention than stocking the shelves. I could stock shelves in the afternoons after school if I didn't get them done on weekends, though that was often the time that Clair oversaw my magical education.

Around noon, the chiming bell on the door announced the first customer.

I looked up, prepared to smile at a familiar face (in a town the size of Topeka, all the faces were familiar) when I met the eyes of an older, harsh-looking woman that I'd never seen before.

I was instantly suspicious; but I tried to be polite. "Hello. Can I help you?"

The woman looked a little bit like a cross between a holdover hippy and Calamity Jane: western style boots, bellbottoms with decorative patches so well worn that they faded into the denim, and a patchwork knitted cardigan that looked like it was made from random bits of potholders past their prime. Her hair was long and frazzled, braided back in a mixture of brown, dirty blond, and yellowish white that reminded me of calico cat. A worn band of leather drooped around her neck. Her eyes were fever-bright and twitchy as they searched the room. "I'm here about a canteen. Is Clair in?"

Odd. Orders didn't come in like that. "She's not." Best to play dumb, just in case it was some random normal un-magical person with unholy luck. "I'm afraid we don't have any antique canteens in stock, I can give you the number of a place in Ft. Worth..."

"When will she be back?"

"Two days."

She looked stricken. "I don't have time for Clair to come back. Just sell me a book or something and I'll make it myself."

Now, as far as I knew, there were only a few people who knew the spell to make the canteen, and most of them were associated, in one way or another, with the Guardian's council.

Clair's customers were vetted and trusted. They were people who wouldn't misuse the magic. You couldn't say that about just everyone, and I'd learned the hard way to be suspicious.

I could sell the woman a book without admitting that magic was real; in the normal course of things, I wouldn't have hesitated, but it had been a rough year. You couldn't just pick up a random coke bottle and pump it full of magic. The object had to soak the magic up, bit by bit, over decades to be able to hold a charge.

Still, if I didn't sell this woman an item to make her canteen, she probably wouldn't get one, and that would mean that when she left Topeka, she'd only have the local ambient magic to work with...not something anyone wanted to chance.

"Let me make a call."

I dialed Kit's number from memory. "It's Gwen. I have an issue at the shop. Can you come?"

Whatever Kit heard in my voice, he didn't quibble. "Are you safe?"

I moved the old rotary phone to the other ear. "I think so."

I heard the snick of metal sliding into sheaths. He was probably gearing up, just in case. Not a bad idea with dragons and who-knew-what-else hanging around. According to Kit, they were very fond of eating *kitsune*. "I will be there in five minutes."

The woman eyed the door longingly. "I really don't have time for this."

"It won't take long."

We spent approximately three and a half minutes avoiding each other's eyes in awkward silence.

Kit sauntered into the shop; the stranger turned, and a sly grin played at the edge of her mouth. "Kit Ulysses. It's been years."

He looked good; he always did: lean muscles clearly defined by his white dress shirt and crisp slacks. It wasn't personal. "Kit" was not his real name. It was short for kitsune—legendary fox shapeshifters from Asia. Kitsune were known for many things, including some pretty amazing feats of magic; but more than any of that, the whole species seduced like they breathed, and nature gave them all the tools to do so. I was immune, thank goodness, because of the magic in my own blood. Though I had to admit, I often felt a little jealous that I hadn't gotten at least one of the magical hair genes.

Kit inclined his glossy head of hair regally at our visitor. "Martha Schmitt... the last time we met was when you talked Clair into joining you in that awful trip to Korea."

Her lips thinned. "Clair decided to go to Korea on her own; she's a patriot."

His eyes narrowed. "She went to make sure you didn't get yourself killed, because she's loyal to her friends."

My hand gripped the smooth wood of the counter. "She and Clair are friends?"

"You'd probably know her by her old code name, Able Hands."

I knew that name. She'd sent information when we were facing down a necromancer who accidentally turned herself into a zombie. I gave her a small smile, but she was too busy glaring at Kit to notice.

She didn't seem to like the tall Asian man much. Her glare would have melted glass when she spat out, "I heard you'd been sniffing around Clair again."

Kit gave her a look, and it was suddenly full of that false heat he could lay on where women were concerned. "I always thought that my dear Clair smelled delicious."

Martha's face flushed. Her lips parted. A light sweat broke on her brow.

She made a slightly disgusted sound in her throat, but both Kit and I had seen her react to his allure. He must have shut it down, because she stumbled slightly.

"What can the humble citizens of Topeka do for you today, Ms. Schmitt?" Kit's tone was cutting, without being in the least inappropriate. I would have loved to have known how he did that, but if I had to guess, I would bet that it would take more than one mortal lifetime to achieve that kind of snark. It was more than natural talent. It had to be the result of serious practice and repetition.

I smiled. "You understand that I needed to verify that you were one of Clair's customers. Pick out a book and I'll give you the usual deal." I pointed to the wall of books on one side of the store and she stomped over without a word.

I felt a little bad about slowing her down when she was obviously in a hurry, even if it had been the smart thing to do. "Do you want a coke? We have Dr. Pepper, Coke, and Sprite."

She kept one eye on the fox and shook her head. "Thanks, but I don't drink anything I don't prepare. It's a simple spell to add things to soft drinks, and you should..." She stopped mid-sentence, narrowed her eyes, and whipped out a tiny compass-like device, seeming to scan her own body. Her jaw tightened.

Kit moved me behind him with one inhumanly fast step.

She glanced at the door, obviously wary, and tossed a moldy-smelling book on the counter for me to ring up. She handed me a five, waved off the change, and quickly performed the spell to fill it with magic. Unless you were using second sight, you wouldn't see much when someone filled a canteen. Other spells had physical effects—you could see something levitating or notice when someone was acting oddly; but despite what Hollywood implied about magic, most of it wasn't showy. The woman simply pushed enough of the flowing power from the town into the book.

She tucked the paperback into her bag, nodded to me, and gave Kit one last disdainful look as she turned to go. Her worn boots clumped across the wooden floor of the shop until she reached the door.

She turned the knob slightly, then looked back at me. "Tell Clair..." She swallowed, hard. "Tell her that if she doesn't hear from me in two days, she'll need to go to my place and pull the records. Greece, 1982. Tell her that some archeologist dug too deep at Delphi. If anything happens to me, I have something set up that will e-mail the most important information."

Kit looked alarmed. "If you need help..." He might not like Martha, but he wasn't the sort to sit by and let something happen to her when she was a friend of Clair's.

"Please." She cut him off. "You reek of magic. Having you along would be like tying a nice juicy steak around my neck when running from wolves." She gave him a tiny smile. "I have a plan. Stay out of my way. You know I work best alone."

And with that, Martha Schmitt turned the knob and hurried out the door like something might catch her if she stuck around too long. I watched through the window as she got into a worn-out sedan and left a puffing cloud of dust as she sped out of town.

Kit didn't even have to tell me to call Clair. I was dialing her hotel before he opened his mouth.

"Martha would never ask unless the situation was important..." I could hear her moving around the hotel room. "And don't bother looking for her. Her magic is almost entirely centered on spells that hide her presence or kill anything in her way. Poor dear can't levitate a teacup, but she's a dab hand with a hoodoo head-shrinking curse. If something is after her, it'll be sorry if it catches up."

"What about Greece?"

"As far as I know, Martha's never been. As soon as we got back from Korea she went back to the boondocks in Arkansas. Even I didn't see her for a few years."

"Do you think she was giving you a hint?"

Clair snorted inelegantly, "Remember back in December when I told you she never put her real name on anything...probably not even the return address on her electric bill? I'd call her paranoid, but it's saved my life twice. Telling me to expect an email if something happens to her is as trusting as she gets."

Kit frowned. "Does she still have that ugly chunk of amber she always wore?"

I related the question to Clair who chuckled. "Wears it on a thong around her neck. Never takes it off."

I closed my eyes, envisioning Martha. "It looked like something belonged on the thong around her neck, it was worn, but there was nothing on it."

Clair said something in German that was probably not fit for polite company. "I'm going to change my flight and head out to her place as soon as I can get away. Ship me a half dozen spare canteens. I'll pick them up as soon as I get off the plane."

"It's already one o'clock. I won't be able to ship them until Monday."

Kit frowned. "I could drive them to her."

I relayed the message. "Tell him not to be silly," Clair replied. "I'll let you know Monday morning if I'll need them. You can overnight them then if I see any reason to stay in Arkansas. I should go. The meeting with the Council is in half an hour. Why don't you and Bradley check the shields tonight?"

"Sure." At least I'd get to spend Saturday night with my boyfriend.

I locked up the shop and headed to the parking lot.

There was a ghost in the driver's seat of my car when I opened the door.

I smiled. "Scoot over, Adam."

He popped out of my spot and reappeared in the passenger side, hair slightly mussed like he'd just pulled a helmet from his black curls. He'd been transparent most of the time when I'd first met him, but now he was clear enough that I could see the mechanic's callouses on his hands. It was one of the benefits of my being his touchpoint, the physical connection that literally tied a ghost to the land of the living.

He was looking at the driver's seat sadly. "I miss driving."

"And I miss DQ blizzards, but I can't eat them every day or my pants won't fit. We'll go driving soon." When we shared dreams, Adam could interact with the real world again; hear, taste, smell, and touch things he hadn't since he died on his way to the Second World War. I put the key into the ignition of the car and it purred to life. "Did you listen in?"

"Of course."

"Can you pop over the Bradley's and see if he'll meet me on Old Mill Road?"

He pouted, "I'm not a cell phone."

I smirked. "Nope. Cell phones don't work in Topeka." The magic interfered with the signal.

He rolled his eyes, but there was a grin playing at the edge of his mouth. "Fine. But the next time you meet me in a dream, I want a picnic. With apple pie."

I smiled warmly at him. I enjoyed the dreams as much as he did. Clair didn't approve, but Adam was my best friend. "Done. You have apple pie, I'll get a blizzard from DQ... something with peanut butter, and maybe bananas."

My incorporeal best friend looked vaguely disgusted at my food choice, but it was his loss. Peanut butter and banana blizzards were delicious. The only thing that would make them better would be if you could fry them.

Adam disappeared as I sped through town. The sheriff looked up as I passed, but I nudged his mind with a little magic and he went back to his two-day-old copy of the paper and ignored my little speeding infraction. (Nudging was a perfectly acceptable way to leave your own thoughts for others to find...and I didn't employ it often, but my car did not like speed limits.)

I beat my boyfriend and my friendly ghost to our normal meeting spot by ten minutes.

Bradley pulled up in his pickup, bounded out like a human version of a Great Dane, and kissed me. I kissed him back until Adam made a half-disgusted, half-impatient noise.

I grinned up at him. I wasn't short, but Bradley was a humongous giant. I'd often wondered if all the magic rolling around town had contributed to his size, but his cousin Sam was even bigger than Bradley was—though they shared the same blond haired, green-eyed genes and general build. They did not share a propensity for magic.

My boyfriend nuzzled my cheek and kissed my forehead as he pulled away. I missed the warmth of his arms immediately. He, being sublimely in tune with the emotions of everyone around him, wrapped a bulky arm around me and gave me a playful grin. "Adam says we need to check the shields?"

"Clair wants us to check. I'm sure Adam filled you in." My best friend and my boyfriend hadn't liked each other in the beginning...at all. However, since Christmas, they'd found a common goal: working together behind my back at every turn, because they did seem to agree that I was a trouble-magnet.

Which was unfair. It wasn't my fault.

Probably.

Bradley took my hand, and our auras merged perfectly. He didn't really need the magical boost to do something as routine as checking the shields that surrounded the town like a giant snow globe. But the feeling of our magic, swirling together, was comforting. It felt like home. I, who had gone my entire life feeling like an outcast because weird crap just *happened* around me, loved the feeling of absolute belonging that I'd found when I merged my magic with his. He seemed to feel the same. He was always the first to offer his hand to bring us together.

Bradley squinted, and I felt his paladin magic reaching out over the town. He wasn't a natural magic-user like me. Bradley was the result of the population instinctively electing him as their collective white knight, because of the swirling energy of the town. When humans live at the center of what amounted to a magical lake, a champion was elected by general (if unconscious) consent. They wanted and needed someone standing between them and the odd things that happened when magic pooled in an area like it did here in Topeka.

And I had to admit, if you were electing a white knight, you'd be hard pressed to find a better guy than Bradley. He was the best-liked guy in school... not "popular" like the kids I'd met in any other school I'd been to. Bradley exuded an aura of gentle happiness, and everyone that was around him felt it. People were kinder when they entered his circle of influence. They smiled more. Bradley influenced the town, and the town influenced him.

I threaded the fingers of my other hand through his. In some ways, he was more powerful, because he could access Topeka's energy in ways no other human being ever could. In other ways, he was less flexible because he couldn't do magic of any kind outside the town.

For all that, he was like a human dowsing rod when it came to problems inside the shields.

"I think we need to drive north." His voice was rough. We piled into his truck, and I scooted to the middle so Adam could ride with us. He could appear on his own of course, but it saved energy, and being a ghost, he didn't have much to spare.

I put my head on Bradley's shoulder and wished I'd packed weapons when I'd made my lunch.

We drove on the gently curving road for about twenty minutes. People didn't realize it, but they instinctively designed and built the roads within the shields. The magic lulled the "normal" people into not noticing it, but it stuck out like a sore thumb if the magic didn't muddle your thoughts.

When we pulled off the road a bit, even without second sight, I could tell that the shields were taking damage. Bradley put out his hands and fed energy into them. Adam and I watched as the slight dark tinge to the shields healed to a healthy color, mirroring the sunny gold of his energy.

I scanned the area outside the shield. I could sense one of the many magical "rivers" emptying into the boundary. This was one of the places within the shield where the magic was more chaotic, as the new magic flowed in and the old magic had to push together to make way.

The flowing energy was inaccessible to most magic users, human or otherwise. *So, what could have damaged the shield?* "I'm going to take a look outside."

Bradley's back stiffened, but he nodded sharply. "Be careful, and don't go too far from the edge. I can manipulate the shield, stretch it to cover you, but only if you stay close."

I held up my hand with the ugly ruby ring I'd started wearing every day. "Don't worry, I've got a full canteen. I could fry a goblin horde all on my own if I had to."

It was Murphy's law of canteens that the objects that were best able to hold magic tended to be the objects I least wanted to wear.

Bradley tried to smile and failed miserably. I reached up as high as I could on my tip toes and managed to kiss his jaw... barely. He was too tall to kiss if he didn't help. He rolled his eyes, because he knew what I was up to, but his smile deepened. I could feel his amusement, and saw that the smile was real. He gave me a gentle squeeze.

"Back in a few."

Walking through the shield was as easy as walking through air... for me. It tended to—well, for lack of a better word, *zap* creatures that weren't keyed into it.

There was a creek meandering around, with a little scraggly patch of taller trees and brush. I stepped out carefully, snaking my power around the area as Bradley repaired the shields inside.

A patch of grass caught my eye, and I hunkered down next to it. We didn't really do spring much in Texas...the weather went bipolar from freezing to sweltering for a couple of weeks instead. Today it was warmish, but it might not stay that way all day. I could smell rain on the horizon, coming from the north. That cold air coming down from the mountains would probably plunge us into one last gasp of winter.

But none of that explained why the grass was black. I picked up a stick and poked it experimentally. Brown, even a washed-out kind of taupe color were pretty common on the cusp of spring.

Black meant that you either had a nasty mold... or nasty magic.

I felt the vibration under my feet and jumped back as the ground opened. I heard a high, screeching noise as something long and dark shot out of the ground, raining dirt clods all over me as I rolled away.

It smelled vile: sickly sweet with a dry, metallic undertone. I gagged and kept rolling... further from the shield, but away from the stench.

I came up on my feet, balanced, and ready to cast. Whatever had shot out of the ground was nowhere in sight. I began inching toward the shield, eyes on the ground. One foot, then two. I could see the shield shimmering only a few yards away.

A snake-like tentacle wrapped around my ankle. I didn't hesitate; I shot a bolt of pure magical energy at it and fried it. It screeched and pulled away. Part of it broke off around my ankle.

I didn't waste time. My feet barely touched the ground as I sprinted toward safety. Adam and Bradley were waiting as Bradley strong-armed the shield toward me.

I felt something wrap around my ankle again. I didn't even look as I charred it and dove through the barrier. Bradley caught me and held me close. I looked back. Whatever it was, it looked like it couldn't cross the shield without a physical body. Most nasty things couldn't.

Adam paced beside us. I could feel that the ghost was distraught, both by his own helplessness in the situation and the fact that he wasn't able to touch me.

Bradley was holding me tight enough for any two men. "What was that?"

I patted his arm. "I don't know what it was." I lifted my leg to show off my grisly trophy. "But I brought a piece of it back."

I turned to Adam, who obviously needed to be doing something. "Can you ask Kit meet us at the shop?" I could have called him, but Adam preferred to be active when there was something dangerous on the loose, and I preferred him to be far away from danger.

"Tell him my mother will babysit if he needs her to." My mother, while not "talented" enough to train, had a knack for knowing when she was needed. It probably came from her own mother being a Guardian. Or from just being a mom. But if Kit asked to drop off the young kitsune, my mom wouldn't complain.

Kit was waiting in the store when we drove up. I dialed Clair's cell and put her on the ancient speakerphone in the office, and explained the attack and the damage to the shields.

Kit wrinkled his nose. The snake-like bit of flesh reeked even to my much less sensitive nose, and acute senses came with the territory when you were a shape-shifting fox. "I know that smell. Unlike Martha, I *have* been to Greece. My family was widely traveled. I toured many countries when I was young and my parents were rallying support for some of their trade negotiations. I know the scent on the thing that attacked you, Gwen."

Clair grouched over the phoneline, "And you know I'm going to whack your mythical head if you don't spit it out."

His lips curved. "Me? Mythical? That's a bit of the pot calling the cauldron black, isn't it?" I heard an exasperated huff from the phone.

My mentor and her not-quite-paramour could argue all day. I decided to be blunt. "What are we fighting, Kit?"

He rose and started pacing gracefully around the room. "You know the temple at Delphi was the most accurate in the ancient world?"

Clair made a noise that sounded like she thought anyone who didn't know that was rather dull (not one for suffering fools gladly, my mentor). "I know that it was dedicated to Gaia before it was a temple of Poseidon and then Apollo."

Kit pulled out one of the many dusty tomes around the shop. One of the ones with a subtle spell to keep customers from accidentally trying to purchase them. "It was probably the site of others before Gaia. It was the site of both volcanic activity and hallucinogenic vapors from the Earth, and a deep pool of magic according to the old tales I heard from a nymph my father introduced me to. No matter which God or Goddess was represented at the temple, the one thing that always stayed the same was this: the oracle was always pictured with serpents." He flipped to a picture of a mosaic that depicted an ancient priestess, surrounded by dark tentacles.

I frowned. "Like the ones that attacked me? I'm not sure I'd call those things snakes."

Kit shook his head. "I do not know. The temple was destroyed before I visited. There was nothing but rocks there... and the faintest hint of that smell."

Bradley frowned. "You think someone has been visiting the temple?"

Kit shrugged. "Some say the temple was destroyed by the last priestess... the Pythia. The status of the temple had declined for generations, quite likely because there hadn't been any earthquakes to open new vents to the hallucinogenic vapors. And then, they say that a powerful woman showed up out of nowhere one day, draped in blue veils and spouting gibberish, claiming to be the daughter of Poseidon. She ruled the temple for seven years, and then, everything was gone. People came for prophecy and found that the temple was in ruins, and that most of the priests were dead."

"Most?"

Kit cocked his head to one side. "They never found the High Priestess and Priest."

Clair sighed. "And, as a guess, let me just postulate that the dead didn't go peacefully in their sleep?"

Kit nodded, though Clair couldn't see him. "They were ritually slaughtered, exactly as the young goats in the temple were sacrificed."

I rubbed the back of my neck. "And you think Martha dug something up... in Arkansas?" I let my tone convey exactly how geographically improbable that theory was.

Kit shrugged and cocked his head to the side. "I didn't say it was a perfect theory."

~

We eventually ran out of new avenues of conversation. Bradley and I left to go get my car, and Adam joined us in the truck again.

He smirked at my boyfriend as I scooted to the middle. "Cozy."

Bradley snorted. "Well it is now." He turned to me. "Remind me again why the ghost gets shotgun?"

I pretended to look offended. "You'd rather have him in the middle instead of me?"

Adam grinned. Bradley rolled his eyes but didn't comment.

We were driving down the dark and twisted country road silently when Adam finally spoke again.

"No one's asking the big question."

Bradley looked at the ghost from the corner of his eye, and then turned back to the road. "What question?"

"Why does the whatever Martha Schmitt was running from want to get into Topeka?"

"You think it's the same thing."

"I don't think that we're under any delusions that something powerful enough to damage the shields showing up here right after Martha left was an accident."

I nodded thoughtfully. Adam should have brought up his concerns to Kit and Clair, but they didn't approve of my friendship with the ghost. He was tied to me, and it was dangerous for both of us. My mentor and even my boyfriend thought I should send Adam on to whatever awaited him when his soul crossed over.

But Adam didn't want to go, and as long as he didn't harm anyone else, I wasn't going to force him.

Bradley pulled over at our normal meeting place and I kissed him lightly and retrieved my car. He waited for me to turn on the ignition and waved as he pulled away.

Adam appeared in my seat. "You aren't thinking of going back out there, are you?"

I looked at him like he was crazy. "Don't be an idiot. Remember, I'm not guardian material. I'm going home. Clair will be back after she finishes in Arkansas tomorrow."

"And the e-mail will come to explain everything."

"If that e-mail shows up, then Martha will be dead."

Adam nodded. "Yes. I hope she knew something that would help."

I drove silently for a long moment. "You think she's already dead, don't you?"

He turned away, looking into the darkness as I sped along the road. "I think she's been dead since she set foot outside this town."

Sundays in small towns generally followed a set pace. Church from ten to twelve and then a nice lunch if the Cowboys weren't playing. My family had only been in town less than a year, and I knew there was a certain amount of pressure for my parents to choose a "home church"; but because my father was both politically astute and a tiny bit lazy, we just made the occasional rounds at all the local churches like we were still looking. We'd never lived in a town for more than three years, so I had no idea how long he could keep it up before people figured out he just wanted his Sundays free to sleep in.

The result was that I didn't have to wake up early and spend half the day in church, and lunch at our house on Sunday was often a sandwich. Bradley would be busy until early evening, since his father had some cable channel that showed "classic" football games and another that did pre-season baseball.

Since I hadn't managed to get much of anything done after noon on Saturday, I decided to head to the shop. I eyed the stack of new products, but since it wasn't a regular work day, I decided to keep the shades down and the closed sign in the window. Kit found me in Clair's office a couple of hours later, surrounded by every book we had on the shelves concerning ancient Greece.

"You should work in the front where there is more light."

I rubbed my eyes. "Where's Todd?" I often babysat Kit's son in my spare time. Kit was not the kind of father who allowed his child to wander alone.

"He's watching that dreadful American football with your paramour. How goes your search little witch?"

"There are a few mentions of the temple and the priestess, but it's all in relation to other myths and tales. All except what's termed 'sacred wars.' Did you know that Alexander the Great's father actually ransacked the temple?"

Kit shrugged. "You'd have a hard time tracing ancient events into present day."

"Well, we can't exactly fly to Greece for the weekend and go dig around in the ruins."

"It wouldn't tell us anything if we did." He picked up one of the books with pictures and began flipping through the pages.

"How do you think Martha got involved?"

"I could not say. She has lived quietly for many years in her hills." Kit let his long hair hide his face. I knew he felt guilty for allowing her to leave; he cared about Clair and Clair cared about Martha. I could tell that he felt like he should have stopped the woman.

"Clair will have a better idea once she gets to Martha's place," I said. "She's flying in this morning?"

"She changed her flight and got to the state late last night, but it's not well populated. She landed in El Dorado and said she'd drive the rest of the way into the Ouachita Mountains today."

I shut my book. "Well, I'm not doing any good here. Bradley said he'd check the shields again on his own, and I asked Adam to tag along and get us if anything went wrong."

"Your ghost is very helpful."

I heard the bite in his voice, so I raised my chin and looked him in the eye. "My *friend* is very helpful."

Kit sighed and changed the subject. "Would you care to keep my son this evening? I think I might go for a run outside the shields."

I felt a moment of gut-clinching fear. "Martha said that you reeked of magic. Remember? This thing, whatever it is, can smell you. What if it's able to absorb magic? Or just eat you?"

He raised a black brow. "Intriguing notion. What makes you wonder that?"

"Because why else would it need to smell other supernatural creatures if it wasn't hunting them?"

"It might be to *hide* from us." He smiled, and his canines were just a bit longer than normal.

He wasn't listening. Time to pull out the big guns. "If you go, I'll tell Clair. And I swear if you ever get the courage to ask her out, I'll refuse to babysit."

Kit's expression darkened. "I don't lack courage, little witch," he snapped. "I don't lack opportunity. I lack a masochistic nature that enjoys falling in love with creatures that live and die like mayflies. Human lifespans make it impossible for a creature such as myself to truly fall in love with a human."

He didn't mean impossible. From the way his jaw was clenched, he meant unbearable. Even with Clair's life being much longer than the average human's, she was never going to live as long as Kit already had; and he was just past his brash youth in terms of kitsune.

"But if you *are* already in love with her, will it hurt any less if you pretend you aren't?"

His lips thinned and his eyes turned very unfriendly. "If you pass your first century, I might allow you to advise me on matters of the heart. For now, forgive me if the words of a child not yet twenty hold little interest for me."

He stomped out, his Italian leather shoes barely making a sound on the hardwood, even when he was angry.

Some days I just didn't know when to keep my mouth shut. I had to hope he was too pissed off to go outside the shields.

~

The phone was ringing when I unlocked the store Monday afternoon. I raced to the phone, nearly knocking over a Tiffany lamp and a Russian tea set as my purse flew behind me.

"Topeka Antiques, this is Gwen, how can I help you?"

"Gwen. Listen very closely to me." Clair's voice was firm, and there was something underneath the serenity in the tone that it took me a second to identify.

My teacher was terrified.

"What do you need?"

"Have you finished unpacking the latest load of antiques?"

"No, I was going to work on them this afternoon."

"It's fine. Better in fact. If that thing had been out of the shielding Martha wrapped it in, we'd be in even *more* trouble."

"What thing?"

"Don't worry. Just go to the storeroom and find a box that has Martha's name on it. Or she might have sent it under the name Able Hands, you know how paranoid she was."

"Was?"

There was a long moment of silence on the line. Her voice cracked. "She took a rather drastic step once she realized what was going on."

I couldn't think of anything that would make her feel better. "Let me go find the package. I'll call you back. Are you on your cell?"

"Yes. I rented a car and I'm heading that way. I just passed Texarkana. I'll be there in three hours or so. Less, if the traffic isn't bad and I can hit all the State Troopers with spells before they see me."

I chuckled. My mentor had the same lead-foot problem that I did. "What about your car?"

"I'll get one of you to drive me to the airport."

I heard a noise from the back room and ducked behind the counter with the phone still at my ear. I whispered, "I'm going to have to call you back."

"Gwen, whatever is wrong, don't you dare..."

I hung up the phone while Clair was still talking. I knew she'd be on the phone with Kit as soon as it disconnected, and I didn't think we should give whatever was in the back more warning than it had already gotten.

I picked up an antique bat from one of the cases. I *really* needed to start carrying more weapons with me to work.

The light switch didn't work as entered the hall. I rolled my eyes. Of *course*, it didn't.

I wasn't as surprised as I should have been to see Martha Schmitt's dead body rifling through the boxes and muttering in Greek as she moved jerkily through the room. She had a box open and I could see a small bronze mirror in one hand. She hissed as she touched the chunk of amber that had been packed into the box to protect it.

I was beginning to suspect that my own particular magic had some kind of connection with dead things. One of the drawbacks to being a magical mutt on the purity spectrum. The other was a distinct lack of pretty, pretty magical hair. I forced myself to focus. If I died trying to contain Martha's corpse, I did not want my last thought to be about jealousy over the people in my life having hair that was ridiculously gorgeous. It would be embarrassing if I crossed over and there was some kind of accounting on the other side.

I edged toward the cabinet where Clair kept the unguent. Martha's dead eyes snapped up when I was about halfway there. Whatever was inside the body, the stench revolted me in a way that left me moving quicker, and slightly nauseous... more so than when I'd smelled the creature the first time. Because the smell was unmistakable. It was the same stench as the thing I'd fried outside the shields.

She screeched and came toward me. I dodged. Her movements

were clumsy. Whatever was driving her body didn't seem to have a good hold on her.

I yanked open the cabinet and pulled out an old margarine tub, I felt her cold hands pull me to her, and I wedged the bat between us. She grabbed my legs and tried pulled me down. The tub hit the ground hard and the lid popped off. Unguent slopped all over the floor.

I cursed under my breath and struggled back to my feet, trying to get enough room to swing the bat properly.

Then I slipped in the unguent, and before I could recover my balance Martha's cold, bony fingers caught my throat. I muttered a few curse words in my head, but it wasn't the first time I'd been choked by a homicidal zombie. I knew better than to panic.

Adam appeared. "Gwen!" He was drawn to me being in danger.

I tried to wave him off, but I could feel him gathering his power to do something dangerous, something that would leave him vulnerable.

Gotta move fast.

I dropped to my knees in a move that was going to leave bruises, but Martha's grip on my throat was broken. More importantly, I got my hands where I needed them to be.

My fingers found the spilled ointment. I scooped up as much as I could and smacked my hand on the arm that was reaching for my throat.

The spirit in the dead body tried to jerk away, but I had another handful ready. I leaned forward and smeared it on her face and into her open mouth.

The noise it made wasn't remotely human. It sounded like a pissed-off T-Rex.

Something dark oozed out of Martha's body. It writhed like a ball of snakes for a long moment and then shot toward Adam in a movement that was almost too quick for the human eye to follow. It surrounded him, darkness covering the faint glow that always surrounded him, even without second sight.

No. You're finished here. I felt a deep peace well up within as I drew on the power around me, to do what Clair had trained me to do from the start. My voice sounded odd when I put all the power I could gather into a single command. "Move on."

The shadow stalled, fighting the command, but that deep peace inside me wasn't afraid or impressed with the remnants of what had once been a human soul. Whatever this thing had done to remain alive, it had damaged the essence of itself.

"Move on."

I felt the barrier between worlds thin, and Adam appeared at my side suddenly, his face raw, so full of a longing I didn't understand. It frightened me. My focus started to crumble.

He looked at that thinning barrier like it was a portal home.

The thing beside us screamed and writhed, fighting the inexorable pull towards the pulsing opening. The creature left three feet of nail marks in the wood floors as it screeched and fought.

At last, it was pulled through.

The doorway lingered for a long moment, almost as if it were asking Adam if he were coming along. He took a step forward, hesitated, and then shook his head. He turned back to me and smiled.

And then the space between worlds was gone.

I'm not sure how long I sat in the floor of the shop with Adam, staring at the place where the worlds had literally ripped open at my command. It might have been five minutes. Judging by the fact that my feet were numb when Bradley and Kit helped me up, I assumed it had been awhile. They called Clair to fill her in.

Adam hadn't moved. I had to shout to get his attention, but eventually he snapped out of whatever headspace that seeing the literal afterlife left him in... at least enough to turn his head toward me.

I could feel an overwhelming sadness in him that had always been absent. I asked him, "Do you want to move on?"

He hesitated for a very long, quiet moment, and then gave me his normal grin. "Not yet."

~

Hell hath no fury like a witch mentor who was absent when the crap hit the fan.

If that wasn't an ancient saying, it needed to be.

Clair was fifteen shades of pissed off about me facing another zombie on my own. She used her anger to cover up her feelings about one of her oldest friends dying.

The facts were easier to put together once we were all together, and Clair shared the email from Martha. Out of the blue, Martha had received the ancient bronze mirror in the mail in Arkansas. The mirror was a touchpoint; and it was possessed and activated, leaving Martha fighting the ancient priestess for control.

Martha had sent the touchpoint to Topeka so that the shields could protect it, but she'd sent her canteen, the amber she always wore around her neck with the mirror to power a spell to keep it safe until it arrived. Nothing like using UPS.

Clair cursed as she paged through the email. "Losing the amber left Martha more vulnerable to the spirit that had inhabited the mirror. The spirit needed the mirror, but it could survive if it fed off Martha. Martha hadn't realized how bad it was before she walked in to get a canteen."

She paused a long moment. "She managed to get out of the shields and write this email, so we knew the story. Then she..." Clair took a deep shuddering breath. "Then she took a massive dose of sleeping pills to kill herself and deny the ghost anything to feed from. But she forgot that the ghost could still possess her body as long as it had the power, and it had enough to get to Topeka and get inside the shield. Once it was here, it had plenty of energy."

Clair had found notes all over Martha's isolated home that detailed the possession from beginning to end. She slammed one of the old books into the table. "I could have helped if she'd just asked!"

Kit snaked an arm around my teacher and held on for a long moment. "It was never her way to ask for help, my Clair."

She stood there, held in his arms, and wept.

~

I stepped out to find Adam lurking in the parking lot. Clair didn't like him being in the store. I smiled briefly. "Penny for your thoughts?"

"She meant to do good."

"Martha?"

"No, the ghost. The Pythia. The priestess. The seer."

"You...communicated with her?"

He gave me a jerky nod, eyes far away. "What was...left of her. She was almost like a poltergeist. The same thoughts ran through her mind, over and over. She had a good reason. When she was alive, she saw a time when being in that form would protect her people. She used magic to turn the high priest into her touchpoint, along with the bronze mirror that Martha found. The dead priests volunteered to fuel the spell." He sighed. "She did eventually save the Greeks, at a battle that turned the tide of an invasion. But after that she lingered, and the longer she lingered, the less human she became."

"She was trapped in an object, without human contact," I said, nodding. "Even people in solitary confinement become less sane if they spend too much time alone. We're social creatures."

Adam shook his head. "You don't understand, Gwen. She devoured her own *soul* to keep going. That's why she looked like that."

My stomach churned. "That's horrible."

"Yes." He looked into the sunset and I could see his jaw clench. "Promise me, if I ever get... odd, dangerous, like that... promise me you'll send me on."

I suddenly felt out of breath. "But... you don't want to go."

His lips quirked. "I *didn't* want to, not before... but now that I've seen it..." He gave me a smile. "It's not a fate worse than death."

I felt tears gather in my eyes. "I'll miss you."

I felt him near me, the air buzzing with the undefinable hum of magic and ghostly energy as his lips brushed my forehead. "You are the best friend I've ever had. And the only person I would ever trust with my soul."

How could I be selfish? Why limit him? I stifled a sob. "Whenever you are ready."

He nodded, looking back into the sunset. I suspected that he wasn't seeing the same thing I was.

"I'll cross over, in my own way, in my own time," he said softly. Then he turned back to me and grinned. "But not yet."

If he hadn't been incorporeal, I would have hugged him.

AN APP FOR THAT

ALYSSA N. VAUGHN

"Moooom, Ludo threw up on my bed!"

The call came from Laura's ten-year-old daughter Wendi, who proceeded to drag the ancient mutt down the hallway toward the kitchen.

Laura, halfway through making lunch for her three kids and less than half dressed for work, groaned.

"Put him in his kennel okay? And be gentle with him! Don't pull so hard on his collar!" she called. "Martin! Jesse!"

Her six- and four-year-old sons came careening into the kitchen, screeching like police sirens. They were still in their pajamas.

"Why aren't you dressed?" Laura cried despairingly. "Ugh, sit down and eat your breakfast, I'll bring you your clothes in a minute."

They noisily attacked their bowls of cereal and Laura took advantage of the moment to run back to her bedroom and throw on the rest of her clothes, managing a smear of eyeliner and a dab of mascara before running into the boys' room to grab their school clothes.

"Mom, my comforter!" Wendi shouted from her room. Laura swore under her breath, but swooped in to gather it up, dumping the boys' clothes on the kitchen counter on the way to the laundry room. Martin had finished his cereal and was putting his bowl in the sink, but Jesse (for reasons known only to himself) was sitting underneath the kitchen table with some of his toy dinosaurs, completely naked.

Laura managed to sort the boys out and sent them off to get their backpacks. She was on the phone with the vet and digging in the fridge for one of her prepackaged protein shakes when Wendi yelled again, this time from the living room.

"Moooooooom, Ludo threw up again!"

"I'm sorry, Laura, you're missing the meeting *why*?" Her boss's voice was like helium slowly leaking out of a balloon—if the balloon could somehow be condescending and passive-aggressive.

Laura closed her eyes and took a deep breath, trying to imagine that the sounds of cars speeding past on the highway were gentle waves. "Rachel, I'm really sorry, but as soon as I left the vet I blew out a tire! The roadside assistance guy said he wouldn't be able to come out here for another hour." Laura would have changed the tire herself, but she couldn't quite bring herself to admit to Rachel that her ex had "borrowed" the jack for some reason and neglected to put it back.

Rachel sighed heavily.

"I can't say I'm not *disappointed* right now," God, Laura wished she could reach through the phone and choke her, "especially since *you* were the one who insisted this client had so much potential for the company. Unfortunately, I can't say I'm not *surprised.*"

Laura felt herself redden. Rachel was enjoying herself.

"Of course, take whatever time you need to get your *personal affairs* in order, but we will need to have a conversation about separating these issued from your *professional obligations.*"

"Thanks, Rachel." said Laura shortly.

"Well, *I* always try to be accommodating of people's needs." Rachel sighed again, and it sounded incredibly self-satisfied. "I'll see you tomorrow morning, bright and early?"

"Yup. See you tomorrow, Rachel."

Laura waited for Rachel to hang up first. The last thing she needed was to be written up for insubordination. Then she leaned back against her van and closed her eyes. She tried to put out of her mind the choice that the vet had presented—pay for Ludo to have an expensive treatment for kidney failure, or have him put down. Maybe as soon as next week.

Martin and Jesse were at least young enough that they wouldn't fully absorb the loss. They would miss the dog and then they would forget. But Wendi would be heartbroken. Would it destroy all the progress Laura, the therapist, and the team at school had worked so hard to make this year?

She checked her phone. She still had almost forty-five minutes to wait.

She thought about calling her mother, but before she could dial, the screen lit up. It was Martin and Wendi's school.

"Hello?" Laura answered with panic rising in her chest.

"Ms. Peña, this is Martin's teacher Mrs. Fredericks."

"Oh, yes. How can I help you?" Laura struggled to keep her voice calm and even.

"I was wondering if you'd be able to come in for a meeting this afternoon, say 2:30, about half an hour before dismissal?"

Laura held back her own sigh of frustration. There went any hope of catching up on work before the kids came home.

"Yes, I should be able to make that. Is there anything wrong?"

"Well, I don't want to worry you but... perhaps it would be best if we discuss it in person." said Mrs. Fredericks slowly.

Mrs. Fredericks made Laura very worried.

"And they think Martin's got dyslexia and maybe an attention disorder." Laura was on the phone with her mother after putting the kids to bed. "They want me to take him to get tested at this center downtown next week."

"Mmmm." Laura wondered if her mother was actually listening.

"I don't know where I'm going to find the money for all of this. The grant we got from that foundation barely covers Wendi's therapy. Tyler's still out of work, so he can't help with anything. I swear, he isn't even looking for a job. He just sits on the couch in his mother's basement playing video games."

"*Solo el que carga el cajón sabe lo que pesa el muerto.*" her mother intoned absently. Only he who carries the coffin knows how much the dead man weighs. Laura held back another noise of frustration.

"You sound like Abuela before you put her in the home." she muttered.

"Hmmm." Her mother didn't seem to react.

"So do you think you could pick up Wendi and Jesse after school on Thursday while I take Martin to this place?"

"Not Thursday, *mija*. I have church. Why don't you take him on Wednesday?"

"Because his appointment is on Thursday, Mama. Couldn't Wendi and Jesse go to church with you?"

"Mmmm... I could take Jesse, but I don't think Wendi will enjoy it."

Laura bristled. She didn't know whether her mother favored the boys because they were boys or because they weren't autistic, but she absolutely *hated* it when she wanted to play Grandma of the Year with only a subset of her grandchildren.

"You know what Mom, I'll just see if they can go home with friends. I don't want to interrupt your night."

"Okay, honey." Her mother was oblivious to the anger in her voice. "And remember, *al mal tiempo, buena cara.*" Put a good face to bad times. Laura rolled her eyes.

"Yeah, Mom. It's just a little hard when so much seems to be going wrong."

"Well, you know what your abuela used to say to me."

Laura did know. It was her least favorite saying; *el buen músico con una cuerda toca.* One string is good enough for a good musician.

"Right, Mom. I gotta get some sleep, I'll call you tomorrow."

"Bye honey!" Her mother sounded happier to say goodbye than she had sounded during the entire conversation.

Laura was still awake at two in the morning. It wasn't that she couldn't sleep. She probably could have slept for days; but she was several hours deep into Internet research. Not for Ludo, or Martin, or the money problem. She was looking at suicide guides—people who gave advice for how to end your life on strange internet forums and twisted little blogs.

Her thoughts frightened her. She knew her children needed her, but every page that talked about pills and razors and God-knows-what-else had some kind of siren-call hold on her mind. She couldn't tear her eyes away from the screen.

Before Tyler had left, she had been able to see someone for her depression every once in a while, maybe two or three times a year. Enough to keep it at bay. Even though he hadn't been perfect—far from it—what little support he offered was enough to keep her steady.

The minutes kept ticking by, and Laura fell deeper and deeper into the rabbit holes of the Internet. She felt hypnotized.

Until she saw the ad.

It looked so out of place in the bottom left corner of the black and grey website. It was bright red, green, blue, and yellow, like a kindergarten finger painting. She wasn't very surprised to see it; most of these sites included someone trying to butt in and offer helpline numbers and the like.

This one seemed so odd, though.

It was for a mobile app. A "life planner".

"Take control of your life!" the text read. "Before you try anything else, try the Complete Control app. Just see how everything falls into place!"

Really? she thought. *For people who want to end their lives, you want them to download an app?* Then she shrugged. *Well, I suppose that's about the same as calling a hotline and talking to some unqualified volunteer who just wants to pray the bad thoughts away for me.*

She couldn't say after how she got from staring at the app to downloading it, but suddenly there it was, open on her phone. It looked like a control panel, with a so many virtual switches and buttons displayed on the screen, she had to scroll to see them all. Weirdly enough, there didn't seem to be a calendar or task list or anything she'd expect to see in a planner app.

"Whatever." Laura set her phone down and settled back on her pillows. If she didn't get some sleep now, she wouldn't be able to function in the morning. The phone buzzed. She picked it back up. It was a notification from the app.

"Try our sleep quality feature?" it asked.

"Sure, why not?" Laura muttered, and hit the confirm button. It brought up a virtual dial.

"How many hours of sleep do you typically need to feel rested?"

"How 'bout a hundred?" snorted Laura. She entered "seven" and hit confirm again.

It asked for permission to access her alarm functions. She granted it.

The app displayed a cartoon mouse climbing into bed and displayed one last message: "Good night!"

The next thing Laura knew, morning light was pouring into the room through a crack in the curtains. She sat up and stretched, and her phone dropped gently from where it had been resting on her chest.

She felt—amazing. Like she'd had a full night's sleep.

She picked up the phone and opened the app. She scrolled up and down for a long while, but couldn't find any hint of the "sleep quality" feature. Not a report or a setting or anything. After a second Laura shrugged, put the phone down, and went to wake the kids.

Rachel was in fine form that morning. She was storming through the cubicles, haranguing the web developers and sending at least one analyst to hide in the bathroom. Laura ducked down at her desk and wished she could disappear into her coffee mug. Her phone began buzzing like crazy, almost vibrating itself off the desk.

Laura grabbed it hastily, quickly popping her head up to see if Rachel had zeroed in on the sound. Luckily, the witch seemed to be too focused on their unfortunate intern to spare a thought for Laura's traitorous phone. Laura glared at the screen.

It was another notification from the new app.

"It looks like you have a meeting in **15 minutes**. Would you like to **confirm** or **reschedule**?"

Laura groaned, remembering the "conversation" she was meant to have with Rachel about "professional commitments". Without even thinking about what Rachel would say when she got the notification, Laura hit the button to reschedule.

The screen showed another cartoon animal getting up from a computer and going to get a cup of coffee. For a life planning app, it sure had a lot of cutesy animations, Laura thought to herself. She did, however, need more coffee. She got up and tiptoed around Hurricane Rachel to the breakroom.

Pilar, from accounting, was already in there, skulking near the ficus in the corner and trying to peer around the door frame without giving away her position. She and Laura exchanged nervous giggles.

"Does she seem like she's running out of steam yet?" Pilar whispered conspiratorially.

Laura shook her head and grimaced.

"Looks like she's going to be haranguing poor Asahi for the next, I dunno, thousand years?" she whispered back as she filled her mug. Pilar rolled her eyes, then craned her neck, trying to get a bead on Rachel.

"If I drop my mug at your desk now," she said, more to herself than Laura, "I might be able to make it to the bathroom before she gets to my section." Laura gave a hesitant thumbs up, and mouthed "Good Luck". Pilar stuck out her tongue playfully and turned to go.

She promptly slammed into Rachel, spilling her scalding coffee all down the boss's pristine white blouse.

"Oh my gosh, I—Rachel, I'm so sorry, I—" Pilar stammered.

"You absolute moron!" Rachel screeched, "You complete incompetent! You-"

"Excuse me," Laura felt her backbone solidify a bit as she stepped forward, "she said she was sorry." Rachel's mouth puckered so hard Laura was tempted to warn her that it might freeze that way. But she stopped yelling. The entire office fell silent as Rachel stomped into her office, grabbed her purse and keys, and marched out the door. No one dared make eye contact with her.

Laura patted Pilar on the shoulder gently, went back to her desk. She'd pay for standing up for her coworker sooner or later, but overall it was a lucky break—for Laura at least. She could finally get caught up without having to waste time being lectured by Rachel, and when they did reschedule their meeting, maybe they could finally get around to talking about those work-from-home days that Rachel had been dangling in front of Laura for the past year and a half.

~

Laura enlisted Wendi's therapist to help talk about the Ludo situation via phone call. It went about as well as Laura expected; Wendi melted into tears, became near incoherent in her speech, and finally crawled into Ludo's crate with him and refused to come out. The therapist gave Laura the links to some articles that might help Wendi adjust, if they were able to stave off the inevitable for enough time.

The boys were oblivious, as usual, happily playing video games in their room, while Laura sat on the living room couch. She read up and compared potential expenses for keeping the dog going and getting Martin the diagnoses and potential medication he might need. She was seriously contemplating sneaking a little vodka inside her diet coke when Wendi, sniffling and still largely unintelligible, dragged herself into the room, her blue and pink porcelain piggy bank clutched in her hands.

She set the pig down next to her mother, blinking at her behind a waterfall of tears.

"F-f-for L-l-ludo." she choked out between sobs. Then turned and ran out of the room.

Laura felt her own eyes welling up.

She placed a hand on the pig, feeling some horrible storm of desperation and fury swirling inside her. Her grip tightened.

Her phone buzzed.

It was the app.

"It looks like you are in the midst of **financial planning**. Do you have **multiple sources of income**?"

"I wish!" Laura laughed sourly.

The phone vibrated again. Laura frowned; she hadn't pressed anything.

The cartoon mouse was holding a phone, making a call. Below the animation, a caption read "**Call Tyler**".

Laura's stomach flipped. That was downright odd. She didn't even remember giving the app permission to access her contact list. Nevertheless, she found herself dialing the familiar number without hesitation.

The voice that picked up was tearful, sobbing. For a minute, Laura wondered if Wendi had come back into the room for her piggy bank. Then she recognized the voice. It was her ex-mother-in-law.

"Peggy?" she asked.

"Laura!" came the strangled reply. "Oh, Laura. It's so awful."

"What is it? What happened?" Laura's unease was growing by the second.

"There was an accident." Peggy's voice broke. "Tyler—Tyler—"

Laura heard a sob, and then another; then a firm, calm voice came on the line. "Ma'am? Are you kin to Mrs. Lawson here?" His deep southern drawl oozed calm and authority.

"I was married to her son." Laura said quietly.

"Would you mind coming down here? She needs someone to be with her right now."

"Of course." Laura agreed without thinking about logistics, what time it was, or hardly anything else. If there had been one good thing about her marriage to Tyler, it had been Peggy Lawson.

In what seemed to be an illogically short amount of time, Laura had bribed her younger brother into watching the kids – he was probably the only babysitter who could cope with Wendi's current distress and found her way to the hospital, where Peggy sat in one of those horribly sterile hospital rooms, filled to the brim with whirring machines softly beeping vital signs. In the bed lay a comatose, non-responsive Tyler.

"He was riding his bike without a helmet," Peggy whispered. "And then some idiot changed lanes on top of him."

It was awful to look at. Laura had always hated Tyler's stupid

Harley, and especially his insistence that he didn't need a helmet. But despite everything, this wasn't something she would have wished on him.

She sat down next to Peggy and held her hand for a long time without saying anything.

"My brother Jack helped me set up one of those Get Funds pages." Peggy said finally, breaking the silence. Laura looked at her curiously.

"Will that help you cover the hospital bills?"

Peggy waved her free hand impatiently.

"Hospital bills are covered. That's not what it's for." She squeezed Laura's hand. "It's for the kids. We know Tyler was a bit of a deadbeat. And if he—even if he pulls through this—"

She stroked Laura's cheek.

"We want you to be better taken care of. I'll do what I can, and so will Jack, but we know it hasn't been easy on you. We just want you to know you can count on us."

Laura's eyes stung and she rubbed at them vigorously. It seemed so wrong to be talking about this at her ex-husband's potential deathbed. Peggy pulled her into an awkward hug, still holding her hand, the arms of the chairs pressed uncomfortably into their sides.

Around midnight, Uncle Jack arrived and the two of them sent Laura home to the kids.

Out in the hospital parking lot, she paused, pulled out her phone, and stared at the Complete Control app.

Then she put the phone away and drove home.

She might be dealing with suicidal ideation but she wasn't psychotically delusional. At least, she was pretty sure.

Laura forced herself to ignore the app for the next week... for the most part.

When it offered the "Do Not Disturb" feature the night before her big presentation, suddenly the kids got through homework, bathtime, brushing their teeth, and tucking themselves in without any problem.

When it asked if she wanted to use the copy-and-paste function on her grocery list, she was too curious not to... and was rewarded with a trunk that had refilled itself after all the bags had been carried inside.

She even tried out the Undo button when she burned the cupcakes for Jesse's class bake sale.

Strangely enough, the app never offered any suggestions concerning Ludo or Tyler, who seemed to be maintaining their miserable status quo for the time being.

It was Thursday, and Laura and Martin had just arrived at the testing center downtown. Sitting in the outdated, barren waiting room, Martin began to get fidgety. Laura reached over and gently took hold of his hand.

"It's okay, my love," she whispered, giving him a little smile. "Everything is going to be fine."

Martin didn't meet her eyes, fidgeting instead with the ring on her finger.

"Hey, it'll be about dinner time once we're done, right? What if we got McDonald's? That could be fun, huh?" she gave him a playful poke in the ribs.

Martin gave her a feeble smile back.

A severe-looking woman came to the door and called Martin's name.

"Do your best!" Laura gave him a thumbs-up.

Martin hurried after the woman to the testing room. Laura settled back stared at the clock (just a few minutes after five), trying to get comfortable in the hard plastic chair, and took out her phone to kill some time.

It buzzed immediately.

"It looks like you are attempting to cope with **imperfect children. Delete and try again?**"

Laura stiffened. "What the hell?!" she burst out, forgetting to keep her voice quiet.

"Delete children and try again?" another notification queried.

An animation of a large rat, dressed like the tester, pounced on a small animated mouse wearing a red t-shirt just like Martin's.

"Holy shit!" Laura dropped her phone and ran over to the reception window. She banged on the flimsy clear plastic, making it shake violently.

"Can I help you?" the receptionist looked alarmed.

"I need to see my son NOW!" Laura yelled. Her hands were trembling.

"Is there a problem?" she asked, taken aback.

Laura's voice became a scream. "There will be if you don't go get him RIGHT. THE HELL. NOW!" She leaned over the counter and into the woman's face.

The ashen-faced woman scurried away. Minutes later Martin came running out looking bewildered.

"What's going on, Mom?"

"We're leaving!" she said shortly.

She grabbed her purse and his backpack, but left the phone sitting on the chair, vibrating.

Her mother called the house phone that night, wanting to know how the tests had gone.

"We left early, Mom. They weren't any good at their jobs. I want the teachers at the school to do it."

"Ah! So why didn't you have them do it in the first place? *Ahogado el niño, tapando el pozo.*" After the child has drowned, they cover the well. Laura bit back a sharp reply.

"This is what they recommended, but it just didn't work out." she said flatly.

"And why haven't you been answering your phone all day long?"

"I lost it." Laura sighed.

"*Mentirosa!* Wendi finally answered it. Crying about the stupid dog."

Laura paled.

"What?"

"The dog! I can't believe you haven't just—"

"No, when did Wendi answer? What time?"

"Oh, I can't remember—"

"When, Mom?!"

"Five thirty, maybe?! Don't yell at your mother!"

"I gotta go. Bye."

"Don't hang up on—"

Laura ran into the bedroom.

There, charging on her nightstand, was the phone.

It buzzed.

"Are you dissatisfied with the **Complete Control** application?"

"Yes." Laura said in a low, deadly voice.

It buzzed again.

"Would you like to uninstall the **Complete Control** application? This will delete all data from the install point to present."

Laura stared at her phone. She was still standing at the end of her bed, a good yard and a half away from it. She was quiet for a long time.

"Yes."

Laura woke with a jerk. It was four in the morning. Her laptop was wedged uncomfortably between her face and the headboard, open to one of the suicide forums. In the corner was an incongruously bright ad, all primary colors.

It was for a help line.

Laura sat up, stiff from being contorted into such a strange position for so long. She stared dully at the ad. It was so cheesy, she wondered how they expected anyone to take them seriously. What were they going to do, sing at her?

Without knowing why, she reached for her phone. She dialed, not the number on the screen, but a number she hadn't called for a long while. The voice on the other end was groggy.

"Laura?"

"Hi, Peggy. I'm sorry to wake you."

"Is something wrong, honey?"

"Yeah—yeah, it is. Peggy, I need help."

GRAND THEFT NIGHTMARE

MISHA BURNETT

The sun was just coming up when I got to the site of the robbery. It was a shop on the inland edge of Shell Beach, a refurbished warehouse that had been subdivided into storefronts. I parked my unmarked cruiser at the curb and took a moment to scope out the street.

Jannson Thaumaturgy Supply. It was tucked in between a law office and an architect. Good neighborhood. Two constables on the job. They'd blocked off the sidewalk with crime scene tape and were standing more or less at attention.

They watched me as I got out of the car and crossed the street, polite smiles on their faces. I pulled out my ID wallet and showed it to the younger one, a tanned blond beefcake. Probably a surfer in his off hours.

"Erik Rugar, Committee for Public Safety," I announced. "Can you tell me what you found?"

The kid stood up straighter and looked puzzled. "Sir?"

The other constable—a sergeant, I saw—explained. "Magic's licensed by the Mayor's Office, kid. Theft of magical items makes it a CPS case." Then he looked to me. "Saw the busted window, called it in, secured the scene. I went around back, but it was all locked up."

I nodded my thanks to him and peered through the window. Someone had smashed the window with a trashcan, which now lay on the sidewalk.

"Dispatch got in touch with the owner," the sergeant said. "He's on his way."

"Thanks," I said. "Any problem with staying until he gets here?"

He shrugged. "Fine by me. Shift's over at eight, if you need us longer than that you'll have to square it with the desk commander. They've been squirrely about overtime lately."

That gave us a couple of hours. "I don't think it'll run that late."

I stepped over the tape and got up next to the broken window. I bent to get a look inside, careful not to cross the line where the glass had been. The kid took his flashlight off his belt and offered it to me.

"Thanks," I told him, and shone it into the shop. It was a mess. Displays had been knocked over, broken bottles and boxes were all over the floor. A cash register had been thrown on the ground hard enough to spring the drawer open.

"This made a lot of noise," I observed. I looked around. No apartments above the shops, just warehouse space. In the middle of the night this place would be a ghost town. "Any idea when it happened?"

"Came through here at three and all was well. Came back at five and it was like this," the sergeant said.

"Got any mobiles in this area?" I asked.

He shook his head. "Naw, just me and the kid on a foot beat. The mobiles are all around Shoreline and Ocean Avenue."

Keeping an eye on the hotels and casinos, no doubt.

The sergeant seemed to catch my thought and grinned. "Gotta protect the tax base. You know how it works. Usually, though, this patch is quiet. I can't remember the last time we had a break-in."

"You figure it was freecasters, sir?" the kid asked suddenly.

I gave him a frown. "Unlicensed mages? I doubt it. There are too many other ways they can get gear, and they wouldn't trash the place like that. I figure it was just punks on a rip. Maybe come up from Leeshore or Pickmantown."

"But what about, you know, countermeasures?" the kid asked. "I mean, it's a magic shop. Wouldn't he be warded somehow?"

"Yeah," the sergeant broke in, "maybe the perps got turned into toads. You want to do a sweep for stray toads, bucky?"

The kid reddened and I wanted to say something to take the sting out of the sergeant's teasing, but just then the magus showed up. He was driving a late model ragtop stanhope—kind of a flash car for the owner of little spell shop, I thought. Business must be good.

He was tall, thin, with a shaved head and a neatly trimmed gray goatee. He wore brass-rimmed glasses with tiny violet lenses; and even though I was sure the call from dispatch woke him up, he was in a charcoal gray suit and carried an ornate walking stick with some kind of carved crystal top. He glanced at the uniforms and then his gaze settled on me.

"I'm Ivor Jannson," he said.

"Erik Rugar, CPS," I showed him my ID wallet. He gave it a hard look and then studied my face to make sure it matched the picture. Satisfied, he gave me a nod.

"Thank you for coming," I said. "I'd like you to do an inventory with me so we can determine what has been taken."

"Yes, of course. I'll need a copy of that for my insurance."

"You can get that downtown," I told him. "From the records department. It usually takes a few days to file it."

He nodded. "Naturally. Can I go in?"

I nodded. "Let's get it over with."

He pulled a complex key from his pocket to open the door. It was a good lock, either a Ferose import or a well-made imitation.

I followed him in, a ghost at his shoulder, watching without speaking or touching anything.

When he pushed the door open a tiny trio of bells rang, on three distinct tones, but the effect was spoiled by the grating of glass shards under the edge of the door.

The place was laid out like most small specialty stores: a display case serving as a long counter, with a swinging half door leading to a narrow space backed by shelves and a door leading deeper inside, to the stockrooms where the trade goods were stored.

The counter had been smashed, the contents rifled. Mostly sorcerous tools, judging from what had been left behind. A set of arthames, a pocket orrery, astrolabes and etheric levels. A package of colored sand had been torn open and scattered across the floor.

At a glance, these were not pros. Their object seemed to be destruction, with theft a secondary goal. The thieves had made off with a few hundred bucks worth of tools and would mostly likely fence them for pennies on the dollar, having no idea of their worth.

Jannson stopped in the middle of his ruined shop and looked around with an icy calm.

"Junkies, I expect," he said, as if to himself. "Guys hopped up on tigerberry or whiteblood." He gave a bitter little chuckle. "People spend good money to do this to themselves. Some world, eh, agent?"

"Could be," I said noncommittally.

Most of the boxes on the shelves had been torn open and dumped on the floor. The combination of alchemicals had formed a bubbling patch of sticky green fluid. We stepped carefully around it to the doorway that led into the back of the shop.

Jannson stopped dead. "No," he breathed.

He darted forward to a wooden packing crate still covered with import stickers. It had been smashed open and packing excelsior strewn around. Jannson dropped his walking stick and started digging through the mess, looking for something.

I let him do it. His prints would be on everything in the shop already.

He stopped looking and clenched his fists, looking up at the ceiling. I saw him take a deep breath to calm himself. Then he looked to me. "We have something of a problem, Agent Rugar." He had recovered his cool self-control.

"What was in that crate?" I asked softly. The import stickers were from Nivose.

"Mandegora," he said, enunciating the word carefully, as if he wasn't sure I would know it.

The crate was more than a foot on a side. "Mandegora?" I repeated. "How much?"

"Twenty-five hundred grams," he answered tonelessly.

"*Two and a half kilos of mandegora?*" I stared at the empty crate. "Uh, do you usually stock that much?" Mandegora was an extremely powerful necromantic reagent, and a Class One hazardous material. Importation of it was strictly controlled.

He sighed. "Do you remember the AA scandal a few years back?"

I nodded. "Of course." Acme Arcana had been the city's biggest wholesaler of magical goods until the chief financial officer had skipped town with one of the staff wizards and most of the bank accounts. During the subsequent investigation it had come to light that the company had been diluting its product with inert substances —usually ground chalk, as I recalled—for years.

"Well, after AA went belly-up some associates and I formed a buyers' club," Jannson said. "We didn't want to get stuck for product like that again. So every couple of months I make a big buy and we split up the product."

"Oh," I said. "You've got an importer's license?"

"Yes, I do," he said angrily. "And I filed a declaration on this shipment. Your office knows all about it."

I held up my hands for peace. "I'm just asking. I had no reason to pull your records, and besides the office wasn't open yet. So who knew that you had that?"

"Nobody." Jannson went back to kicking through the packaging, as if the mandegora might still be hiding there someplace.

"What about your partners?" I asked.

"They knew I was going to order, but not the details. I just asked my partners if they wanted the same amount, and they said yes, so I got in touch with my people in Nivose. No one on this side knew it would be here last night."

"I'd still like to talk to them," I said. This case had just been upgraded from a simple burglary to a significant threat to public health. I looked at my watch. Almost six. "And I'll need to call this in, ASAP."

Jannson waved his hand at his desk. The drawers had been rifled, but it was mostly intact. I picked up the phone and checked for a dial tone, then called the night duty desk.

The duty officer's response, once I explained the situation, was short and sweet. "*Shit.*"

"Any instructions for how to proceed from here?" I asked.

"We've got to get it off the street and now," he said. "I'll get it on the hotsheets city-wide and send the lab boys to your location. But you're lead on this until the chief gets in."

He paused, then went on. "I'm going to have to kick this up to the Lord Mayor. Be a hero for me, Rugar. Locate the package. If they've opened it, secure the scene, and I mean the whole damned scene. Block the street. Even breathing in the fumes from that crap can be lethal."

"Got it, Control," I told him.

"And I'll pull the file on this shop, make sure the permit is on the level. Get me that list of his partners. Maybe one of them decided to cut out the others."

"Will do," I said, "But judging from the scene here, we're looking at a gang of dumb thugs, probably junkies. I'll bet they have no idea what they have."

"Let's hope they don't decide to screw around with it," he said without much hope. "You've got your marching orders. Get on it." I told him I'd check back in when I had something to report and hung up.

I had heard Jannson moving around in the front of the shop while I was on the phone. He came back wearing a pair of gray leather gloves and holding a shard of glass.

"Okay," I told him, "We've got a forensics team headed over. I'll need you to wait outside until they get here."

He shook his head impatiently. "We haven't got time for that." He held up the glass and I saw a smear of blood on it. "I can track them with this."

"This is a police matter," I said automatically. "We'll handle it from here."

"Agent Rugar," his voice was low and calm, but I could hear the undercurrent of tightly controlled anger, "it takes about nine grams of mandegora to produce a galvanic response in dead tissue. Thirty-five grams is sufficient to reanimate a human corpse. Every minute that we sit here and wait for the witchfinders increases the odds that shipment will end up in the hands of someone who knows how to use it, whether that's Territorial separatists, Theosophists, or the Blind Jokers."

I thought it over. He was right, of course.

"Let's go," I said. "I'll deputize you as a special consultant for the Mayor's Office on the way."

We went out to my cruiser; I swept the coffee cups and takeout food cartons off the passenger seat for him and he got to work. He pulled some kind of complex eyepiece out of his jacket pocket and peered into it.

"South," he said. "Take the Coast Parkway."

I pulled away from the curb and headed to the Parkway. "Put on your seatbelt."

The trail led us to the Standing Stones exit. Leeshore.

Guided by Jannson's directions I threaded my way through the rat warren of narrow streets lined with decaying buildings. I caught the strobing lights of cruisers when we were still a couple of blocks away.

"I know that you're the wizard," I told Jannson, "but I'm going to bet that's the place."

Jannson looked up and slid the ocular off his face. "That doesn't look good. And, yeah, this looks like where the trail ends."

Constables in Leeshore don't patrol in pairs, they patrol in teams. Even so, the presence in front of the building seemed extreme. Three cruisers, parked slantwise to block the street, an ambulance sitting at the curb with its lights ominously off, and a large unmarked van that was probably Crime Scene Investigation.

I parked half a block away and got out. I walked slowly to the crowd of uniforms around the front entrance, my hands empty and in plain sight. I waited until one of them headed over to stop me.

"Erik Rugar, CPS," I said. "I'd like to talk to the lead on the scene. I may have some information for him."

"Badge?" the constable asked. He was a big unfriendly looking man, and his uniform was tactical, with armor patches across his chest and a machine pistol on his hip.

"In my jacket," I said, and moved slow to get my ID wallet, then held it out. He took a hard look at it before waving me through the line.

"Who's him?" the constable asked as Jannson moved to follow me.

"Civilian informant," I said. "The source of the intel."

A momentary cold glare, then a nod. "Go on in. The brass is upstairs."

One of the other constables spoke up as we got to the door. "This is a bad one. Don't puke on the evidence, okay?"

A few grim laughs followed us inside.

This place had been an elegant townhome back in the middle of the last century, when Leeshore was home to merchant captains and shipping moguls. It hadn't aged well. Somebody had cut the place up to make a cheap flophouse, putting in plywood partitions and doors scavenged from other buildings. The front hall opened onto a narrow stairwell. I went up listening to the voices from the upper floor. They had the hushed tones that even hardened cops use in a room full of death. The house stank of old food and unwashed bodies, but the stench of blood overwhelmed everything.

"You don't have to go up," I told Jannson softly.

"I need to see," he said.

On the second floor there were five doors. Four of them were closed. Light bloomed suddenly from the fifth—a flashbulb. As I got closer I could see the back of a man in a suit.

"Excuse me," I said as I got closer.

The man turned. "And what's this?"

I held out my ID wallet again. He scanned it and nodded.

"Okay, Agent Rugar, I'm Captain Grigor Marduke, Leeshore Major Case Squad. You want to tell me why CPS is on my doorstep?"

I gave him a rundown of the break in at Jannson's shop and the missing mandegora.

He frowned at me, then turned and waved to someone inside. His bulk mostly blocked the door, behind him I could see a small dingy room and a lot of blood. When he turned back to me he held a big plastic evidence bag. Inside it was a steel container the size of a big saucepan, the sides festooned with warning labels. The lid was off and I could see that it was mostly empty.

I stepped aside to let Jannson see the bag.

"That's it," he said softly. "Did you find the contents?"

"Not exactly," Marduke said, and stepped aside to let us into the room.

The room was a typical junkie crash pad, too many beds crammed into too small a space. The windows had been covered with layers of cardboard, but one of them had been smashed open, letting in what early morning daylight filtered in from the airshaft. The floor, cheap linoleum laid inexpertly over old wood, was spattered with blood. So were the walls, and the cardboard on the remaining windows. So was the ceiling.

There were three lumps on the floor that I first took for blood-soaked rags. Then I saw the hair and skin and realized that they were —or had been—human bodies.

They lay too flat and too limp, as if boneless.

Nausea flooded my belly. Beside me Jannson whispered, "I've seen enough."

He turned and hurried down the stairs. I heard his retreating steps and I felt like going with him. Instead I took a measured step back and tried to breathe the less foul air of the hallway.

"What happened here?" I asked.

Marduke shrugged. "Ask your wizard friend. All I know is I've got three bodies—well, part of three bodies, anyway. It's going to be hard to ID them. See, they've got no bones. Looks like somebody filleted the poor bastards. And from what the neighbors said about the screaming, I'm guessing it happened while they were alive."

"I'll...," I felt sick. "I'll go ask Jannson what he thinks happened."

"Do that," Marduke said. "And then let me know. Because I have never seen anything like this before."

I managed to get down the stairs without throwing up and then took a couple of deep breaths on the porch until I felt like my guts were under control. I looked around and saw Jannson by my cruiser, smoking a cigarette, his face pale.

"Do you know what happened?" I asked softly.

"Those poor dumb bastards," he said. "Stupid, stupid, *stupid!*"

"What did they do?"

He looked up, dropped his smoke on the sidewalk and ground it out. "They ate it. Can you imagine that? Chemically pure mandegora and they thought it was some kind of drug. They saw the Nivose import stickers and figured it was maybe maidensbreath or something. So they sat around and ate it out of the jar."

I felt cold. "What would that do to a person?"

He closed his eyes. "There's a necromantic procedure. Illegal as it gets—blackest necromancy. Automatic death penalty. A living person is forced to consume mandegora. It regalvanizes parts of their body, specifically their bones. It's how you construct a marrowfiend."

"A marrowfiend?" I repeated. It wasn't a word I knew.

Jannson opened his eyes and looked at me. "It's a self-willed necromantic construct. Like a ghoul, only it's made of bone."

"A rawhead," I said.

He nodded. "Yeah, rawhead is another word for it. That's what they did, they made rawheads. Out of their own bodies. While they were still alive."

"But..." I tried to process that. "Where are they?"

"That's the big question, isn't it?" Jannson laughed. It wasn't a happy sound. "Off the top of my head I'd say the nearest graveyard, or maybe a slaughterhouse. See, they're going to want more bones to incorporate into themselves. It's how marrowfiends grow. They don't have to be human bones, any animal bones will work. The more they get, the stronger they are."

"We've got three rawheads loose in Leeshore?" It was worse than I had imagined. Much worse.

"That's the size of it," Jannson agreed. "And since they weren't created on purpose, they've got no control spells on them. No way to stop them except to destroy the bones. All of them."

"Can you track them?" I asked. "Or at least the one you have blood for?"

"No. Not a chance."

"We can get more blood. Fresher." I gulped. "There is plenty upstairs."

"You don't understand," he said. "It's not the blood that's important, it's the life energy. The trail I followed to here was the trail of a living person. Whatever's left of the man isn't alive any more. It may still have some blood from the original, but it's a new creature—a necromantic construct. It doesn't leave a trail of life energy. I need to work out another method."

I nodded. "Then we track it the old fashioned way. We listen for the screaming."

We headed back to the building to tell Captain Marduke the bad news.

The flophouse had no working phones, of course, so Marduke had to use one of the cruiser's radios to contact his dispatch, who set up a three way call with the CPS duty desk. I had a feeling that a lot of chief constables were about to have their breakfasts ruined.

The CPS duty officer told Marduke he was calling out the Necromantic Response team, and in addition he promised to request aid from Pickmantown, Quayside, and Marsh Parish. Then he told me to place myself under temporary command of Leeshore Constabulary for the duration of the crisis.

Marduke would be running the onsite CP from this location, treating it like a manhunt for escaped prisoners. After that was hammered out he turned to Jannson.

"Can you give me and the boys the Radio Science Weekly rundown on these marrow fiends of yours? How do find them, how do we kill them, things like that?"

"They aren't alive, so you can't kill them," Jannson began. "And they don't have a differentiated internal structure. They're like golems in that way. You're going to have to smash them, break them up into pieces."

"Shotguns, then," Marduke observed, "and riot sticks."

Jannson frowned. "Will riot sticks break bones?"

"They do when my boys are swinging them," Marduke said, smirking. Then, louder, "Okay, you heard the man. We find these things and we hit them hard. CPS has the Spook Squad on the way and we'll get some warm bodies from across the canal. All of us are going to be using big iron, so be careful—make damned sure of your target."

Two of his constables wrestled a big sheet of oilskin across the hood of the the car and I saw it was a detailed map of Leeshore. Marduke pointed and started assigning search areas. When he finished with that he looked to us.

"You looking for a ride home?" Marduke asked Jannson. "My men are kind of busy right now."

"I want to help, sir," Jannson said. "I may be able to track the constructs from what's left in that jar."

"We've got the Necro Squad coming," I pointed out. "They've got mages who specialize in this kind of stuff."

He shook his head. "Nobody specializes in a mandegora overdose. You need all the magic support you can get."

"I can't guarantee your safety," Marduke warned.

"I'll take my chances," he said. "This mess started with me—I need to see it through."

Marduke gave him a long cold look, then reached into the cruiser and pulled out a handheld radio and offered it to me. "Channel one goes to dispatch, channel three comes here. If you get a trace, you call it in. Do not attempt to engage. Are we clear on that?"

"Absolutely," I told him.

Jannson nodded gravely. "Yes, sir."

Another appraising look, then Marduke handed over the plastic bag with the steel canister. "Good luck," he said.

Jannson got his ocular back out and fiddled with it. "Mandegora gives off a powerful signature, and there's not likely to be any other source for it nearby." He pointed down an alley. "That way."

I headed where he pointed, my hand on my gun and sweat running down my neck all the way to my shoes. "How far?" I whispered.

"Not sure," he whispered back. "A quarter mile, maybe less. Maybe much less."

The alley twisted and turned. A trashcan had been overturned, garbage spread across the street. I looked at Jannson, who nodded.

"One of them was here," he whispered.

Up ahead another trashcan fell over with a clatter, the lid rolling across the brick pavement. Something was rooting around in the can.

"One of them is still here," I suggested. Carefully I unclipped the radio, made sure it was on channel three.

"We're got one in sight," I said into the radio. "It's in a trashcan behind..." I looked around for landmarks. All these dirty alleys looked alike.

Jannson pointed to a filthy awning that hung in tatters. I could just barely read the old lettering.

"...we're behind a place called the Crystal Cove Hotel. Or used to be, I think it's closed now."

"Yeah, closed up for years. Okay, I know where you are. Keep it in sight if you can, I'll get the boys on their way."

A *thing* came out of the fallen can. It looked to be about the size of a big dog, dirty white spattered with red streaks. It clicked when it walked. I stood as still as I could, scarcely daring to breathe. Beside me Jannson was a statue.

The bone-thing headed slowly down the alley, away from us. If it didn't stop soon we would have to move to keep it in view. But it came to an overflowing can and stopped, knocked it over, and began digging in the garbage.

I had expected something like an animated human skeleton, but this thing was just a mass of bones all jammed together without any order. It had four limbs of uneven size and a lumpy body. It didn't seem to have any head, although I could see a smooth dome that was probably the top of a skull protruding from its side. As I watched, it uncovered the remains of someone's chicken dinner. One of its limbs, tipped with bone appendages more like spider legs than fingers, started carefully pressing the chicken legs to its side, where they stuck.

Then thunder roared from further down the alley, and the thing blew apart into fragments. Three constables came into view. The one in front worked his shotgun and ejected a spent shell, then fired again. I backed up, pulling Jannson with me. Bits of bone rained down all around.

On the ground the bits were rattling against each other, like the alley was a skillet that someone was shaking to make sure his food didn't burn. The three constables approached the pile of fragments carefully, shotguns pointed down at the mass. Gradually, the rattling slowed down, and the pieces no longer cohered into a solid structure as before.

"What do you think, magus?" one of the constables asked without looking up. "Are we done here?"

Jannson peered through his ocular. "I'm not sure," he said slowly, "I'm still getting a—"

The second rawhead dropped down on the back of one of the constables and his shotgun roared. The man next to him went down in a heap, cursing.

By reflex I had my pistol out, but I had no shot. The second rawhead looked like a potbellied monkey with three short limbs and one absurdly long one. The long arm was wrapped around the cop's neck, the others clawed at him, shredding his uniform. Already his face was running with blood.

The unwounded constable dropped his shotgun and pulled his riot stick off his belt. He smashed the rawhead at the shoulder where its long arm joined its body. The joint came apart with a crack and the rawhead fell at their feet.

Right into the pile of bone fragments from the other one. They clung like iron filings to a magnet and in an instant the thing nearly doubled in size.

A shotgun roared and the thing leapt to the wall of the narrow alley. It scrambled like a squirrel up and over the rooftops and was gone.

I never had time to aim, much less fire.

The unwounded constable took off down the alley after it. The one who had been clawed shouted, "Tenzig! Wait!" But Tenzig never slowed.

I turned and almost tripped over Jannson. He was kneeling on the ground, cutting the uniform pants of the constable who had taken the shotgun blast. He worked fast and seemed to know what he was doing. "It's superficial," Jannson said after examining the wound. He folded the cut cloth and laid it on the wound. "Keep pressure on it until the medics get here."

Then Jannson turned to the other constable, who shook his head.

"I'm fine," he insisted. "It scratched like a whore, that's all. Get after Tenzig," He turned to face down the alley and raised his voice, *"Since he's a goat-herding territorial who's too dumb to wait for backup!"*

"Make sure you tell the medics about the marrowfiend," Jannson advised. "They'll need to scour the wound site. It hurts like a son of a bitch, but it's better to be safe."

The constable nodded and turned to me, holding out his shotgun. "Take this, and call the captain when you find my partner. Stupid cowboy."

I took the shotgun and headed down the alley at a trot. I thought Jannson might stay with the wounded men, but he followed me, scanning through his ocular.

I heard the wounded man calling in on the radio. "Captain, this is Cale. Me and Oussig are down, need medical, at the back door of the Crystal Cove. We got one hostile, but a second got away. Tenzig is in pursuit. The CPS man and the civilian are following Tenzig, they'll advise if the hostile is sighted."

Marduke's voice came back flat and tinny. "Are you stable? We've got a hostile cornered at the Green Dolphin Tunnel, all available are headed there."

"Take your time, we ain't bleeding bad."

"Copy that, Cale," Marduke said and then went on to direct his other officers, a mix of anagrams and unfamiliar street names. I turned it down until it was just barely audible.

The alley was full of overflowing garbage cans. It was tough to tell, but I didn't think that anything had been rummaging through them searching for bones.

"So you're a medic, too?" I asked Jannson.

"Huh?" he was concentrating on whatever signals he saw through the ocular. "Oh, no. I worked as an ER orderly to pay for school. Summerisle General. You pick up the basics."

There was a dark silhouette waiting at the next corner. As we got closer I saw it was Tenzig and he was motioning us to come on. We hurried to join him.

"I heard Cale say you were coming," he said. "Can you find that thing?"

Jannson pointed with his cane across the street to the loading dock of a brick building that covered half the block. On the upper floors I saw rows of small windows, grimy and covered with bars. "In there," Jannson said.

Tenzig nodded. "I was afraid of that."

"What is that," I asked, "a warehouse?"

Tenzig shook his head grimly. "That's the back entrance of the Angel Street Hospital."

Angel Street was the city's biggest charity hospital. Overcrowded, underfunded, long overdue for remodeling, it was where the city sent people who had nowhere to go. I'd never been inside the place, myself, but I'd heard stories from other cops. They weren't good stories.

Tenzig broke open his shotgun and loaded it, then held out his hand for the one I carried. While he was attending to it I called in.

"Captain Marduke, this is Erik Rugar of CPS. We've located the third rawhead—it went inside Angel Street Hospital. Officer Tenzig is with us. Please advise."

There was a pause. Then, *Shit. We're all committed on Green Dolphin. The damned thing got into a meat market—it's the size of a horse. I'll inform Angel Street. Do not go in there without backup. Watch the perimeter, but do not engage until I can free up some tacticals for support. Do you copy, Rugar?*

"I copy, sir," I said.

Jannson shook his head. "With all due respect, your captain is wrong. We have to go in there. If we give it time to... harvest those patients it'll take artillery to take it down."

Tenzig nodded. "Yeah, we're the cavalry." He offered me one of the shotguns. "You coming, Rugar?"

"We have to." I took the shotgun and started across the street. The others fell into step beside me.

Tenzig looked over at Jannson. "Tell me that stick shoots lightning bolts or something."

Jannson gave a grim little smile. "Not when there are cops around."

"I got really poor powers of observation," Tenzig said. "How about you, Public Safety Man?"

"All I care about is stopping this thing," I said.

We got to the dock doors. I expected them to be locked, but Tenzig pulled one open easily. On the other side was a wide dirty corridor, brightly lit by a row of caged bulbs. A dirty wheelchair with a broken wheel sat against one wall.

Someone screamed, a sound so twisted by agony that I couldn't tell if it were a man or a woman.

"Upstairs," Tenzig shouted, then ran for an unmarked steel door. He shoved it open and headed into a narrow brick stairwell, me and Jannson close behind him. One flight up we heard the scream again and Tenzig paused a moment to fix its location. He nodded to himself and charged further up the stairs.

I was starting to flag and got to the top just in time to see the door to the hallway swinging shut. I hit it and went through puffing. Jannson was even farther behind.

Tenzig was headed down the corridor, towards a sign that read "Exotic Diseases." Another sign below it listed quarantine procedures in bright red capital letters. I didn't waste time reading it. The screaming was starting up again and coming from that direction.

A turn in the corridor brought us to a metal gate stretched across the corridor. Two orderlies with rubber gloves and cloth masks were struggling to hold the gate closed against a dozen patients in thin white gowns.

"Clear that gate!" Tenzig roared.

Startled, the orderlies turned to stare. One of them started to say, "These patients are infectious, they are in quarantine—"

Tenzig lifted his shotgun and fired into the ceiling. Plaster and glass from a shattered light fixture rained down. The orderlies hit the ground.

I got ahead of Tenzig and unlatched the gate and yanked it open. The patients had retreated from the shotgun blast as well, giving us a clear path into the ward. They started jabbering and pointing. We went that way. Another round of screaming began.

An archway led us into an open patient ward. It was a slaughterhouse.

The rawhead was still formed like a misshapen monkey, humpbacked and crooked, with one arm longer than the other three limbs, but it had gotten bigger.

Much bigger.

It towered in the middle of the room, nearly brushing the fifteen-foot ceiling. Its body was more red than white, its stolen bones running with blood. All around it lay the bodies of its victims, flat as discarded rags.

I stared, overcome with horror. Tenzig didn't hesitate. He darted forward and started shooting, the shotgun blasts a series of punishing thunderclaps in the enclosed space, as fast as he could work the slide.

I started forward, then thought better of it. I'd wait until he ran out, then fire to cover his reloading. I wondered how many shells he had in his pouch. We were going to need a lot.

The blasts were chipping away at the rawhead's bone body, but it was so massive that it was shrugging them off. Against the thunder it came forward and Tenzig backed up, still firing.

Then his shotgun clicked empty and I raised mine and fired. It wasn't my weapon of choice, but it was a target that was hard to miss, especially as it was drawing closer.

I felt Jannson grab my shoulder and tug me back to the door. "Get it into the hallway," he shouted beside my ear. Tenzig shuffled along beside us, reloading.

The ceiling of the hallway was lower, and the rawhead had to bend over the squeeze through the door. Its featureless head smashed one of the caged bulbs and it didn't seem to notice.

Jannson moved to the middle of the hallway, facing it. "Get back, you two!" he shouted and raised his cane. A jet of brilliant flame flashed from the crystal top, slamming into the rawhead's torso.

The rawhead shambled towards Jannson, moving as fast as its misshapen body and the tight hallway would allow. Jannson backed up at a brisk walking pace, easily keeping the distance between them.

As he walked he kept up the jet of flame. The blood on the rawhead sizzled and cooked off, filling the hallway with an acrid stench.

Tenzig raised his reloaded shotgun. I put my hand on his shoulder.

"Let's see how this goes," I said, then held out my hand for more shotgun shells.

The rawhead and Jannson continued their slow retreat down the hallway, joined by the stream of white fire. The outer layer of bones on the rawhead's body yellowed and then blackened from the heat, but it didn't seem to be doing it any real damage.

Still Jannson kept up his sorcerous assault, pouring fire onto the thing. Tenzig and I followed, but the rawhead was paying no attention to us.

Soon, though, Jannson would run out of either magic or hallway, and we had to be ready to take over. I could see the strain that Jannson was under, his hand holding the cane beginning to shake.

The rawhead was covered with boiling blood now, the stink of it monstrous. The whole front of the creature was heat blackened and the spot where the fire was hitting it glowed dull red.

It wasn't dying, though, and it still advanced with a steady, murderous pace.

Jannson gave a gasp and fell to his knees, the fire winking out. Then, as Tenzig and I came forward to renew our assault, the mage lifted his wand and fired one last burst of flame, at the ceiling directly above the rawhead's superheated body.

The fire sprinkler erupted into a deluge.

In a moment the hallway was full of steam. We could hear the rawhead's body cracking, a thousand sharp sounds like ice shattering on the surface of a pond. Inside its shroud of steam the huge creature seemed to be coming apart, breaking into smaller chunks.

Somewhere up ahead, past the steam cloud, Jannson shouted, "Now! Don't let it reform."

Tenzig and I walked together into the steam, shooting anything that moved. Eventually the steam cleared and we ran out of ammo, but the stolen bones lay still.

Marduke had some choice words for the three of us when he showed up. They had taken out the one at Green Dolphin Street and come to the hospital *en masse*, but it was all over by the time they got there. I got an official reprimand for disobeying the direct order given by the commanding officer of a cooperating agency. But then, I also got a commendation for merit under fire and saving civilian lives. They balanced out.

Jannson received an official complaint for carrying an unregistered class two thaumaturgic weapon, and a second for failing to take appropriate precautions to safeguard the mandegora. Both complaints were eventually dropped, though, and he kept his license.

I might have helped with that, a little bit.

TRUST

JAKE LITHUA

Calem trudged ahead of his mule up the steep path into the hills, sweat trickling into his eyes and staining his green linen tunic. The heat made him uncomfortable; he was far happier secluding himself in his father's cellars, a candle and a book of Qanaa'thi lore in hand, than he was outside. But more than the heat, Calem felt the hostile gaze of hidden eyes, somewhere in the hills ahead. Any moment he expected to feel a spearhead sink into his belly.

He could not feel how many were waiting for him, nor where they were; his skill with the Ciphers was still poor. Though Father had already mastered the Ciphers by the time he was thirteen, and Calem's older brothers were safely competent at that age, Calem was already sixteen and still the Ciphers told him little. But now, the Cipher of Receptiveness told him enough: dangerous men were waiting ahead, and they hated him.

Is that why Father sent me here alone? To kill me off, like culling the runt of the litter? Immediately Calem dismissed the thought; family was everything to Father, as it was to all Qanaa'thi. Without a land of their own, scattered amongst the gold-skinned Eridari people (who hated and feared them for their uncanny mental powers), the Qanaa'thi had learned that you could only truly rely on family.

Still, Father had some cavalier ideas about child-raising. Having escaped with his family across the seas to New Erida, the skilled merchant wanted to open trade with the natives. And he had inexplicably sent his youngest son to make the first contact, which was why Calem was sweating his way up this overgrown hillside, leading a mule heavily laden with trade goods. *Father is wise*, he thought, *but this is a terrible idea.* "You won't need guards, Calem. You'll be safe, Calem. The Greens are honorable towards guests, Calem. It will be a good experience for you, Calem." Hah!

The unseen watchers must have come to a decision, because there was a high-pitched whoop and cold-eyed men with dusky green skin rose from the ground just in front of Calem, casting aside mantles of woven leaves and branches that had disguised their presence amongst the high bushes. They wore only animal-hide pantaloons and rawhide sandals, and the occasional bracelet of bone or copper; on their bare chests they each bore a tattoo of a black triangle, and a coiled mark that resembled a serpent. Suddenly Calem found a thicket of sharpened wood spears leveled inches from his throat.

Calem shrank back against the flank of his mule, which eyed the Greens with bored curiosity. "Peace!" he cried out. "I come in peace! I'm here to trade! Peace!" He had learned the Green language in two weeks thanks to the Ciphers' power, listening to the former plantation slaves who scratched out their living in a slum just outside of the colonial capital of King's Landing. (Of course, Father could have done it in two *days*.) *These* Greens were nothing like the broken castoffs of the plantations; they were strong, and they radiated malice.

One of the men strode forward slowly, importantly. He wore a colorful sash and bracelets of bone beads, and carried a heavy club covered with carvings and inlaid with tiny gems. "Peace?" he repeated, mockingly. "With the Yellows? The invading people that burns our homes, kills our men, sells our women?" He raised his voice, speaking to the others. "What shall we do with this Yellow fool, who has intruded in the territory of the Snake clan?" Ugly mutters and laughs were the response.

Calem's insides were churning, his blood thundering in his head. *Need to concentrate.* He focused his mind's eye, struggling to call on the Cipher of Harmony. The symbols flickered unevenly in his inner sight, reflecting his agitation; but soon they quieted his mind and prepared him for action. When he felt a bit calmer, he took a deep breath and said, "I am no Yellow. I am of the Qanaa'thi people, and I am here to trade."

The man snorted. "Trade? And you bring a single mule?" He snapped his fingers, and three of his men pushed forward and started to ransack the mule's saddlebags. Calem did not react. *Father warned me this might happen. Can't show them I'm afraid.*

"This is a poor cargo indeed," the leader said scornfully as the Snake men began laying out spices, iron knives, gold necklaces, and bolts of Kirian silk on the ground. But then the tallest of the three let out a cry, unwrapped a long thin bundle and held up an iron-tipped spear. It was unmistakably an Eridari element-forged weapon: the spearhead glittered unnaturally blue and green in the daylight, almost seeming to hum.

The spear was of average quality, forged by a mere journeyman elementalist for a common soldier of the Fifth Colonial Regiment— who decided to "lose" it one day, with Father's prompting; but it would be a far better weapon than anything the Greens could make on their own. Or so Father had hoped, and part of Calem's task had been to find out. It seemed Father was right again; the Greens let out cries of wonder as the tall warrior turned it over in his hands, his eyes wide.

"Bring that to me," the leader barked, eyeing the others. "*I* shall choose who gets the spear. That is our law."

The tall warrior stared at him balefully, caressing the spearshaft in his hands; but he finally muttered a curse and brought it forward, and the leader snatched it from him. "Very well, Chief Roganath," the warrior said. "Be sure to choose quickly."

Roganath nodded in acknowledgement, and turned back to Calem. "Only one?"

Calem smiled. "Only one—for now. My father can send more, if you trade for them. But the price will be high; these spears are from the Imperial Regiments, and are not easy to get."

The chief's eyes narrowed. Quietly, he said, "What sort of price?"

Fighting the urge to lick his lips, Calem said, "I come for silver amber."

The chief recoiled and a murmur went up from the others. Silver amber was unique to these hills, and its powerful magical properties were poorly understood by the Empire. Roganath's lips thinned. "A high price indeed, boy."

"Or we could kill him, and take his goods," the tall warrior said loudly. "I know of no Qanaa'thi people. He looks like a Yellow, he smells like a Yellow, and we can't trust a word out of his lying mouth."

"You could kill me," Calem said, outwardly calm, struggling to recall his language studies. "But then you will get no more element-forged spears."

The warrior spat. "Spears? We have our own spears. The Yellows think they just can walk into our land, after what they have done? No. We answer with blood!"

"Lanorak! You are being hasty." Roganath did not raise his voice, but the tall warrior closed his mouth, looking abashed. Then the chief turned back to Calem, frowning. "Still, Lanorak is right. This spear is pretty, but we are mighty warriors even without such weapons. It is hardly worth sparing your life over the empty promise for more, at a high price that we cannot pay."

He leaned the spear against his shoulder and pointed to the lowlands. "You see," he said, almost apologetically, "the Yellows always want more slaves: men for the plantations, women as servants or pleasure-toys for their war chiefs. And scum like the Leopard clan attack our settlements and take our women and children to sell." The others hissed, their auras shot through with hate and fear. "So what silver amber we do have, we need to give as peace-gifts to other clans. Otherwise, our men will never find women of their own. And women are scarce all throughout the hills, thanks to the Yellows, so we must give gifts to many, many clans."

Calem nodded. He saw the flaw in the chief's logic, and the opportunity. "But need the peace-gifts be of silver amber? Or can they be anything valuable?" Roganath said nothing, but he lifted an eyebrow. Calem smiled. "Mighty chief, don't you see? Trading with us will leave you richer than before, not poorer! You give us something you desire less, and we desire more, in exchange for something you desire more and we less. We are both better off, and you would be able to make peace with more clans than before."

Roganath hesitated, considering, but Lanorak laughed bitterly. "Did you hear him? He's a Yellow dog for certain. This is what they said to us; and then they took our medicines and the lore of how to make them, and gave us beer and thin clothes and shiny trinkets and *nothing* useful. No weapons, no tools, not the secret of their talking scrolls. And they do not exchange their women for ours, oh no!" A dangerous growl went up from the others and Roganath nodded automatically, his expression turning grim. Lanorak snarled, "No,

Yellow women are too good for the Men of the Hills! They steal our women instead of exchanging for them. They do not see us as equals to trade with; they see us as goats to be milked, and fed a little grass now and then before slaughtering. This boy is just the same. I say we cut off his head and send it back to the city as a gift!"

His heart fluttered in his chest; his palms felt clammy. For a second, Calem thought his throat would close and he would choke on his own panicked flesh. But then Father's voice sounded in his ear: *Offer people what they most need.* It was his fundamental rule, and the basis for enduring commerce. Calem took a deep breath and set aside his rising terror. In his mind he augmented the Cipher of Harmony with the Cipher of Victory, made his voice firm, and said, "What if I could get you Yellow women for your men?"

Sudden silence. Lanorak stared at him openmouthed. Roganath was carefully expressionless, but Calem could perceive the sudden blaze of hope that burned in his heart, and that of a half dozen other men around him. The chief fixed him with a flat stare, and said, "How?"

Good question. He invoked the Cipher of Insight and saw a way. "Not all Yellows live in fine houses. Some women have little and suffer for it, even here in the colonies; and they want a better life than the cities can offer. Perhaps they might want to live with you in the hills, if you can offer them more than the cities and farms can.

"Make me your prisoner," Calem continued, fighting the urge to lick his lips. "Bring me back to your settlement. Let me see how your women live. Then I can send word to my father, and we will bring you women who want the life of the Hill Folk."

Roganath's lip curled. "You would *sell* your women?"

"Not at all," Calem improvised hastily, intuiting the grave insult implied. "It would be just the same as marrying a woman from another clan. And besides, as I told you, I am not Yellow. I am Qanaa'thi."

Roganath suddenly smiled. "Just the same, you say?" He gave Calem an appraising look and began to chuckle.

"Ridiculous!" snapped Lanorak. "This boy hasn't passed the Test of Manhood. He isn't fit for our women. And he has no ancestors to bind, so we couldn't trust him even if he were!"

Yet Roganath's chuckle became a deep belly laugh. He bent over and slapped his chest several times, his laughter loud and raucous. Finally he straightened and cleared his throat. "What is your name, boy?"

Yes! "Calem, son of Aliron."

"Welcome, Calem son of Aliron," the chief said formally. "I accept your goods as a peace-gift, offered from the Qanaa'thi clan to the Snake clan. You may stay with us as a protected messenger; soon you will take the Test of Manhood, and we will negotiate the exchange of women. If your women come as promised, then we will give you a suitable peace-gift of our own, and you may go back to your clan in peace."

Calem bowed deeply. "You are gracious, great chief." Then it hit him. *Wait. "Exchange of women"? I am not fit for their women?* His mouth went dry. What had he just agreed to?

"Are you mad?" Lanorak burst out, almost frantic. "He has *no ancestors!* We can't *trust* him!"

"*Women*, Lanorak," Roganath snapped, his humor gone in an instant. "He offers us *women*. We can't trust him yet, but perhaps we will find a way to trust him later." Then he shrugged. "And if he cannot provide the women, then he is a false messenger and we kill him anyway."

Calem and the hunting party climbed up faint paths through the underbrush, snaking between tall pine trees and large, jagged gray rocks that erupted from the ground. Calem soon struggled to breathe, a painful stitch lancing through his side, and he leaned against his uncomplaining mule; but the hillmen hardly seemed to notice the strenuous climb. A few shot him contemptuous looks as his breath heaved, and Lanorak laughed out loud. An hour later, sweat streamed down Calem's face and stung his eyes, and his thin linen tunic and breeches clung to his flesh. His calves and thighs burned, for all that

Calem tried using the Cipher of Strength to fortify them; he had always been poor at using Strength.

And then Roganath let out a low, warbling bird-call. The call was repeated from somewhere in the thicket ahead of them, and the hillmen all let out relieved smiles. "Safe for another day," Roganath said; they continued forward, and as if by magic the hill settlement appeared in front of them.

Small huts clustered around outcroppings of rock and nestled underneath low trees. They were built from bundles of thin pine branches lashed together, covered with a blanket of brown needles; from a distance, they blended in with the forest perfectly. Roughly in the center of the huts, under an animal-hide canopy some ten feet across, piles of yellowed bones were arranged on rock pedestals around a low obsidian block, perhaps an altar. Calem shivered as he realized that few of the bones were animal. A human skull, its dome caved in from some mighty blow, leered at him from its perch.

As the party entered the settlement, women and children emerged from the huts and appeared from deeper in the forest, some of them leading goats on lengths of woven cord. Calem struggled not to stare and a blush rose in his cheeks; like the men, the women wore only leather pantaloons, very different from the elaborate dresses and mantles of Eridari women. They were silent, but comfortably so, waiting for some signal before greeting their men.

Finally, an old man emerged from a low tent of animal-skin with strange symbols painted on its sides. He wore a blood-red headdress of beaded leather and carried a carved staff, its knobby head trailing strings of what looked like bleached knucklebones. His eyes were wild, cunning; Calem viewed him with the Cipher of Receptiveness and nearly gasped aloud. Strange magical energies swirled around the man, greasy and alien, feeling of death.

This must be one of the shamans, masters of the Hill People's necromantic magic, so it was said. Oddly, Calem could also detect a whiff of the elemental magic favored by the Eridari. He had never seen a non-Eridar who could use it; but Father always said that all forms of magic were in principle available to everyone. Some nations seemed to have affinities to particular modes of thinking, was all—and of course, the Ciphers were superior to all of them, which is why the Qanaa'thi kept them secret. If anyone revealed the mysteries of the Ciphers, the Qanaa'thi would soon find their greatest weapons used against them.

The shaman's eyes found Calem and he stopped, frowning; but he soon strode to the chief and smote his staff upon the ground, the knucklebones rattling. "How went the spirits, this day?" he called in a loud, reedy voice.

Roganath responded formally. "The spirits have guided us true, in the hunt and in all things."

"Welcome, then, beloved of the spirits," the shaman replied, and at last the people relaxed into a happy chatter as the hunters rejoined their village.

One older girl of perhaps fifteen, wearing silver armbands and a brightly colored Eridar belt around her waist, approached Roganath and embraced him. "Any wounded, Father?" she asked.

"No, Sakina," the chief replied, smiling fondly. "We don't need your skills today, thank the spirits."

Calem noted that fewer than half of the hunters seemed to have wives or children; the others, Lanorak included, merely lounged around the central altar, butchering the hunted animals or else pulling out bone dice and playing with each other. But they all kept an ear cocked as the shaman went on in a more normal voice, pointing to Calem and scowling. "Who is this Yellow, Roganath? Why have you brought him here?"

"He is Calem, son of Aliron. He says he is no Yellow, and he offers to trade with us for silver amber," Roganath said, tensing slightly.

The change in the shaman was terrifying. To Calem's magical sight, black anger seemed to roll off of him in waves, mixed with no small amount of fear. "Never!" he snarled. "*I* am the keeper of the silver amber, and I say it is our clan's birthright! Kill the boy for his presumption and be done!" He took a step towards Calem and raised his hand, as if to smite him then and there. Calem froze; the Ciphers fled from his mind.

"Boragos," the chief said gently, "he offers to exchange women. *Yellow* women." From his seat near the altar, Lanorak scoffed loudly but said nothing. Sakina gazed sharply at her father, then gave Calem a cool, appraising look.

Boragos breathed heavily. "How can he?" he said at last, his voice rough. "I feel no ancestors about him."

"Perhaps you can find a way to teach him regardless," Roganath said, "as he prepares for the Test of Manhood."

The shaman stared at him, then suddenly let out a nasty laugh. "Very well," he said. "Let us see if this boy can become a man." Calem relaxed. *I guess he won't kill me just yet.*

The chief nodded, then turned his head. "Lanorak, come!" Lanorak rose warily from his dice game and approached. Roganath held out the element-forged spear. "You are the fiercest warrior of the Snake clan. Take this weapon for yourself, that you may take the skulls of our enemies!"

Lanorak caught his breath, and took the spear-shaft gently as the other hunters whooped and gathered around him. The spearhead caught the light and gleamed bluish-green. Lanorak thumped his chest with a fist. "Thank you for your mighty gift, great chief!"

"And of course, you will train Calem to grapple," Roganath said smoothly.

Lanorak chuckled ruefully. "Ah, you are indeed a wise chief." He shot Calem a vicious look. "Perhaps the boy will even live long enough to take the Test."

Fantastic. Both of my teachers want to kill me.

It was late in the day, and the clan gathered for their evening meal. Before joining them, Calem was stood before the central fire and his shirt removed; Lanorak painted a red band around his left arm, and Boragos a blue band around his right. This marked him as a student, apparently. Calem's exposed flesh felt cold in the deepening gloom, and he had to fight the overpowering urge to cover up his scrawny chest with his hands.

As the clan huddled close to the fire, Roganath made a short speech welcoming him as a messenger from the Qanaa'thi clan; it seemed that all the young girls in the village were shooting Calem covert looks. A few giggled. He blushed again. *Did I really just agree to marry one of these girls, sight unseen? What will Father say? What if I don't like them?*

What if none of them like me?

The food at least was excellent. The Eridari often traded with the Hill Folk for exotic delicacies unknown in old Erida, but it seems the Greens kept the best for themselves. In hollowed-out gourds, Calem was served chunks of roasted goat meat flavored with spices, roots and vegetables that he had never seen before; in horn cups, the Snake clan poured out sweet juices that quenched his thirst. *Far better than the coarse bread that common Eridar eat*, Calem thought. *Perhaps some Eridari women would want to live here just for the food!*

As the Hill Folk retired to their huts, Lanorak caught Calem's arm. "You will sit vigil tonight before the altar," he said with a smirk. "Sleep not, and think upon the task that lies before you, for tomorrow you begin your path to manhood."

Calem said nothing and allowed himself to be guided to the center of the bone displays. Inside he smiled wryly; Lanorak could not know that Calem had often gone without sleep, especially since turning thirteen. Father had come to believe that all Calem lacked to master the Ciphers was a single moment of clear understanding— and was increasingly frustrated that his son was having such difficulty. Nights of endless meditation were a frequent prescription.

Admittedly, Calem had never had to meditate while staring at piles of human bone before.

Ah well. Let's try the Ciphers again, shall I?

～

Calem presented himself at dawn before the shaman's tent, as instructed. His eyes stung and his limbs were heavy with cold and weariness. But when Boragos emerged, he snapped, "You are wasting your time," and strode past him without breaking stride, his knuckle-bone staff rattling.

Is this some kind of test? Calem trotted after the shaman, invoking the Cipher of Harmony. "Master Boragos, I have been placed in your care," he said, as meekly as he could. "Whatever I need to learn, I promise that I will."

"You *promise*," the shaman mimicked nastily, heading away from camp and further up the hills. "You have no ancestors to be bound by your promise, so I don't believe you. And that is the heart of your problem, and why you *cannot* learn the spirit magic."

"What do you mean, I have no ancestors?" The shaman ignored him. Calem's jaw tightened. He sprinted forward and turned so that he faced Boragos squarely, his eyes burning. "Are you breaking your word to your own chief, man of the hills? Is this how *your* honor can be trusted?"

Calem had been trained since birth to control his anger, as were all Qanaa'thi. Anger clouded the mind, caused needless destruction. Anger obscured the vision of the Ciphers and left one weak. Still, there was a time and a place for feigned displays of anger. *Not that I'm pretending much.* If he did not pass whatever test Roganath meant for him, he would be killed as a false messenger. In casting him away, the old shaman was condemning him to death.

Steady, Calem. Anger clouds the mind. Go beyond the what, ask why.

Boragos gazed at him impassively, then gave his staff a little rattle. "Very well, boy. Listen well, for this is your only lesson from me. All Men of the Hills learn to call on the spirits of their fathers and fathers' fathers. Those spirits give them strength in battle, or wisdom in council. Men of greater skill can even command the spirits of their slain enemies." A slight smile touched his lips, and Calem shivered. The shaman stared at him with cold eyes. "Let me show you."

Calem quickly invoked the Cipher of Receptiveness, and almost wished he hadn't. Swirling around the shaman were formless presences, the dried husks of souls; the greasy feel of them nearly made Calem retch. Boragos let his eyes unfocus, and then Calem felt a sudden wordless command pulse out of the shaman's mind.

Three of the spirits drifted closer and seemed to merge with his own; Boragos let out a low growl, then spun and punched his fist clean through the trunk of a nearby tree. Fragments of wood exploded out of the trunk. Calem cried out and stumbled backward, his eyes wide.

Boragos smiled smugly and allowed the spirits to go free. He brushed splinters of wood off of his unmarked hand. "But even the weakest boy among us must be able to call upon his own ancestors," he continued as if nothing strange had just happened.

Calem slowly came forward again, cursing his earlier fright. The shaman squatted down away from him, carefully harvesting a greenish-reddish moss from the side of the tree's stump and depositing it into a satchel hanging at his side. "But the Yellows are different from us," he went on without turning. "I can feel no ancestors beside them. There is no one for them to call. Nor do I feel your own ancestors. Perhaps they abandon you when they die, or perhaps you do not know the way to appease them in their death. Perhaps they cannot come with you across the great ocean. Regardless, you have no ancestors to call on, and thus I cannot teach you the lore of the spirits. You will never pass the Test of Manhood."

Calem digested this. "Are there no other spirits to call on?" he said at last.

Boragos turned, his eyes narrowing, and he shook his head. "They will be beyond your power. Boys of the clan learn the necessary skills with their own ancestors, who *want* to give them aid. If you try to call on the spirits of other fallen warriors, they will destroy your mind."

"I might surprise you," Calem said quietly. "And it seems I have no choice but to try."

"Try on your own, then," the shaman said, and rose. "No man of the Snake clan will help you. Roganath would have done better to kill you at once."

He set off deeper into the forest, leaving Calem staring after him nonplussed. The shaman was difficult to read, even with the Ciphers. *Anger, and hatred, and fear? Why? I have done nothing to him. Why fear?*

He shook his head. *If the door is locked, try the window.* It was one of Father's sayings. There would be some other way to pass this Test, even if the shaman tried to block him. For now, he went to find Lanorak.

The hill settlement was already humming with activity when he returned. Men were crafting bone knives or sharpening the tips of their spears; women pounded on dried nuts and root vegetables with large rocks, forming a paste which they then fried near the fire, or else churned butter from large heavy skins of goat's-milk. Others were weaving large nets, perhaps for fishing or hunting, while old women and new mothers tended the children.

Calem eyed them. The women were working hard, but nothing like the grueling labor of the plantations. They chatted with each other as they worked and exchanged gossip or told stories. *If this is the worst that women have to deal with in the hills, even Eridari women might see this life as attractive.*

A few men, perhaps too high-status to spend time on menial tasks, were playing dice in the central clearing. Lanorak was among the dicers, and he frowned when he saw Calem approach. "What, is the shaman done with you already?"

Calem nodded. "He gave me a task to do later. For now, I am in your care." *More or less true.*

The tall hunter disgustedly tossed his dice aside and rose. "Come," he said, and led Calem to a small clearing just outside the settlement where the tall brush had been hacked away, leaving a flat muddy area partly covered with low grasses and ferns. Lanorak ran a scornful eye down Calem's slight frame. "You are weak, Not-Yellow. Does your clan not teach you to fight?"

Calem ground his lip between his teeth. "The Qanaa'thi fight with our wits and our magic, more than our muscles."

The hunter's lip curled. "See what good those do you when I snap you in half, boy. This is likely a waste of my time; our sons spend *years* learning to fight, dreaming of the Test of Manhood; or even better, hoping to kill an enemy of the clan in battle, so that they become a man immediately without the Test. You cannot learn our arts in a few days."

Again! Fury bubbled up within Calem's belly, despite all his training. *What is wrong with these Greens?* But Lanorak continued, "Still, I told my chief I would teach you, and so I shall. We begin with the stance. One leg forward, lean into it."

The hunter shifted to a slight crouch, his weight mostly over his forward leg. Calem tried to copy him; Lanorak abruptly shoved him backward, and Calem tumbled into the mud with a yelp. "You lack stability," Lanorak said, as his student scrambled to his feet, sputtering. "Your legs are your base, like the roots of a tree. Draw your power from the earth, not from your puny chest. Again!"

This time, Calem remembered to invoke the Ciphers of Receptiveness and Strength, though his agitation made them flicker in his mind. He observed Lanorak's stance keenly and copied it more precisely. The hunter nodded. "Better. Now, clinch with me, thus." He positioned himself in front of Calem and put one hand in back of Calem's head, and the other behind his elbow. Calem mimicked him. "We will circle, you and I," Lanorak said. "As we do, do not lose your root even while you shift your feet. You must be stable at all times. If you lose your stability, I will put you in the dirt again. Begin!"

Over the next two hours, Calem's body was jarred and battered from repeated tumbles into the forest soil. His legs were swept from beneath him, he was flipped over Lanorak's back to thud painfully, his arms were twisted behind him until he cried out in pain. The Ciphers helped, but even when his technique was correct Calem could do nothing to stop Lanorak from tossing him around like a sack of wine. His limbs were too weak, his reflexes too slow.

Still, Lanorak's initial scorn softened as they grappled. Aided by the Ciphers, Calem learned the techniques quickly, and the tall hunter seemed surprised and pleased. After yet another impact into the ground, Calem lay where he fell, his tired muscles screaming at him in unaccustomed ways. "Come now, up you get," Lanorak said gruffly. "Pain makes you stronger, and your weakness is the main thing holding you back." Calem gazed up at him and nodded slightly. Then he grunted and heaved himself back up.

But during the next fall, Calem slipped and his arm struck the ground at an angle. Pain lanced through his arm and shoulder, and he cried out. Lanorak instantly let go and stepped back. "Can you stand?" he asked. Calem nodded, gritting his teeth; holding his arm with his other hand, he scrambled to his feet. *Cipher of Victory for pain, right?* The thought was remote; he seemed to be floating.

"I'm all right," Calem said. "We can go again."

Lanorak shook his head. "Don't be stupid. You've gone so pale, no one would ever mistake you for a Yellow. You need healing."

Calem was guided back to the settlement and sat down on a mossy log, hissing in pain. He expected Boragos to see to his injury, and was half-afraid the shaman would take the chance to murder him; to his surprise, it was Sakina who Roganath summoned. Soon the chief's daughter came running swiftly from the west, where a river wandered its way down the hill. She bent over him, examining his arm with a businesslike expression. Calem bit back a grunt as Sakina prodded his shoulder with unnecessary force.

She straightened, wrinkling her nose. "It's just a sprain. I am busy, and the Yellow hardly needs healing."

"Daughter," the chief said gently, "I need him healthy. And you are the strongest wise woman we have left." He touched her cheek. "Do this for me." Sakina scowled, but nodded and sat next to him, her fingers lightly touching his arm.

Though the nearness of a pretty girl was distractingly pleasant and he almost blushed again, Calem struggled to keep his mind clear. *Boragos never mentioned* women *using spirit magic. Is it different?* Despite the blinding pain, Calem invoked the Cipher of Receptiveness so he could sense when Sakina opened herself to the spirits.

When she did, he drew in a sharp breath; she did not use human spirits, as Boragos had done. Instead, tiny gossamer presences flowed towards her from the very bracken and underbrush they sat among, almost invisible to Calem even with the Ciphers. Sakina's channeling was delicate, precise; she did not try to forcefully direct the spirits, merely guided them gently as their power flowed into her hands and bathed his shoulder in glowing silver light.

At once, the pain began to fade. Sakina's fingers danced, and Calem could feel the torn sinews of his shoulder knitting back together as if she were sewing them herself. The sensation was bizarre, but it did not last long. Two minutes later, the silver light winked out; Sakina exhaled, nodded once, let her hands drop, and without speaking rose, spun on her heel and strode back to the river, panting like she had just run for miles.

Calem stared after her. *That was incredible. Could Father have done that with the Ciphers? Perhaps, but I've never even learned how to heal a bruise!*

Roganath watched him, and smiled proudly. "Yes, my daughter's magic is strong. In a time of peace, she would have studied with our wise women and eventually become a healer of legend." He sighed. "Now, the wise women are dead or taken; and she must learn what she can on her own."

"I've never seen better," Calem said truthfully.

The chief shot him a sudden look. "Do not think that Sakina will be the woman we exchange, boy! I like you, but not quite that much. She will marry a great hunter or powerful shaman from another clan, not a wandering merchant."

Calem's jaw dropped. "Uh, great chief," he babbled through suddenly clumsy lips, "I, uh, never even thought of your daughter in, in that way!"

Roganath grunted, though a smile played around his lips. "Well, start thinking about *someone* in that way. Messengers are protected for three days, traditionally. We shall need to discuss the exchange soon." He clapped his hands. "Now back to your training, boy!"

Calem had another idea. He made excuses to Lanorak, saying that he had to perform his task for the shaman; instead, he followed Sakina to the riverbank, where she tended to a woven fishing trap. She had rolled up her pantaloons and was standing calf-deep in the water and facing away from him, still panting and dripping with sweat; she swallowed cool water from a gourd and wiped her mouth. Without turning around, she said, "What do you want, Yellow?"

He suppressed a flash of irritation. "Thank you," he said. "Your magic was incredible."

"I didn't do it for you," she said flatly. "I only obeyed my father's wishes."

Calem blinked, and examined her with the Ciphers. Her emotions roiled with contempt and hatred. *Why?* Trying again, he said, "Your father wants me to take the Test of Manhood. But Boragos will not teach me the ways of the spirits, because he says I have no ancestors. He does not think I can learn to call other spirits, the way you did."

Sakina turned, one eyebrow raised. "And?"

It was so hard to look her in the eye. Calem never could look straight at beautiful girls, always flinching away as if from the bright sun; and now, the contempt radiating from her face made it all the more painful. Calem took a deep breath and squared his shoulders. "Please teach me."

She stared at him, then spat.

Calem ignored the crushing feeling in his chest and went on. "All I ask is one hour. If you don't think that I can learn after that, then you can send me away and I will have to deal with your father the best I can. But I promise you, I *will* prove myself to you in that hour."

Sakina laughed. She pointed off to the west. "Over there is the Leopard clan. If you are lucky, you could find one of them to kill, and then you'd be a man without taking the Test. If they don't kill you first; perhaps you will find a blind Leopard, or a lame one."

"I don't *want* to kill anyone," Calem said, his shoulders tensing. "I want to learn the spirit magic."

She cocked her head, her lips curled in a bitter half-smile. "And why should I help you, Yellow? So your kind can steal the women you haven't managed to take already, or kill?"

"For the last time, *I am Qanaa'thi, not Yellow.*" The words burst out of him as if by themselves. Calem's jaw set and he was breathing hard; his hands tightened into fists. "The Yellows have murdered my people for *centuries*, Sakina. We survive because our magic is powerful, and because we make sure that the Yellows and the other peoples of the Great Continent need us too much. We find what they need, and trade it to them in exchange for a small measure of wealth and safety."

Sakina's mocking smile faded, and she gazed at him thoughtfully.

"I came here to trade for silver amber with the Snake clan," Calem said, his frustration bubbling to the surface, "to *help* you, to make us both better off. Unless I learn the spirit magic, there will be no trade and no women from the lowlands, which means no future for the clan." He stared at her, struggling to invoke the Ciphers of Harmony and Victory amid his anger. "If you teach me, Sakina, you save your people."

She let out a long slow breath. "I am a woman," she said. "I cannot teach you men's magic. And teaching you women's magic is forbidden. If the clan learned of it, they would kill me."

Calem grimaced. *I didn't expect that!* Thinking quickly, he said, "You don't have to teach me women's magic—just how to call the spirits. The rest I can figure out myself."

Sakina frowned. Instead of answering, she knelt crosslegged on the riverbank and began mending a hole in the trap's weave. The girl's hands moved slowly, automatically, as she stared off in the distance. Finally, she said, "And what will you give me in return?"

"*Give* you?" Calem stared. "Saving your clan is not enough?"

She set aside her trap and rose again, another half-smile on her face. "You are a trader, you said. Trade with me then. Teach me some of your magic, and I will teach you mine."

Calem gasped. The Ciphers were the most sacred secret of the Qanaa'thi. Revealing them would be blasphemous. Unbidden, the thought flashed across his mind *she will use them against me.* "My people's magic is difficult to learn," he said, struggling to regain his calm. "And I myself am poor at it. I could not teach you much at all, even if I were allowed to."

Her eyes narrowed. "Oh? So *I* can risk death and reveal forbidden things, but you will not?" Sakina sniffed and spun on her heel. "Alas," she said, and shouldered her trap. "And I was about to agree to train you after all." She began striding up the path.

He bit his lip furiously, weighing his options. *The Ciphers have been secret for many centuries. Even if I die, it would be worth it to protect that secret. My forefathers have paid the blood price before, and I would betray them if I did otherwise. I don't have the right.*

On the other hand, we are the first Qanaa'thi in the colonies. If we don't find allies, my whole family is at risk, and so would be any Qanaa'thi who followed us.

Maybe I could trust Sakina to keep the Ciphers secret with her?

His breath sawed in his throat as she walked further and further away. At last, Calem decided; he shouted, "All right! All right! I'll do it!"

Sakina turned back to him with the first real smile Calem had seen on her face. "Good," she said. "Meet me here at midnight, and we will begin."

～

That afternoon, Calem was given a small hide tent to use at night. His aching body cried out for sleep, but Calem drew on the Cipher of Strength and ignored his fatigue. He had more work to do.

After another sumptuous evening meal around the central fire, the people of the Snake clan gradually dispersed to their huts. Calem too crawled into his tent, but fought off sleep. Instead, he meditated on the Ciphers, preparing himself for the lesson ahead. *What will calling the spirits even be like? Will it be so different from Qanaa'thi magic that I won't understand it, even with the Ciphers' help?*

At last, midnight came. Calem quietly left his tent, his breath catching in the chill air. He struggled to find his way through the forest in the dim moonlight, terrified that he would blunder into a bush and wake the camp. Finally he managed to reach the riverbank, where Sakina waited for him. Without a word she took his hand and led him deeper in the forest, far away from prying eyes.

At last, in a hidden clearing, they faced each other sitting cross-legged. Calem took a deep breath. "Before we start, swear to me that you won't reveal this to *anyone*." His stomach churned; acid stung his throat. "I'm already breaking the taboo by teaching you."

Sakina nodded. "I swear by my ancestors. So long as you don't reveal my teachings either."

Calem taught her the basic exercise for meditating, called Opening the Door. She learned quickly, remarking that it was similar to the meditation she had to learn to call the spirits. Then, Calem talked her through the technique of Scribing the symbols in her mind's eye, beginning with the simplest Cipher, Calm. Annoyingly, Sakina quickly attained a state of serenity that was far more complete than anything Calem had yet managed.

"It's like the spirits," she said, smiling beatifically. "I give way before the Cipher, and it works its will."

"Fine," Calem said, nettled. "It's your turn. Teach me about the spirits, then."

"Very well," she said. "Answer me this: if one can work magic with any spirit, why then do we begin with those of our ancestors?"

"Because they are more likely to cooperate?"

"No, in fact." Her eyes danced. "That is just something we tell young children. Human spirits have their own personalities, as they did in life, and they do not always cooperate. The real reason is that the *learner* is more likely to trust an ancestral spirit not to harm him.

"That is the key to the spirit magic: trust. You call on a spirit, then give way before it and let it work through you. You trust in its goodwill."

This alarmed Calem. "But what if the spirit attacks you?"

Sakina shrugged. "It's not likely with simple spirits, those of grasses and small plants. And even dangerous spirits can only enter you if you call them in—unless you are fighting another spirit-caller, of course. But a skilled spirit-caller can call a stronger spirit, like a wolf or even a defeated enemy, and avoid harm." She pointed to a dark-colored flower beside them. "Now. This blood-blossom has a spirit close by. Can you feel it?"

Calem invoked the Cipher of Receptiveness and reached out. Above the flower, he dimly perceived a presence, seeming to his magical senses like a second ghostly flower hovering in the air. He nodded.

"Call it to you."

He did, but Sakina shook her head. "You're blocking it. It can't come in. You need to relax, to open yourself."

Sighing, Calem tried again. The spirit drifted closer, but still hesitated. "Make a space for it in your heart," Sakina said, in a low singsong. "Allow yourself to give way. It cannot hurt you; it is a friend. It brings healing. Open yourself."

It was worse than the Ciphers. Try as he might, Calem could not open himself up correctly. Sakina grimaced. "What are you afraid of? It's just a little plant."

"I'm not afraid of a plant," Calem said lamely.

"No," Sakina agreed. "I think you're afraid of letting go at all. You've got your mind in a death-grip." She sighed. "Come back tomorrow night. Teach me more of the Ciphers, and we can try again."

~

The next morning, at the end of yet another bruising session of Lanorak's ruthless grappling instruction, Calem heaved his aching body to his feet to find that Roganath was watching from the edge of the clearing. "I must borrow your student, Lanorak," the chief said. "We must discuss the exchange, and the peace-gift."

Lanorak nodded, a sour frown flickering across his face. "Have him, then. And do not give up our amber cheaply."

Calem followed Roganath to the central shrine, which was surrounded by lounging clansmen, but his footsteps stuttered as he saw Boragos waiting for them. The shaman gave him a thin-lipped smile as they sat. "So, you wish to take our silver amber."

A hush fell, and Calem could feel the eyes of the surrounding clansmen. The trap was obvious. "No, shaman," Calem said carefully.

"I wish to exchange women with the Snake clan, and to give a peace-gift. If the clan wishes to give its own peace-gift to the Qanaa'thi, I will be honored to accept it."

Boragos narrowed his eyes and did not reply; but the onlookers relaxed and smiled approvingly. Roganath chuckled. "You learn quickly, boy. Let us talk of women. We do not know the Qanaa'thi clan; how many are you? How many women does your clan wish to marry?"

No escaping it, then. Father will have a thing or two to say when I come back with a Green wife! "There are thousands of us across the sea," Calem said, "but to my knowledge only my family has yet come to these lands. My father and older brothers are all married; only I lack a wife."

The shaman snorted. "One family. What kinds of peace-gifts can a clanless family provide, even for a single wife?" Roganath shot him a sharp glance, but said nothing.

He keeps trying to trap me. Why? "Forgive me, but we are still discussing the exchange of women." Everyone present knew that the peace-gift and the exchange were inseparable, but the fiction had to be maintained. Offering to *buy* a Woman of the Hills would probably get Calem killed right then and there. He went on. "And we can adopt Yellow women into our clan, to exchange for the Women of the Hills."

Roganath leaned forward. "We know nothing of these women. Are they strong? Healthy? Beautiful of face? Do they have the Yellow magic?"

"I cannot say," Calem said, spreading his hands. "My family will have to seek them out first."

"Then a single Yellow woman is not enough. Besides, we Men of the Hills are better than the Yellow dogs. I say that you must bring three Yellow women, in exchange for one woman from the Snake clan."

Calem gazed at the chief, called on the Cipher of Insight, and thought. *The poor women back in King's Landing work their fingers to the bone carrying firewood and washing clothing for the legions, and still don't* get much to eat. *They live in hovels, and they take what lovers they can. If Father can't convince a few to try life in the hills, then I'd be amazed.* "Great chief," he said, "I say that the women of the Snake clan are beautiful and wise. I should not offer less than *four* Yellow women for a single Snake woman."

Roganath inhaled sharply. "You have offered an exchange, and we will consider it," he said rapidly, rushing through a traditional phrase. "And now, the Snake clan offers a peace-gift to the Qanaa'thi: one hundred beads of silver amber." Beside him, Boragos glowered, but held his tongue.

Yes! Calem had figured it out. By offering *more* women, he had impelled Roganath to offer a peace-gift in order to even the scales. *Now how does negotiation work here? I need to provide more avenues for discussion.* "The Snake clan is generous. The Qanaa'thi offer a peace-gift: an element-forged spear, like the first one I gave you."

Roganath's eyes glinted. "Such a gift does not befit the greatness of the Qanaa'thi. I say that your clan is wise and powerful, and would give no fewer than three spears."

Ah, that is how to say it. Well then, prepare to meet the son of Aliron the merchant! Calem smiled. "I say that the Snake clan is mighty and has strong magic. You would give no less than a thousand beads of silver amber."

Boragos stiffened. "You ignorant boy," he hissed, "do you have any idea how long it takes to find harvest a *single* bead of amber? And you ask for a thousand!" His fingers twitched, as if longing to snap Calem's neck.

An uncomfortable murmur went up from the onlookers. "*Boragos,*" the chief said in a shocked voice, staring at him. "You are shaming us." The shaman pressed his lips together and lowered his eyes, breathing heavily. The chief turned back to Calem. "A thousand beads would be a rich gift. I say that your clan would give no less than six spears, twenty iron knives, and a hundred iron buckles."

Now Calem was in his element. He and Roganath went back and forth, probing, testing, trying one offer after another. In the end, they settled on a "gift" from Calem of four element-forged spears, thirty iron knives, and a hundred iron buckles, corresponding to a "gift" from the Snake clan of five hundred silver amber beads and ten pounds of raw garnet and turquoise. At last the chief said, "It is offered," and Calem echoed him. The surrounding clansmen slapped their thighs and whooped.

Then Boragos said loudly, "Very well. Where are your women?"

Calem stared at him. "What?"

"Your women, boy! Where are they?" The shaman crossed his arms, his lip curled.

This will be the hard part. "Great chief," Calem said slowly, "it would shame us if we cannot bring you strong, beautiful women. But the women of King's Landing know nothing of the hills and do not know why they should join you. When I return to my father, let a Woman of the Hills travel with me so that she can tell the women there of the advantages of this life, so that the best of them will want to enter your clan."

Roganath frowned. "You will have no wife until the exchange happens."

"I understand. She will not be my wife; she will be a protected messenger from the Snake clan to the Qanaa'thi."

"A messenger?" Boragos scoffed. "Or your slave, to sell to the Yellows as soon as you leave our sight?" Roganath gave him a troubled look. This time Boragos did not yield. He turned, addressing the rest of the clan. "I am the keeper of the silver amber, and I say that we know nothing of the Qanaa'thi. Until we see Yellow women, we have only words; and the boy has no ancestors to bind." Some of the clansmen nodded; Lanorak was sitting nearby, a scowl on his face.

"Shaman," Calem said, focusing on the Cipher of Calm, "I cannot snap my fingers and have women magically appear. And my father already sent a peace-gift with me, which your chief accepted; Father will want to see a small part of your own peace-gift. You are great and powerful, and I say that you would send no less than a hundred beads."

The shaman stood. "No."

Roganath rose as well, frowning. "Boragos..."

"I say no! We cannot trust him. If he means us well, let him go alone and empty-handed, and return with the women. I am the keeper of the silver amber, and I say no!" He stalked away back to his tent. At the entrance, he turned and called out, "And all of this means nothing unless he passes the Test of Manhood!" And he disappeared inside.

Roganath sighed. "We will discuss this further. It is a hard thing you ask, to let a woman travel to the Yellow city." He shook his head. "For now, return to your training. Boragos is right; you must complete the Test before sundown tomorrow."

Calem's stomach lurched. "Or what?"

"Or you will not be fit to marry a woman of the Snake clan, and you would be a false messenger." The chief grimaced. "And then we cut off your head."

By midnight, when Calem and Sakina met again by the river, Calem's head was pounding from exhaustion. His arms and legs felt like jelly; he stumbled when he walked and nearly fell right into the river. Sakina shook her head and *tsked*. "Have you been practicing?"

Calem stared at the ground. "Yes," he muttered, "but I don't think it has helped. I can't summon so much as a blade of grass." Somehow, admitting this to Sakina was worse than having to tell Father, over and over, that his control over the Ciphers was still weak.

"Very well," she said, as she led him back to the hidden clearing. "First teach me more, and then we will see what I can teach you."

Calem decided to teach her the Cipher of Strength; it was tricky to master, and there were relatively few ways she could abuse its power. Yet once again, as soon as Sakina figured out the knack of Scribing the symbols in her mind, a greater flow of strength permeated her body than Calem had ever managed to invoke. She giggled as she lifted a large rock that must have weighed nearly as much as she did. "This magic is remarkable! It's a wonder that you Qanaa'thi haven't conquered the world already."

"Not trying hard enough, I suspect," Calem grumbled.

Sakina heard the edge in his voice and set the rock back down. "Come, Calem," she said softly. "Your turn. I'm going to teach you to let the spirits in. Correctly this time; we will start at the very beginning."

She rose; Calem made to stand as well but she said, "No, stay there." From her satchel she produced a long, thin piece of woven plant fibers. She knelt behind him and before he realized what was happening, she had blindfolded him.

Calem's mouth went dry. "What are you doing?" Blinded, alone in a strange forest with a powerful spirit-caller, he suddenly felt raw and vulnerable.

"No talking," Sakina said. "No moving. Keep your hands on your knees." She rose, small twigs and leaves crackling underfoot. "Whatever I do to you, you must not move or react. But this is not about *ignoring* what you feel; it is about accepting it, embracing it, not resisting. Do you understand?" Calem nodded, his pulse rapid, his breathing shallow. *Not safe! Not safe! Danger!* He scribed the Cipher of Calm and tried to slow his breathing.

A sudden light touch against his back. Calem gasped and leaned forward. "Wrong," Sakina said behind him. "That was a little twig. It can't hurt you. Give way, Qanaa'thi. Don't fight it." Calem licked his lips and straightened up again, cursing himself. Then Sakina poked him again, and he yelped. She sighed. "Give way. Don't be so rigid."

For nearly an hour, Calem suffered an endless series of touches and pokes. None hurt, but they made him flinch anyway. He was growing sore and his headache pounded in back of his eyes, his patience strained to the utmost. *I can deal with pain. This is nothing compared to the grappling. I won't give up.*

"It isn't about endurance, Calem," Sakina said at last. "You can sit there for days and still not learn the lesson. Give way. Accept. Embrace. I'm not going to wait all night for you to understand." Still, her tone was teasing.

As time passed, Calem slowly understood. Each new sensation came, and he considered it, tasted it, let the feeling develop texture.

He allowed each feeling to fill his entire mind, and then drift away like a cloud. Time ceased mattering; it was only himself and Sakina's touches, the smell of the air, the feel of the grass beneath his haunches and legs.

"Better," she said, some time later; he felt the blindfold loosening, and blinked rapidly. "Now, call the blood-blossom spirit again. It's been waiting for you."

With his magical senses, Calem reached out and found the flower spirit from last night; he was startled to feel it hovering almost in front of his nose. He called, and the spirit approached. Its touch lingered against his mind, and Calem opened the way, making himself into the spirit's home. He felt its joy flowing though him, and more: a current of healing magic, whisper-light and delicate. Without a focus, it flowed through his fingers and diffused into the world around them, taking a bit of his headache with it.

Sakina clapped. "Very good!" Her voice was excited, pleased. "I knew you'd be fast, once you had the right idea. You've already been trained in magic; you just needed to trust yourself."

"That was fast?" The spirit gave a questioning thrum, and Calem bade it farewell with a pang of regret.

She laughed softly. "Calem, most men never learn to call non-human spirits at all; and you did it in two nights!"

Calem breathed in deeply, feeling more deeply at peace than he could ever remember. "You're pretty good at the Ciphers yourself," he remarked, surprising himself. "I don't think I said that before."

They shared a tired smile.

~

After more practice, Calem and Sakina returned to the village only a few hours before dawn; but Calem couldn't sleep. He was too excited. He remembered what Sakina had said about the Ciphers being just like the spirits. *Could this be it? What Father's been waiting for?*

Opening the Door, he scribed the Cipher of Calm; this time, he relaxed his mind and opened himself up, as he had done with the spirits earlier. To his surprise, the Cipher flooded his mind and soul, and he sank deeply into it and felt it channeled through him. Elated, he tried the Cipher of Strength. Its power too flowed through him, and his sore muscles felt as though they could bend iron bars. Calem invoked other Ciphers one after another. Each time, he found that they granted him far more power than before, far more naturally, almost instinctively—like they had become a part of him, as easy to use as his own eyes or hands.

The sun rose to find Calem deep in a meditative trance, filled with elation. Magic flowed from the Ciphers as if he were bathing in a stream. *I'm not at Father's level, not yet; but it doesn't feel impossible any more.* Even better, with the Cipher of Insight to guide him, Calem called tiny spirits to him again and again, letting them into his heart, feeling their energies hum and pulse through his body. *Today they will test me,* he thought, *and today I will prove myself in their arts.*

At dawn, Calem presented himself to Lanorak. The tall warrior started slow, going through the preliminary warmups, but Calem raised his palm. "Please, Lanorak. I have only a little time. I must know if I am ready for the Test; never mind the teaching, and grapple with me now."

Lanorak raised his eyebrows. "After the thrashing I gave you yesterday, you're probably too sore already to pass the Test. Don't wear yourself out beforehand."

"I might surprise you," Calem said, smiling grimly.

"Oh really?" Lanorak gave him a skeptical look, but he crouched in a fighting stance. "If not, boy, you are going to regret it."

For answer, Calem invoked the Ciphers of Strength, Insight, and Receptiveness all at the same time. Then he called three nearby pine-tree spirits and welcomed them inside of his body, feeling their power pulse through his limbs.

Lanorak inhaled sharply. "You *have* learned to call the spirits," he whispered.

"No thanks to Boragos," Calem said evenly. "Shall we?"

"A moment," the warrior said. Calem felt the Lanorak's own summons, and a much stronger human spirit manifested and merged with him. He bared his teeth. "If you want to use spirits, then spirits we shall use. *Now*, let us begin."

They clinched, and immediately Lanorak tried to sweep Calem's back leg. This move had worked every time yesterday; this time, with the Ciphers Calem could feel the bigger man's muscles as they coiled in preparation for the strike. Even before Lanorak moved Calem reacted, pivoting his body and dissipating Lanorak's energy harmlessly. The warrior grunted in surprise, and his eyes widened when Calem drove his shoulder into Lanorak's chest.

One with the Ciphers, Calem was able to read every tense muscle in Lanorak's body as they grappled, and every flow of spirit energy. It was as if Calem could see the future. His technique was still rudimentary, but improved rapidly as they fought; the Cipher of Receptiveness now let him copy a move the first time he saw it, and refine the details every time thereafter.

After his initial shock, Lanorak was not caught flat-footed again. He moved warily, no longer trying to surprise Calem, relying on his ancestor's strength and power to seize a momentary edge and develop it further. He had a better feel for the rhythm of a fight; he could still goad Calem into overextending and then counterattack, and even Calem's preternatural reactions could not save him from being thrown off-balance. But with every throw, Calem could see better where his mistakes had been.

Now that Calem no longer felt hesitant in his moves, he found grappling to be surprisingly fun. The feeling of wrapping his arm around Lanorak's throat, or slithering out of a hold, or trapping Lanorak's arm and controlling it, tapped into some deep instinct that had never had a chance to express itself before. *I can face him, man to man.*

They grappled again and again, and Lanorak's expression became totally blank, focused. *He's using everything he has. He's not holding back.* Once, Calem saw an opening and swept Lanorak's front foot, following up with a short hard shove to the shoulder. Lanorak fell hard, spinning downward to strike the ground.

Calem had an instant to savor his victory; then Lanorak grunted and rolled back to his feet, eyes narrowed. "Good," he said shortly. "Now watch carefully. *This* is how we fight using the spirits." And he returned to the clinch. Calem gasped as Lanorak's ancestral spirit seemed to reach out from his body, stabbing at him with incorporeal fingers.

There was a Cipher to ward off magical attacks, a necessity when living among the Eridari. *But I haven't used the Cipher of Shielding for years! And then only in practice!* Calem struggled to Scribe the unfamiliar symbols in his mind, and Lanorak struck, barreling forward and slamming Calem through the air. He landed with a teeth-rattling jolt.

Lanorak stared impassively. "However you learned the spirits, you did not learn how to fight with them," he said. "Use a spirit to fight a spirit. That is the best way. Again."

Calem shook his head to clear the ringing in his ears. "Is fighting with spirits part of the Test?"

"No," the warrior replied. "But I am curious. Again, boy."

A half hour later, both of them were panting and dripping with sweat. Calem's tree spirits had fled long before, not used to being attacked by other spirits; but Calem had finally remembered his lessons with the Cipher of Shielding, and it functioned as well against hostile spirits as it did against elemental magic. *I need more practice, but it's better than being sliced apart by angry ghosts!*

Lanorak stared at him silently. Abruptly he said, "What did you mean before, about Boragos? Has he not been training you?"

Calem shook his head. "He refused because I have no ancestors, he said. And he would not teach me to call for other spirits."

Lanorak scowled. "Then he wants you to fail the Test, and be killed. I saw what he was like, when you were discussing peace-gifts."

"Why?" Calem burst out. "I have done nothing to him!"

"The ways of shamans are strange," Lanorak said, shrugging. Then he changed the subject. "Did the chief discuss sending a messenger back with you? Will you be able to get more trade goods?"

Calem eyed him, and said carefully, "I thought that you did not wish to trade."

Lanorak chuckled. "I don't. I still think you mean to bleed us dry." He fell silent for a moment, grimacing, then said in a low voice, "But my spear is a problem. We need more of them, and soon."

"The element-forged spear?" Calem raised an eyebrow. "How is it a problem?"

"The problem is that I have the only one in the clan," Lanorak muttered, glancing down. "The others are envious, you see. Until we have more of those spears, it will cause discord."

"Surely you don't think someone else will steal it?"

"No!" Lanorak looked appalled by the very idea. "But they are my clansmen. There must be friendship between us, or we all suffer."

Calem gazed at the hillman and perceived that he was telling the truth. *Could he become an ally after all?* "The chief has not yet said anything. I don't know if he will agree."

Lanorak grunted in disappointment. "Then he must be convinced. Swear to me that you will protect our messenger, and that you will return with more spears, and I will speak for you."

Calem's eyes widened. "You would trust my word? Even though I have no ancestors to bind?"

For a long moment Lanorak said nothing, staring at him. At last, he said, "You have courage, and I think that you have honor. I will trust your word."

Calem squeezed his eyes shut and sagged back against the tree trunk in relief. Without opening his eyes, he made a fist over his heart and said, "By the sacred truths of Qanaa I swear to you, Lanorak of the Snake clan, that I will protect the messenger who comes with me with my life, and I will return with more spears to give to the clan."

"I hear it," Lanorak said gravely, "as do the stones, as do the trees, as does the sky. Come; let us see about the chief."

Roganath was kneeling at the head of a group of hunters in front of the low altar, which now held a steaming, bloody liver. (From a hunted animal, Calem hoped.) On his right side, Boragos chanted tunelessly in an unknown language, prodding the liver with a sharp stick and peering at it. Then he grunted, satisfied, and raised his hands. "The omens are good," he said.

The hunters relaxed into smiles. Lanorak seized the opportunity, kneeling on Roganath's left and pulling Calem down next to him. "And so they should be," the hunter said loudly. "Calem of the Qanaa'thi has just passed the Test of Strength."

Boragos started, his eyes narrowing to slits. But Roganath smiled broadly. "So quickly! Could you not have waited for the full ceremony?"

Lanorak shrugged. "The messenger has little time. You know my ancestors, and you know the weight of my word. I have tested Calem, and he is a true warrior of the Snake clan."

"Then it is so," the chief replied. "Boragos?"

The shaman glared. "Very well; if we are trampling on the traditions of our ancestors, let us be done with it." He turned to Calem. "Call a spirit, boy, if you can."

Smiling, Calem extended out his magical senses. At the edge of the clearing was an old spruce tree; several tree spirits hovered nearby, and Calem called to them. Two answered and entered into him, their power circulating with every heartbeat. He exhaled. "Are you satisfied, shaman?"

The shaman's eyes bugged. "This is woman's magic!" he cried hoarsely. An uncertain murmur went up among the clansmen. Lanorak winced.

"It is *my* magic," Calem said firmly. "You would not teach me to summon human spirits, so I learned what I could. Do I pass the test, shaman?"

"No," Boragos snapped. "The Test of Manhood is to summon a human spirit. You have failed, boy. You are not fit for our women, and your message is false."

The clansmen went dead silent. Calem paled. *What now? Is he going to kill me in front of everyone?* All the aches of his body suddenly came crashing over him at once. *I've never fought for my life before.*

Roganath frowned. "Boragos—"

"Do you gainsay me?" the shaman snarled. "I judge the Test, not you!"

"You do," the chief conceded. "But surely you understand what is at stake here?"

"Better than you, it seems!"

"Great chief," Lanorak cut in. "Surely Calem of the Qanaa'thi is not a false messenger. He has learned much in only three days. We cannot demand more from him justly. I say that he return to his clan, with a woman of the Snake clan as a messenger. Before he returns, he can learn on his own how to summon a human spirit, as the shaman requires. Then he can pass the Test and the exchange can go forward."

Roganath and Boragos turned in surprise. "Do you speak for him?" the chief said. "Did you not want to kill him when we first met?"

"I did, and yet I speak for him now," Lanorak said. "Heed my words, chief."

"I do heed them, and here is my word," the chief said quickly. "We will give Calem son of Aliron a peace-gift of one hundred beads of silver amber for his clan, and have him escort a woman of the Snake Clan to the Yellow city. Then he will return with his women, and he can then take the Test of Manhood."

A great wave of relief washed over Calem. "Thank you, great chief," he said. "Your trust in me does me honor."

But Boragos burst out, "No! I refuse! I am the guardian of the silver amber, and I say that I will not give the boy so much as a single bead!"

"Boragos, it is the clan's decision," Roganath said, brows lowering. "Abide by it. This will secure our future."

"No!" Boragos scrambled to his feet, his voice becoming a scream. Startled, the others rose as well. "This is sacrilege! An insult to our ancestors, and I will not allow it!"

Calem stared at him. The shaman's anger was obvious, but beneath it lay something else: fear, and shame. *What does it mean?*

The chief's face had gone cold. "Do you defy the clan?" he said in a low, dangerous voice.

The shaman laughed wildly. The sound sent a chill down Calem's back. "No, you old fool!" he cried. "I am protecting the clan—by defying *you*! Now witness my power!"

And with that, he raised his hand and magical energy surged from him. Calem's eyes widened; it was not spirit energy, but the elemental magic of the Eridari. And it came from a ring on the shaman's finger that Calem had not noticed before, with a glittering blue gemstone.

Roganath stiffened and began to call his spirits; but in an instant, a lance of bitterest cold shot from the shaman's ring and pierced his chest, leaving his bare skin rimed with frost. A horrified cry went up from the clansmen and they fell back from Boragos, leaving an empty space around him; somewhere, Sakina screamed. Roganath stared blankly at his murderer, then slowly sank forward and collapsed on the ground, dead. His heart had been frozen.

Calem was paralyzed by horror. Lanorak hissed and drew a bone knife, but recoiled in fear as Boragos snarled and brandished his ring. "Submit, you dog!" he hissed. "I'll destroy you, as I did Roganath!" He raised his voice and addressed the rest of the clan. "You know how I loved Roganath like a brother, how many years we have fought at each other's side! Yet today, he was corrupted by that foul Yellow boy! He would have given up our sacred treasures, for a handful of empty promises—and I, the guardian of our silver amber, could not let it happen."

He turned to Calem, his voice deepening. "So now, boy, leave the Snake clan while you can. Your message protects you, for now. But if you ever show your face again, I will kill you myself."

"*Murderer!*" Sakina pushed her way through the clansman, shrieking in fury, tears running down her face. "Men of the Snake clan, do justice and kill Boragos! He has murdered my father, and I call for justice!"

"It is not murder to protect the clan," Boragos growled, holding up his ring and allowing blue energy to coalesce around it. The clansmen muttered in fear. Lanorak clenched his fists, his gaze moving between Sakina and Boragos, but he did not move. "And as for *you*, traitor's spawn," the shaman spat at Sakina, "I am not done with you. Don't think I don't know how the Yellow learned our magic."

Sakina swayed and nearly fell, her tearstained cheeks pale. In an instant, everything was clear to Calem: the shaman needed her dead, or she would always pose a threat to him. Whether he truly knew or not that Sakina had broken the taboo, it was a convenient pretext to have her executed.

And all Calem had to do was to leave safely, and let it happen.

No.

"Boragos, you are a liar and a murderer," Calem called out in a clear voice, and the clansmen turned to him. "And to prove it, I challenge you to single combat, before all the clan."

The shaman's face went pale with anger. "You? Challenge me? You are no man, for me to face your challenge!"

"Yet I can become a man," Calem replied, smiling coldly, "can I not? By defeating an enemy of the clan in battle?" He pointed. "*You* are an enemy, and I will rid the clan of you."

A murmur went up from the watching clansmen. Sakina cried out, "Would you dare refuse his challenge, you coward?"

Boragos said nothing, breathing harshly. At last he snarled. "Very well, boy. I'll crush you myself."

They made their way to the clearing where Lanorak had held his training; the clansfolk crowded together at the edges of the clearing, leaning against tree trunks or climbing thick branches to see better. A wrinkled old man painted Calem's face with white and red stripes; as he did the same to Boragos, Sakina appeared next to Calem. "Be careful," she whispered. "His magic is powerful. He will kill you if you hesitate."

"I won't." His tongue seemed strangely thick.

"He was going to let you go." She squeezed his hand, and a

whisper of power pulsed through her palm. "Fight well, Calem." Not trusting his voice, he nodded.

Soon, Calem and Boragos stood thirty feet apart, in the center of the clearing. The watching clan waited tensely. The shaman's eyes burned; his aura roiled with fury. Calem's stomach churned. At the same time, a strange new feeling grew—a sort of wild exhilaration. Every sinew tingled, as if Calem had become drunk with strong wine. *He is my enemy, and he did murder. I will face him and triumph.*

The wrinkled man stood between them and raised his arms. "May the spirits favor justice!" he called out, and then scuttled to the side.

Immediately Boragos gestured with his glittering blue ring and blasted Calem with frost. His eyes widened when Calem invoked the Cipher of Shielding, and the Eridani magic splashed harmlessly into the ground in front of him. Frozen grass crackled beneath Calem's feet as he advanced.

The blast had been powerful, its force sending a lance of pain through his temples as he struggled to keep the shield up; but Calem dared not let it show. *Act casual. Make him angry.* "You should know that my people have been fighting against elemental magic for centuries. It won't do you much good against me." Calem dissipated another bolt and sauntered forward, masking the effort that it cost him. The shaman growled and gave his ring a furious glance.

The ring is the key, somehow. I've seen its like before, but where? Calem invoked the Cipher of Insight, and with a sudden thrill he remembered. "That's an interesting ring you have there," he said loudly. "It looks like a Eridani power vessel. I wonder how you got it, shaman."

"Shut up," Boragos hissed, and sent another bolt of frost toward him. Calem blocked it and slowly strode closer, deliberately laughing.

"It seems quite powerful. The kind of thing that an Eridari high mage would craft, to allow an untalented nobleman to use elemental magic as if it were his own. And for you to be given it, you must have paid a high price."

"Shut up!" the shaman screamed. He blasted at Calem with icy energy with all of his strength.

"Did you pay with the clan's silver amber, perhaps?"

An ugly growl went up from the watching clansmen. Boragos went pale and glanced at them. Calem saw his chance, quickly scribed the Cipher of Victory, and sent a pulse of power against the shaman's mind. Experienced in mental combat, Boragos repelled the crude attack, but now Calem had the initiative. *I can't give it up again. I have to finish him now.*

"You did, didn't you?" he said, striding up almost within grappling range where he was halted by a flurry of ice. "And you murdered your own chief because there was no silver amber left to give me. You stole it, and traded it to the Yellows for power. And no one could ever find out."

"I'll tear out your lying tongue," Boragos said hoarsely. He summoned his spirits, so many that Calem could not count them all, and snarled as if he were a savage beast.

There. He was close enough now. "And I, your greed-sickened eyes," Calem said, and leaped at the old man.

It was a mistake. Old he was, but the spirits gave the shaman incredible strength and speed. Lanorak had been good at grappling, but Boragos, driven mad by fear and hate and desperation, clutched at Calem with iron fingers that stabbed at his flesh. Even with the Ciphers letting him sense his foe's attacks before they happened, Calem could barely avoid having his arms snapped by his enemy's relentless power. The onlookers were deadly silent, their fear mirroring Calem's own. Sakina was digging her nails into her arms, deathly pale.

Then Calem was a hair too slow, and the shaman seized his arm and wrenched with terrifying force. Calem cried out as his shoulder gave a wet pop and searing pain pulsed outward. Boragos smiled thinly, and then gave a wordless command. Suddenly Calem was overcome by a wave of terror, forced upon his mind by the spirits reaching out from Boragos.

Dozens of incorporeal presences struck, shredding their way through Calem's shield and slashing him with invisible knives that left real wounds. Calem jerked as long gashes opened in his shoulders and chest. His skin was slick with blood and sweat. Calem invoked the Cipher of Strength, but Boragos giggled and twisted his injured arm cruelly. A red haze covered his eyes and his legs went weak.

Calem dropped to the ground, gasping, and Boragos almost casually put him into a chokehold. The shaman drove his face into the forest floor, and began to crush his throat. "Soon, boy," the shaman whispered in his ear, "I will rip your spirit out of its body. And then you will serve me, forever."

You will serve me. Calem's eyes widened. Of course; the shaman's power came from fallen warriors, perhaps dozens of them, collected over many years. There was no way that Calem could fight that much raw magical strength.

But there was someone else who might.

Roganath, come to me. The murdered man's spirit was still hovering nearby, unwilling to accept his death. Calem called again, desperately. *Roganath, I need you. Help me punish your killer. Please, give me your aid.*

Roganath's spirit approached. It floated in front of Calem's dimming eyes, but came no closer. *Give me your body, and I will come,* a silent voice in his mind whispered.

Though his death was upon him, Calem was chilled by a new fear. *Will you leave once Boragos is dead?*

Sakina needs me, the spirit said plaintively. *I can't leave her. You are dying anyway. Give me your body.*

Calem struggled to think through the dark curtain that seemed to envelop his mind. His lungs were on fire. The scent of forest loam and Boragos's sour breath filled his nostrils. *Your spirit magic alone won't be enough to beat the shaman,* Calem responded frantically. *You need my Qanaa'thi magic as well. Otherwise, he wins and your daughter is in danger.*

Sakina needs me.

Sakina is powerful and brave, Calem replied. *She learned well from you and all her teachers. Trust in her, Roganath.*

And you? If we kill Boragos, will you take the clan from her?

The thought had never occurred to him. Even as his heart fluttered in his chest, his brain spent a precious instant considering. *Rule the Snake clan. Warriors at my command, their riches in my grasp, their women free for the taking. At last I will receive my due.*

The instant passed. It was a silly idea. Calem was a merchant, not a ruler of men. *No,* he answered. *I swear it by the sacred truths of Qanaa.*

Then let us take revenge, you and I.

Roganath merged with him. It was a far stranger experience than calling plant spirits; Calem's consciousness seemed to fragment, overwhelming him with a swirl of fleeting memories from another life. For a moment he was submerged in Roganath's emotions—anguish over his death, love and fear for Sakina, fury at Boragos.

Kill Boragos.

The old chief called, and his *own* spirits appeared from all around them. They merged with Calem and suddenly he felt a tremendous jolt of new strength and power. He twisted in Boragos's grasp and broke the chokehold, then pulled the old man off-balance so he tumbled off to the side. Fresh air flowed through Calem's damaged throat, and it tasted like the finest mead. Gasps arose from the watching clan.

They both scrambled to their feet, Calem panting for breath. "Roganath," the shaman snarled. "I should have mastered your spirit the moment I killed you."

"Your mistake, betrayer of the clan," the chief spoke through Calem's lips. The gasps grew louder. Sakina cried out wordlessly.

Boragos let out a screech, and pointed. All of his spirits boiled out of him at a rush, surging toward Calem in a terrifying storm of magical decay. Roganath's spirit froze in panic, but Calem invoked the Cipher of Shielding and stood firm. The spirit attack hit his shield and did not penetrate it; spirits clawed at the shield impotently, letting out inaudible moans.

Now, boy.

Calem nodded. He invoked the Cipher of Insight; then he split his shield in two and drove the halves out and back, forcing a path between the attacking spirits. Boragos's eyes widened, and he called for his spirits to return. Calem didn't give him the chance. He leapt forward and swept the old man's feet from under him. Boragos fell; Calem knelt down with him, wrapped his arms around his head, and gave a sharp jerk.

Crack. The oncoming cloud of spirits suddenly halted, confused. One by one, spirits began to drift away, fading even from Calem's magical sight. Calem glanced at Boragos; the old man lay limp, his head lolling back at a strange angle, his eyes sightless. His neck had been broken.

Calem rose, his chest heaving, his shoulder burning, blood seeping from the long gashes in his skin. *I'm alive. I won. I actually won!*

You did well, Calem. Remember your oath. The chief's presence suddenly left him; Calem reeled as his mind was his own again. It felt odd, like returning to a childhood home and finding it smaller than he remembered. The incredible strength left his limbs and he nearly fell.

For a moment, no one spoke. Then Lanorak called out, "Does anyone here doubt that Boragos was a murderer, a betrayer, an outcast of the clan?"

Sakina strode forward next to Calem. "He spilled my father's blood," she said, her voice hard, the tears drying on her cheeks. "Though Calem of the Qanaa'thi, his blood is avenged!" The others slapped their thighs in agreement in a staccato rumble.

"Then let Calem of the Qanaa'thi be counted a full man," Lanorak replied, "by right of victory in battle!"

A chorus of ululating cries went up, and Calem suddenly found himself mobbed by grinning clansmen who clasped his hands, slapped him on the back, or simply pushed through the throng to touch his arms and shoulders.

It hurt terribly, but Calem could barely notice. He seemed to float on a cloud of pure joy. The sleepless nights, the endless bruising from his training, the terror of his first mortal combat and the agony of his wounds, it all seemed to condense into a single shining jewel of triumph in his mind. *I won, I won, I won, I'm going to live, I won!*

"That's enough!" Sakina snapped. "He needs healing, you brutes!" The clansmen fell back, abashed, and she guided Calem back to the center of the clearing and helped him lie on the grass. The clan watched Sakina work her magic for a time; then they gradually drifted back to the settlement and their daily work, leaving the two of them alone.

The magic flowed from Sakina's fingers and the pain slowly began to recede. Calem sighed with relief. "Thank you," he said.

"I would do this for any of our warriors," Sakina replied gently. "Would I do less for the man who avenged my father and slew a mighty foe?"

Her words pulsed with a new admiration. It swelled within her heart even as her grief threatened to overpower her. Calem reached up with his good hand and squeezed her fingers. "You taught me to call the spirits," he said. "It saved my life."

She snorted. "And don't forget it! For I surely will not."

Then Lanorak squatted down next to them, his face grave. "Thank you, Calem. Were it not for you, I am sure that Boragos would have killed me the first chance he had."

Calem nodded. "You were his greatest rival to lead the clan."

Lanorak blew out his cheeks. "What of your peace-gift, the silver amber?" he said. "We have searched for it, and there are fewer than thirty beads left in the shaman's cache. If he stole the rest, then you have no peace-gift and we are disgraced!"

Calem thought, then smiled. "His Eridari ring was bought with that amber. Give that to me instead."

The warrior inhaled and seemed to struggle within himself. Sakina gave him a sharp glance. "Will you tell him, or must I?"

Lanorak sighed and held the ring out in his hand, along with a bulging leather satchel. "It is already yours, Calem. You won it, along with all of Boragos's personal possessions, by defeating him in the challenge."

"Oh." It was all he could say. Rings like that were fabulously rare and expensive. It glittered dangerously as Calem slipped it onto his finger. *I doubt even Father has one like it!*

"What can we do?" Lanorak spread his hands. "We have nothing to give you that can compare to the silver amber."

Calem touched Sakina's hand; she understood and paused her work. He rose, hissing at the pain, and faced Lanorak. "Give me a single bead of amber as your peace-gift," he said. "You can collect more while I am gone, and give me the rest when I return."

The warrior gazed at him, relief shining out of his eyes. "You trust us that much?"

"I do," Calem said, and smiled. He clasped Lanorak's hand, and the warrior returned his grip firmly.

"Wonderful," Sakina said briskly, and forced him back to the ground. "Now go away, Lanorak, and *you*, lie still so I can heal you. You must regain your health before we go to the Yellow city."

Calem nodded and lay back down; then her words registered. "We? You're coming with me?" Lanorak smirked as he turned to go.

"Of course," she said, returning to her healing. "You wanted a woman to tell of our ways to the Yellows; who better than I? Besides, before we get married we should spend more time together."

His body went rigid with shock. "*Married?*"

"Well, yes," she said, suddenly flustered. "You did agree to marry one of us, after all. And I thought... well..." She blushed crimson and glanced down. In a low, faltering voice, she said, "Unless... you don't... want me?"

Calem's mouth was dry. "Um, do you, do you need to mourn for your father first?"

"I can do both, you know," she said, her voice brisk again. "And my father trusted you in the end, so why can't I?"

Calem rose again, ignoring his hurts, and pulled Sakina to her feet as well. She was powerful and fierce and beautiful. And she wanted to marry *him*? A slow smile bloomed across his face. "I, uh... I think I can get used to the idea."

ABOUT THE AUTHORS

Oren Litwin is a political researcher and author who recently discovered that it's just as much fun to publish other people's stories as it is his own. This anthology marks the launch of his new project Lagrange Books, which will be focusing initially on short-story anthologies in several genres. Oren is also an associate editor at Liberty Island Media. He lives with his family in Northern Virginia.

Misha Burnett: Misha has been writing poetry and fiction for around forty years. During this time he has supported himself and his family with a variety of jobs, including locksmith, cab driver, and building maintenance. His first four novels, *Catskinner's Book*, *Cannibal Hearts*, *The Worms Of Heaven*, and *Gingerbread Wolves* comprise a series, "The Book Of Lost Doors." Major influences include Tim Powers, Samuel Delany, William Burroughs, and Phillip K. Dick.

Michael Connon: Michael has written for TV, radio and the stage. His short stories have won awards in the UK and US and have been published in several anthologies. He currently lives in the North East of England with a black cat which he feels is appropriate to this collection.

Steve Cook: Steve is an author and teacher. Previously, his work has been published in *Amygdala* magazine, *Cogs In Time 3*, *Avast, Ye Pirates*, and *Broadswords and Blasters 2*. He publishes free flash fiction twice weekly on his Patreon, 'Giant's Reach', and short stories once a month.

L.C. Gibson: L.C. is a retired Marine Officer who currently works at one of those three letter agencies that you love to hate. He lives in Northern Virginia with his wife and a spoiled rotten rescue dog of uncertain antecedents.

Jake Lithua: Jake was forever corrupted at the age of 5, when he discovered his father's *Dungeons & Dragons* Basic Set. Ever since, he has been interested in telling stories of heroism and courage, fantastical or real-world. His short story "The Most Powerful Weapon" is published in *The Odds Are Against Us*, by Liberty Island Media. He lives far too close to Washington DC for anyone's good.

Will Neely: Will is a musician and author. This will be his first time in print.

J.S. Rogers: J.S. has been writing since she could get her hands on a pencil and paper. These days, she writes as a freelancer for her day job and pens fiction by night. Her fiction has previously appeared in "Untethered: A Magic iPhone Anthology." She can be followed on Twitter at @j_srogers.

Aaron Smith: Aaron is a family law attorney practicing in San Diego, CA where he lives with his wife, son and two pitbulls. He has previously been published in Microhorror.com, *Liberty Island,* PJ Media and had short stories published in the anthologies *California Screamin'* and *Trump Utopias and Dystopias*. His story "Meat Market," has been selected for the forthcoming anthology *MCSI: Magical Crime Scene Investigation.*

Max Sparber: Max is an author from Minneapolis. His speculative fiction has appeared in "The Best of Strange Horizons: Year One" and "People of the Book: A Decade of Jewish Science Fiction and Fantasy."

Wondra Vanian: Wondra is an American who lives in the United

Kingdom with her husband and an army of fur babies. A writer first, Wondra Vanian is also an avid gamer, photographer, cinephile, and blogger. She was a multiple Top-Ten finisher in the 2017 Preditors and Editors Reader's Poll, including in the Best Author category.

Alyssa N. Vaughn: Alyssa is a writer and teacher from Dallas, Texas. She enjoys knowing the locations of obscure shops with unusual wares, but her favorites are always the ones with books. You can follow her on Twitter @msalyssaenvy.

Vanessa Wells: Vanessa lives with her family in an enchanted forest... in Texas. She spends her time battling infestations of plot bunnies (and dust bunnies, but that's a different matter entirely). She's currently working on the next trilogy in the Seventeen Stones world, a new prequel to Topeka, and a series of science fiction shorts called Area 52.

www.ingramcontent.com/pod-product-compliance
Lightning Source LLC
Chambersburg PA
CBHW021225250626
47155CB00008B/2937